Melek Han

Thirty years in the harem

or the autobiography of Melek-Hanum, wife of H.H. Kibrizli-Mehemet-Pasha

Melek Hanum

Thirty years in the harem
or the autobiography of Melek-Hanum, wife of H.H. Kibrizli-Mehemet-Pasha

ISBN/EAN: 9783743337640

Manufactured in Europe, USA, Canada, Australia, Japa

Cover: Foto ©Raphael Reischuk / pixelio.de

Manufactured and distributed by brebook publishing software
(www.brebook.com)

Melek Hanum

Thirty years in the harem

THIRTY YEARS IN THE HAREM:

OR, THE

AUTOBIOGRAPHY

OF

MELEK-HANUM WIFE OF H.H. KIBRIZLI-MEHEMET-PASHA.

LONDON:

CHAPMAN AND HALL, 193, PICCADILLY.

1872.

LONDON :
BRADBURY, EVANS, AND CO., PRINTERS, WHITEFRIARS.

CONTENTS.

—◆—

CHAPTER I.

CHAPTER V.

CHAPTER VI.

CHAPTER VII.

CHAPTER VIII.

CHAPTER IX.

CHAPTER X.

CHAPTER XVIII.

CHAPTER XIX.

CHAPTER XX.

CHAPTER XXI.

CHAPTER XXII.

CHAPTER XXIII.

CHAPTER XXIV.

CHAPTER XXV.

CHAPTER XXVI.

CHAPTER XXVII.

CHAPTER XXVIII.

CHAPTER XXIX.

CHAPTER XXX.

CHAPTER XXXI.

CHAPTER XXXII.

CHAPTER XXXIII.

CHAPTER XXXIV.

THIRTY YEARS IN THE HAREM.

CHAPTER I.

My family—My mother's marriage.

My maternal grandmother, who was from the isle of Chios, married an Armenian, a banker patronized by the then reigning Sultan Selim III. (1789—1807). He was very rich, and—what is always a perilous matter in the East—he was known to possess a fortune.

The Janissaries were, at that time, the tyrants of the country. They were a source of universal terror, so resolutely did they devote themselves to the most shameless depredations—to the most cruel measures of vengeance, and to acts the most arbitrary.

My grandfather one day received a warning that the Janissaries had formed the design of paying a visit to his house in order to lay hands upon his treasures. Fear got the better of his courage ; his reason was disturbed. Ascending to the terrace-roof, common to the generality of old houses, he precipitated himself to the ground. When he was taken up, horribly mutilated, life was found to be extinct.

The announcement which led to so lamentable a result was unquestionably false, for the widow, the son, and the three daughters of the deceased were left in peaceable possession of his effects.

The family resided at Constantinople, in the suburb of Galata, between the quarter named *Salibazar* (the Tuesday bazaar) and *Azab-Capou* (the Refuge). The house they lived in was of great antiquity. Built by the Genoese, it was the property of a celebrated physician, named Hadji-Mustapha. It was laid out in four flats, each comprising four or five bed-rooms and a spacious reception-room. As it stood on a considerable elevation, an agreeable prospect was enjoyed, even from the first floor, ranging over the White Sea, the tower of Leander (called by the Turks the Maiden's Tower), and Scutari, with its forests of lofty cypress.

The reason why the Turks call Leander's Tower *Kiz-kulesi*, or the Maiden's Tower, is referable to a singular legend :—

A certain Sultan dreamt that his daughter would

perish from the bite of a serpent. The muned-jims (soothsayers), when consulted as to the means of preserving the princess from the fatal calamity that menaced her, could suggest nothing better than to construct, out at sea, the tower in question. The young Sultana was confined in this tower, with several of her ladies to bear her company. One day, whilst surrounded by her attendants, and seated upon the highest storey, she was amusing herself by watching the boats passing below, when she remarked in one of them some magnificent fruits, especially grapes, for which she had a great longing. In spite of the Sultan's prohibition, who had ordained that nothing whatever should be allowed access to his daughter, she purchased a basketful of the beautiful, fresh, and rosy grapes which she found so tempting. A cord, let down to the boatman, enabled the basket to be drawn up; but scarcely had the princess laid her hand upon it when a serpent, gliding out, bit her in the arm. Every care was lavished upon her, but to no purpose; she expired after a few moments. So · difficult is it to escape the destiny which is in store for us.

My grandmother, as I have said before, was in easy circumstances; so her house was tastefully furnished. On the three sides of each room other than that which contained the doorway, were ranged large divans of cloth or velvet, supplied with cushions. Ancient Turkey carpets covered the floor in winter; in the summer they were replaced by mats. Fresco paintings of flowers adorned the walls, and the air was cooled by vases of water placed in niches. Every room had a chimney; whilst in modern houses people warm themselves solely by means of huge chafing-dishes resembling Roman braziers, or by means of the *tandour*.

This last-named system of warming is so peculiar as to be deserving here of special mention. To make this original stove, a large iron foot-warmer is placed under a kind of flat, circular wooden chest, lined with sheet-iron, and about a foot-and-a-half high. It is pierced at intervals with holes sufficiently large to allow persons sitting on it to pass their legs underneath. The whole is covered with stuffs more or less rich, according to the resources of the owner. In the centre is placed a circular table-cloth, or covering, of silk or cashmere. Before each of the persons who take their seats on this novel divan is a drawer, in which fruit and other things can be placed.

The inmates, male and female, of the same house can all seat themselves in this fashion and remain for many hours, without perceiving any attack of cold. Their heads alone are visible, for their bodies, up to their shoulders, are under cover. When the • circle is composed of young girls they become extremely animated, tease each other, throw fruit and nuts, and excite themselves by playful interchanges of kicks and blows. This kind of entertainment is sometimes attended with serious results, as the foot-warmer occasionally gets overturned, and sets fire to the house. Fires are of frequent occurrence at Constantinople, and their origin is often merely the upsetting of a *tandur*.

My two aunts and their brother were already married when my mother (who was named Constance), although twenty-five years of age, found herself still free, at a time when women in Turkey married at fourteen.

It was not that numerous opportunities did not present themselves. Extremely intelligent, she had received but little education, as is customary in the East in the case of girls. She only knew her mother-tongue, Greek. Tall, and with magnificent black hair, her dark complexion and dauntless carriage gave her an air of energy which was not belied by

her character. She had preferred to remain single
sooner than put up with an unsuitable match.

As my mother's house was situated in the native
quarter, where very few Europeans made their
appearance, those who did venture into that neighbourhood could not fail to excite remark. A young
European was frequently seen to pass, of tall stature
and of graceful bearing, always armed with a long
and slender sword. The ladies of that quarter
amused themselves by looking at him through the
wooden grating of their *djumbá.* One evening,
when my mother had half opened the wicket contrived in the thick lattice, in order to obtain a better
view of the stranger, the latter stopped to survey her,
and was struck with the beauty of her countenance.
Next day he appeared again before the window, and
threw my mother a note in French, in which he
avowed his passion for her. She caused him to
explain himself through the servant of a Marseilles
merchant, who moreover told her that she knew the
author of the letter to be a Frenchman, named
Charles Dejean, living at Constantinople on the
proceeds of a considerable quantity of valuables
which he possessed, and which he was selling by
degrees.

Satisfied with these particulars, my mother replied

in a note, which she sent him the next time he passed through the street, that she accepted his addresses, and that if he would demand her in marriage of my uncle, she was ready to marry him.

* Next day the Frenchman called on my mother's brother, who could speak a little Italian ; they came to an understanding, and my uncle being assured of his sister's consent, she was married to M. Dejean before the French consul. This occurred in 1810.

I was the second daughter, issue of this marriage, and I was born three years after it, during the temporary absence of my father, who had been compelled to take a journey into Wallachia. He had been there only a short time when a pestilent epidemic, which was prevalent in that country carried him off in the course of a few days. Thus it happened that I never saw my father.

My mother was a fervent Catholic, and had the reputation of being the most saintly woman at Constantinople. She had, however, very great trouble with me, on account of my resolute and wayward nature. There was an extraordinary incident connected with my birth, and to which my mother attached great importance. A severe pestilence having broken out in Constantinople, and several of her relations having died of it, my mother

became so alarmed that she removed from the city to
the little village of Kandili, about two leagues off.
The loss of her relatives and fear of the plague had
such an effect on her that sudden and unexpected
symptoms of maternity manifested themselves. She
knew no one, and there was no doctor in the
place.   In this sad state she sent her servant to
seek a nurse, or some one to come to her aid.
The servant had not gone far down the street when
she saw an old woman hobbling along, and leaning
on a stick.   She stopped her, and asked if she
knew of a nurse who would come to her mistress.
The old woman instantly replied, " I will come
directly."   Without saying another word, she followed the servant back to the house, and was
present at my birth.   After muttering a great
many prayers and benedictions over me, in an
unknown tongue, she took her departure with
that extraordinary taciturn ·and prompt manner
with which she had entered.   On leaving the room,
however, it was remarked that she took from two
capacious pockets handfuls of wheat, and strewed
them on the floor as she walked ; she scattered
the grain down the staircase and throughout the
house.   This was thought very strange ; however
no questions were asked, as it was expected she

would come back in the morning to be paid for her services. But she never returned, and my mother frequently sent all over the place, far and wide in the country, to search for the old creature, but she could not be found; in fact, it was denied that such a person had ever been seen or heard of. My mother being very credulous, entertained the firm belief that her nurse was a good old fairy-midwife, who had kindly given her services. I believe corn and wheat are, in all countries, emblematical of abundance and plenty; if so, the kind intentions of the stranger (whether in the flesh or not) in the supernatural sprinkling of the grain have often failed to be faithfully accomplished. My poor mother, who had but too frequent cause to correct me for my wild doings, always ended her reprovals by saying, " I can do nothing with you ; I am certain that old woman bewitched you at your birth, for you are not like other children." I readily own to being of a very remarkable nature, endowed with a restless temperament and untiring energy—qualities that have enabled me to endure many hazardous events and vicissitudes that any ordinary mortal would certainly have succumbed to.

My sister, who was of a very gentle disposition, bore

a strong personal resemblance to my mother; I differed entirely from both of them, as well from a physical as from a moral point of view. I was told that my features and my character had much similarity with those of my father.

All counted we were twelve children in my grandmother's house. Though the youngest, I assumed a certain authority over all the others; they listened to me, and obeyed me more readily than their own parents.

From the age of eight years I was specially remarked for my facility of learning and my high spirit. The master who came to teach us to read French and Greek, always questioned me last, although the youngest, and he seemed perfectly astonished to find that every day I knew my lessons better than did my elder companions. At the same time I was so boisterous that I could not be kept in order against my will; so far did I carry my pranks that I would often come home with my dress all in rags, from climbing the very tallest of the trees in our garden.

During the summer we left Constantinople to pass the season at Prince's Islands. It was in this semi-peaceful and semi-boisterous manner that my early years flowed on.

CHAPTER II.

WHEN I was thirteen years old, my mother sent me to a school kept by a Madame Barbiani, to learn a little embroidery and the rudiments of a simple education, such as at that time was ordinarily given to girls in the East. Having little or no taste for study, I learnt next to nothing during my stay, which lasted two years, as my nature could ill brook restraint of any kind; school discipline least of all. I was now a little more than fifteen, when one day my mother surprised me by saying she intended me to accompany her to an evening party. I was delighted at this, it being my first introduction into society. I must confess to a degree of vanity when I caught sight of myself attired for this grand occasion. How, indeed, could I be blind to the beauty I saw reflected in my mirror? I felt quite satisfied with myself, and went off highly elated. A new life was about to open before me.

That evening proved an eventful one. Amongst the guests there was a gentleman, lately arrived in Constantinople, who had been in the suite of Lord Byron during his sojourn in Greece. He was a tall, fine-looking man, of distinguished manners, intellectual, and a good linguist, speaking Greek almost like a native. Within a brief period, he asked my mother's consent to become my suitor. She at first hesitated, an account of his being a Protestant, but eventually, acceding to his repeated wishes, we were married soon afterwards by a priest of the Greek Church, my husband having a dislike to the ceremony being performed by a Catholic priest. This union, contracted so hastily, was not of long duration. There existed no sympathy between us, either in taste, temper, or habits. My husband was a serious, stern, and learned man, and I was a giddy, uneducated girl of fifteen ; the disparity in our respective ages also contributed towards estrangement, and at the expiration of five years we mutually agreed on being divorced.

I left Constantinople soon after, and being desirous of visiting Europe, I placed my children under the care of an amiable relative residing in

Rome ; and there I remained for several months, without feeling much change in the life compared with that I had been leading ; for, owing to the curious habits of my friends, who were strict devotees, I spent the time in almost as utter seclusion • as though I were in a Turkish harem.

My desire to escape from such thraldom, therefore, grew stronger every day, and the want of some fixed income on which I could depend in the future alone detained me. My husband at this time contemplated another marriage, and made overtures to me by which he hoped to obtain my acquiescence. I was informed that at Paris I would find deposited in the hands of a relative stipulations which, if I signed, would secure for me ample provision for my future maintenance, if I would consent 'to live in that capital; and thither I went, with a heart full of joyful anticipations. My dreams of happiness, however, were cruelly dashed when I found the conditions attached to the agreement I was to sign totally repugnant to my feelings as a mother. In this extremity, the change from the seclusion at Rome to an equally dull lodging in Paris was not to be endured. At Rome I found society endurable, and even sympathetic, but in Paris I was' thrown amongst unfriendly strangers. I almost sunk under

the weight of my difficulty.   Then it was that the
happy idea came into my head of laying my case
before the Turkish Minister, and appealing to him
for his aid and sympathy.

At this period Féty-Pasha was Ambassador for
Turkey at the court of Louis-Philippe.   My cousin
presented me to his Excellency, who received me
very graciously.   Féty-Pasha was a Turk of the old
school — an honest, good-hearted, and perfectly
straightforward man.   Such a one is rarely to be
found now-a-days in Turkey.   He was rather a
fanatic, but I have no right to blame him on
that account.   In purity of mind and manners he
was a bright example.   He told me he was
delighted to see me in Europe, and that he would
do all in his power to render my stay in Paris
agreeable.   "But," he continued, "I shall not be here
many months longer, as I intend returning to Constantinople, as I am going to marry a daughter of
the Sultan Mahmud."

A few days after my arrival, the Ambassador
sent me an invitation, by his secretary, to a ball at
the hotel of the Minister for War.   This was my
first ball in Europe, and I was greatly charmed and
astonished at the elegance and brilliancy of the
salle-de-danse; the dresses of the ladies absorbed

my attention, and above all I was puzzled at the
stooping, extraordinary posture of the French
gentlemen, who, hat in hand, advanced towards the
ladies with such a strange gait that I imagined they
were all rather lame and deformed. Great, however, was my surprise and pleasure on seeing
Reshid-Pasha, an old friend, talking to Féty-Pasha
as they were seated side by side on the ottoman.
As I knew Reshid-Pasha and his family intimately
at Constantinople, I went up to speak to him ; he
was very glad to see me, and told me he was going
to London, where he was appointed Ambassador
from the Porte. He added also, for my information,
that he was very pleased at the idea of going to
England, and that the young queen of that country
was very pretty and clever. He then made me
laugh very much by drawing my attention to the
same peculiar gestures of the French gentlemen I
had already noticed. "Look," said he, "Look at
them, with their hats in their hands, going up
to the ladies and entreating them to favour them
by dancing with them. How different it is with
us. We Turks, on the contrary, remain seated on
our divans, and expect the ladies to come and ask
us to grant them the favour of a few words." "I
hope," he went on to say, "that you will not be

persuaded to dance, for you know we could not endure to see you do such a thing." I said I had no idea of doing so ; but as soon as Reshid and Féty had taken their departure I accepted every invitation for quadrilles, and even waltzes, and I must confess that I passed a most charming evening. I heard with sincere regret, some years afterwards, that poor Reshid-Pasha had been poisoned by some of his enemies at Constantinople. I have often lamented his loss, for in all my after troubles up to the time of that lamentable event, he was always my friend, and ever ready to afford me his good advice and commiseration.

Soon after my first appearance in the salons of Paris I made the acquaintance of Kibrizli-Mehemet-Pasha, who was then military attaché to the legation. From our first interview the Pasha paid me great attention, and wherever we met in society he strove to make himself agreeable. These assiduities were soon followed by an offer of marriage, which I was rather disposed to accept, but I hesitated on account of my suitor's creed and nationality. I also felt a dread of the harem, the seclusion of which seemed to me an awful prospect. However a second and third offer proved irresistible, for Kibrizli-Pasha had gained my affections. I therefore decided on accepting him, thinking that, with his love, it would be far better for me to be in the harem even to remaining in Paris. It must be re-membered that I was then only twenty-two years of age, with no experience of the world, and deprived of my natural protector.

On the occasion of a grand *bal-costumé* given at the palace of the Tuileries, I received an invitation, and had an opportunity of seeing the good Louis-Philippe and his interesting family. It was a very brilliant affair, and the diversity of costumes dazzled me greatly. I was, however, surprised to find that a description of the costume I appeared in had been given in the French journals the following day, and had been much admired. My English lady readers will perhaps like to know what it was like. It was a Greek costume, which I had brought from Constantinople, and consisted of a very full and rather short skirt of pink silk, embroidered with gold. A white Broussa silk waistcoat, trimmed with Turkish point lace and large hanging sleeves of the same material. A green velvet jacket embroidered with gold, and a crimson *tarboosh*, or Greek cap, embroidered with pearls and long pearl tassels. My hair drawn off the forehead and fastened with a diamond pin, was allowed to fall in two long thick plaits. The ornaments consisted of a necklace and bracelets of diamonds, rubies, and emeralds, of Greek patterns. I was invited to dance several times, but of course was obliged to refuse in the presence of so many Turkish gentlemen; so I contented myself with looking on. At last S.A. Le Duc d'Orléans advanced and asked me for a waltz, and as etiquette forbade me to decline this mark of favour, I rose and took a few turns with my royal partner. The conversation of the Duke was very amiable, and he did me the honour to admire my costume, telling me that it was the prettiest in the room.

My stay in Paris was not of very long duration, for the departure of Féty-Pasha for Constantinople obliged me to follow the fortunes of my betrothed, who was the Pasha's *aide-de-camp*. I took with me a servant, a young negro, who had come from Bordeaux, and to whom I gave the name of Mustapha.

CHAPTER III.

On my arrival at Constantinople I waited on
Féty-Pasha. He referred me to one of his friends,
whose hospitality he had bespoken in my favour.
I therefore took up my residence in the palace of
Haïder-Effendi, which was situated in the quarter
of St. Sophia.

In this palace resided fifteen or twenty ladies,— '
mothers, step-mothers, aunts, sisters, cousins, step-
sisters, and other relatives of the master of the
house. It was a spacious abode, and luxuriously
furnished.

We passed the time very pleasantly together, in
conversation, dancing, music, listening to and telling
stories; in fact, seeking to entertain ourselves in
every way we could imagine.

It was then the time of the Ramazan, the Mussulman Lent. During this season their religion forbids them to eat, drink, or smoke all day long. At midnight a crier goes through the streets, beating a large drum (*daul*), and rousing all the inhabitants. The women then make ready the repast, for it is allowable to eat and drink till day-break. Then another cry goes round, forbidding them to take anything; they rinse their mouths, and sleep till nightfall. As I did not at all like to take my meals at night and sleep in the day-time, I used to put certain articles of nourishment on one side, and eat them secretly in the course of the day. This scheme was not my own invention, for very many people, including Pashas, do not scruple to provide for themselves in secret. At the same time, when they appear in the streets by day they keep up the farce, and assume the languid and fainting air of one suffering from starvation.

All through this month the rich keep open house. They receive all comers, and every poor person, after making his repast, is dismissed with a small present of money wrapped in a handkerchief.

During the nights of the Ramazan, the Mussulman youth of both sexes spend their time in wandering through the streets of Stambul, visiting the mosques, and frequenting the cafés and other places of amusement. They usually carry small lanterns of different colours—green, red, blue, &c. The effect produced by these masses of lanterns, casting a mysterious glimmer, was extremely original and attractive.

A Circassian lady, named Nazib-Hanum, the adopted daughter of the Sultan's sister, came on one of these nights to pay us a visit. She was of a spirited and playful disposition ; and, as for myself, I may venture to say, speaking for both, we were a good match.

Turning to me, she said, " If you are willing, my dear, let us go and dress ourselves up like men (for women are not allowed to enter the mosques), and we will go together to St. Sophia, to see the festival which is held to-night."

Putting on male apparel, and carrying small lanterns, we went to the mosque. On entering it we were completely dazzled. The columns were decked from top to bottom, with lustres of coloured glass; the Sultan's band was performing ; and the crowd was so dense that it was almost impossible to get in. After remaining for some time prostrated like the celebrants themselves, we wished to retire, and tried to find the door by which we had entered, but as there were a great number, we found our way out by a different one from that which we were seeking.

Presently, we heard two young men behind us call out, "Beyler! beyler!" that is to say, "Gentlemen! gentlemen! don't go so fast; come with us to a café, and take some refreshment." At these words, supposing that they had discovered our stratagem, we quickened our pace, without replying. They persisted, however, in following and speaking to us.

Seriously alarmed, we hurried on faster and faster. "I fear, my dear," said my companion, "if we are pursued much longer I shall be obliged to stop. These men must have suspected our trick, and are now pursuing us in earnest."

Wearied of this pursuit, we saw approaching us an old man of venerable appearance. We accosted him, and begged that he would escort us to the house where we were staying. Our followers asked him if he knew us. "They are strangers," he replied, "whom I am conducting to their home." When we returned we were worn out with fatigue. Nazib-Hanum stayed that night with me. In the morning she left, inviting me to visit her at the palace on the following day.

I went, accordingly, and she showed me over the ladies' apartments and those of the Sultan. The divan in her chamber was of red velvet, embroidered with pearls. Afterwards she made me seat myself in an immense room, and then Essemah-Sultan, the sister of the Sultan Mahmud, a lady already of considerable age, joined us. She was accompanied by several young ladies, one half of whom were dressed in male attire, and took her seat on a large gilded chair.

Some of them began to dance, and the princess invited me to follow their example. I was dressed in a magnificent costume, and mingled with the other young women. Nazib-Hanum, who had introduced me, accompanied us, in the most enchanting style, on a kind of guitar. Then there was a cry of " The Sultan ! " We were going to withdraw, when his sister invited us to remain, saying, " His Highness will be much pleased to see you thus."

Mahmud looked at us for some time, and then offered his hand to Nazib-Hanum, my chaperon, and took several turns about the room with her, conversing in the most animated manner. Returning to Essemah-Sultan, he told her that it would greatly oblige him if she would give him that young lady. She refused, saying that, if she gave him what he asked, he would keep to his new wife for three or four days, and then she would have to pass the rest of her life in a corner of the palace. He thereupon retired, and betook himself to his repast.

He did not appear to be a long time over it, for almost immediately after his departure we had all the dishes brought us that had appeared at his table. I was not sorry for this, for I had tasted nothing since morning.

When bed-time arrived Nazib showed me to her chamber, where a bed had been prepared for me beside her own. I was in bed, when I heard a knocking at the door. A young woman had come to ascertain whether she had found any letter. Opening a little wicket formed in the lattice of the window, she drew in a string, to which was attached a letter. She forthwith burst into peals of laughter, and quickly wrote another, which she fastened to the string and let down.

Calling the treasurer, she said to her in great glee : "It is the little rascal whom we have met so often that has written to me. I have replied that

I shall be happy to see him, and that he will see us to-morrow on the promenade, in the principal passage of the Bazaar."

On the morrow Nazib-Hanum took the princess's carriage, and I accompanied her, while two pretty little slaves dressed like men were following us on horseback. We soon saw a young gentleman approaching, who threw into the carriage some flowers, and a note. The young Circassian alighted, furtively spoke a few words to him, and contrived to hand him a letter unobserved.

This person was a Greek merchant of the Bazaar, of whom Nazib was enamoured. He was in no way remarkable for good looks, and as to money, he was a mere pauper, an adventurer who was seeking to make his fortune by marrying one of the court ladies. It must be said that Nazib was playing a dangerous game, for in selecting a Christian for a lover she ran the risk of being thrown into the Bosphorus in a sack weighted with shot.

Some time afterwards the news was spread that she had taken flight. This is how she managed it. She wrote to her lover to come to her, on a certain day, with a boat all ready before the palace, on the side nearest to the sea. Through some of the Greek women who are allowed into the harems to sell various articles to the inmates, she procured European clothing, including a thick veil to disguise her features. She took with her some diamonds and other valuables, which formed part of the marriage trousseau presented to her by Essemah-Sultan, who had intended shortly to give her in marriage. Taking advantage of the circumstance that European ladies frequently paid visits at the palace, while their husbands waited for them outside, she passed rapidly before the guards, who remarked among themselves that she bore a strong resemblance to the adopted daughter of the Sultan's sister. With the utmost coolness she took the arm of him who was awaiting her ; they got into a boat, embarked on board a vessel that was moving off, and took their leave of Constantinople and of Turkey.

The next day Essemah-Sultan sent for her protégée to go and pay homage to the Sultan Abdul-Medjid, her nephew, who had just come to the throne. In spite of all researches they were unable to discover the hiding-place of the young Circassian. It was only after a considerable interval that they learned she was married at Galatz to the lover who had carried her off.

After her marriage with the Greek, Nazib-Hanum had to endure many vicissitudes. Her husband made away with all her treasures, and ended his career with his bankruptcy. The poor woman was left a widow with twelve children. Finding it impossible•to live and support her large family, Nazib decided on seeking refuge among her former masters, and returned to Constantinople, an old woman and in rags. The Turks, instead of reproach-• ing her for her conduct, received her kindly, and they furnished her with the means of subsistence up to the present day.

The princess was a woman of strong passions, but, at the same time, of a most cruel disposition. She exercised great influence over her brother, the Sultan Mahmud. It is related of her that she• used to amuse herself by collecting together in her presence ten young Greeks duly shaved and painted, and making them dance in female costume. On several occasions her brother, hearing of the debauches to which she gave herself up with these dancers, had them seized and put to death, whereat his sister seemed to be not in the least degree affected.

Once, while taking a walk in the country, seeing a young peasant of prepossessing appearance, she

invited him to come to the palace with some
flowers, and other trifles.   Once admitted, nothing
more was ever heard of the unhappy youth : he was
massacred, after having afforded a pastime to this
capricious and cruel woman.

CHAPTER IV.

THE Ramazan once at an end, my lover, Kibrizli-Mehemet-Bey hastened to make the necessary preparations for the celebration of our marriage. Féty-Pasha, who had taken us under his protection, bore the greater part of the expense, and assisted us by every means in his power.

It was now the day following the night called Kadir-Gedjessi, which precedes by three days the termination of the Ramazan. During this night the minarets are illuminated with blackened lustres, forming verses and other sentences from the Koran. The Sultan repairs, with great pomp, to one of the mosques, amid the glare of torches, escorted by troops, preceded by bands of music, and accompanied by the great officers of state. The Turkish ladies take advantage of this occasion to

D

go out, and to converse more freely than they could in the daytime with those who drew near to their carriages to pay them compliments, and present them with bouquets and bonbons.

In the course of this day an old lady, the wife of the imam who was to celebrate our nuptials, called on me in her carriage and took me to the house of my future husband, which stood on an eminence overlooking Tophané. This building, surrounded by a garden, was very small; it comprised only three bed-chambers and a reception-room, forming the harem, besides a small chamber for the use of the men, or *sélamlik*. From this elevation there was a magnificent view. At our feet was the Bosphorus, and in the far distance, on the opposite shore, the smiling hills of Scutari. The furniture in the Oriental fashion, was of the greatest simplicity.

After accompanying the Sultan to the mosque, Kibrizli-Mehemet-Bey arrived, followed by a general and another officer of rank, and the imam or priest. The nuptial ceremony is very simple in the case of those who have been married before. The lady draws near to the door of the harem; the bridegroom and the imam are on the other side. The latter asks each of the parties three times whether he or she respectively will take the other in marriage ; on receiving a response in the affirmative thrice repeated, he recites a few prayers, and retires after taking a glass of sherbet. The witnesses then take their leave, the husband enters the harem, offers his hand to his bride, and remains alone with her.

In the morning the husband goes out, and his wife avails herself of his absence to bring forth her most beautiful attire. She adorns her head with a rich head-dress decked with brilliants, and placed over her loose-flowing locks, and dresses herself in long sweeping robes of silk embroidered with gold.

Our establishment was limited to an old woman and a black slave. All the windows were guarded by wooden gratings, some of them having in addition small balconies surrounded with trellis work, called in the language of the country *djumba*. We could see out of these windows without being seen. I could perceive that our garden was very fine, and, moreover, that there were four small doors giving access to the houses of some of our neighbours.

These doors presently opened, and admitted numbers of ladies, young and old, accompanied by their children, both girls and little boys of from six to eight years old. They entered my chamber without ceremony, to see, as they said, the new comer.

They made me the subject of their comments :—

" This lady is indeed beautiful, Mashallah!" said one.

" Are you a Turk or a Circassian?" enquired another, on coming near me.

" I am a Georgian," I replied.

" Have you not a sister?" asked a third; "because I have a son to whom I should be happy to give a wife such as you."

" I have no sister."

After each question they conversed together, either in Turkish or Circassian. As some of them left, others came in, and plied me with questions as idle as the preceding, without giving me a moment's truce.

Seeing that they lived in the same quarter with myself, and that they were all the mothers or wives of officers, I treated them with due consideration, and avoided giving them umbrage. I did not dare to take any repose in their presence, and feared I should offend them if I begged them to retire. They only left me towards nightfall.

Prudence constrained me to act in this manner. Indeed, the promotion of the officers is independent of any fixed rule; favour and caprice dictate their selection; the women also employ themselves actively in the matter, on behalf of their sons, their brothers, and their husbands. As they visit a good

deal, they try to ingratiate themselves with the
wives of the ministers or the generals in chief, and
these speak in favour of their protégées, when they
find themselves alone with their husbands, and, by
dint of importunity, obtain from them the steps
which they desire. It is nothing unusual for a
young man of five-and-twenty, who has never seen
active service, to be nominated general of brigade
or division, or promoted to some important naval or
military post. It is easy to understand that, with
such an organisation, the Ottoman troops lose the
benefit of the personal valour of the soldiers who
compose them.

Soon after our marriage, my husband received,
through the interest of Féty-Pasha, the title of *bey*,
or colonel, and three or four months afterwards, that
of *liwa*, or general of brigade. On this occasion he
had the honour of a visit from his general of division,
Gueuzluklu-Réshid-Pasha. After the customary
salutations, the latter imparted to Mehemet-Bey his
determination to marry. He begged my husband to
call me close to the door, so that, without being
seen, I could hear what he had to say on this subject.
Having no family connections, being a native of
Georgia, he was desirous that I should take upon
myself, in his behalf, those duties which, in the

choosing of a wife, ordinarily devolve upon some female relative.

As he had lived in Europe, he explained that he wished his wife to be tall and slender, as Europeans generally are, and that she should, moreover, have an agreeable expression of countenance.

I immediately entered upon the campaign; I dressed myself to the best possible advantage, and went, in succession, amongst all the families of equal rank with that of the general. In conformity with established usage, I contrived my visits of this kind in the following manner :—

I presented myself at the door of a house where I knew there was a marriageable daughter. "What do you want, Madam?" "I wish to see your young lady." Forthwith I was introduced into the drawing-room, where I sat down on a divan, whilst the young person was getting arrayed in her finest clothes. She made her appearance, saluted me with the handkerchief which she carried in her hand, and, with her eyes always fixed on the ground, proceeded to sit down on a seat placed in front of mine, and arranged expressly for her. Then coffee was brought in a small silver cup. The young lady stays all the time while it is in course of drinking; as soon as the cup is empty she withdraws; so that it is taken as slowly as possible, in order to afford a thorough inspection of that which one has come to see.

As soon as she has disappeared, one of her relatives, her mother or eldest sister, enters and inquires what one thinks of the young lady. To such a question one most naturally makes answer in the most eulogistic terms. Then the lady explains what the damsel is possessed of, both in clothes and jewelry, and states the amount of her dowry.

However, it does not do to trust implicitly to ' these representations. It often happens that after promising more than they are able or willing to give, the parents, when once the marriage is concluded, furnish a provision greatly inferior to what was held out in the first instance. There are no means of compelling them to fulfil their promise, because a contract previous to marriage is a thing unrecognised, and contrary to all received usages.

On taking my leave, I assured the family that I would explain everything to the person who had commissioned me, and that I would let them know if the match proved acceptable to him.

Every evening I gave my husband an account of my visits, and he reported the same to Gueuzluklu-Réshid-Pasha, who showed himself very hard to please. In one case he found too many relations ; in another not sufficient fortune : this one was built on too large a scale, or had blue eyes, whereas he preferred black ; that one was too old. In fact, not one of them could secure his choice. For twenty days I ceased not to assail the houses of the ulémas, the generals, the ministers and all the high dignitaries.

Weary of so much going about, and such useless applications, I resolved to speak, on behalf of the Pasha, to the very next damsel whom I happened to visit. · He had sent me, with this view, a bouquet, enriched with a magnificent diamond. I entrusted it to a Circassian whom I took with me, and directed my steps to the palace of Hafuz-Pasha, situated at Stiniah,· on the Bosphorus. His own wife came to receive me. Though about fifty years old, this lady had a magnificent arm and hand, of which I still preserve the recollection. She made me come into the drawing-room, where I found great delight in her conversation, on account both of the charming sweetness of her voice, and the spirit and brilliancy of her remarks. To hear and see the mother could not but dispose one favourably towards the daughter.

The latter soon appeared. She was tall, full of health, with regular features, and fair complexion ; she had a hand and an arm as beautiful as her mother's, but her hair and eyebrows were red, and her eyes were of a light chestnut colour. This was by no means what Gueuzluklu-Réshid-Pasha wanted, for he was seeking some one slight, and with black hair and eyes.

Tired of having gone to no purpose into so many houses, I decided at once in favour of this young lady, whose fortune was, moreover, very considerable. I placed on her head the present I had brought her, saying that his Excellency took her for his wife. When I returned home I rendered an account of my embassy, taking care to say nothing about the red hair of the betrothed maiden.

Some days after an apartment, superbly furnished, was prepared at the residence of Hafuz-Pasha for the future bride and bridegroom. I went to see the young lady, to ascertain whether she had procured suitable wedding attire. I took with me a skilled Greek woman, who died her hair, eyebrows, and eyelashes black, and this, added to the natural fairness of her skin, gave her a very agreeable appearance.

In spite of this precaution I had some fear as to

the result; indeed Gueuzluklu-Réshid-Pasha had threatened to discard his wife after the very first night, if he did not find her to his taste, and to make serious complaint of the matter both to my husband and myself.

The next morning Gueuzluklu-Réshid-Pasha came to the house, and, so far from making any complaint, highly commended my choice. He appeared well satisfied with the charms of his bride.

Some time afterwards he was appointed to the command of a military expedition, sent out to reduce the Koords to submission. When he set forth on this enterprise he took his wife with him, and so pleased was he with her that he never cast her off, nor took any other wife in addition. On his death, which occurred at Bagdad in 1864, he left her a considerable fortune.

CHAPTER V.

His former superior having departed, my husband had over him no longer a friend but an enemy, their political opinions being different. The chiefs successively in command belonged, in fact to a court clique, composed of worthless and corrupt individuals. There was first a son-in-law of the late Sultan Mahmud, Mehemet-Ali-Pasha, and then came Riza-Pasha, formerly chamberlain to the late Sultan. Both of them hid the real state of affairs from Abdul-Medjid ; their sole care being to augment their fortunes. On the contrary, Mehemet-Pasha was contented with his rights, and tried by every means to ameliorate the condition of his country.

Abdul-Medjid, when he came to the throne, had applied himself ardently to the furtherance of the

civilizing movement inaugurated by his predecessor,
Mahmud. He saw plainly that the old system
threatened the empire with certain ruin. It was,
in fact, entirely based upon the formidable militia forces of the Janissaries—men of indomitable
courage, and of unbounded devotion to the interests
of the nation, and whose authority kept the people
in complete subjection. Unhappily they were not
content to play a subordinate part to the Sultan;
they wished to be his masters, and it was this that
worked their destruction. When once this militia
was put down, means must be found of giving a
new basis to the Ottoman organization. The Sultan
thought that this could only be obtained through
the reform of abuses.

Of a character extremely gentle, and little formed
for strife, Abdul-Medjid met with invincible resistance to the execution of his designs from the old
Mussulman party, very numerous to this day, but
at that time represented by an immense majority,
both amongst the government officials and the
people, who believed the safety of the empire to
consist in the rigorous application of Mohamedan
principles, the abasement of infidels, and their extermination both at home and abroad.

The Sultan, paralysed in regard to his projects

relative to internal administration, was thrown into
consternation at the progress which foreign policy
was making at this epoch, in seeking to profit by
all the misdeeds of the Ottoman government towards Christian populations, by extending dominion
over them. In utter despair he saw that his efforts
would be powerless to retard the fall of the power
of the Osmanlis.

His ministers, far from endeavouring to revive ·'
his hopes, persuaded him to forget, in sensual
delights, the sombre thoughts that assailed him.
" You are our Sultan," they would say ; " to you
belong repose and pleasures ; the bustle and fatigue
of public affairs are our portion." While speaking
thus, they made it a rule to offer their master, as
frequently as possible, the most sumptuous repasts,
at which they induced him to drink copiously ; in
this manner they habituated him to the immoderate
use of wine and other strong drink, and led him to
abandon to themselves the reins of government.

They also endeavoured to distract him from
public affairs, by favouring his natural taste for
luxury and dissipation. They provided him with
as much money as he asked for, knowing that they
could have their own way as long as the sovereign,
confining himself to his palace, knew nothing of

what was passing out-of-doors, except through their own reports.

The Sultan's love for his wives—and very numerous they were—was ruining the country. They contrived at once to gratify their caprices, whatever might be their object. They availed themselves of it to obtain from him the most costly presents. Covered with diamonds, and attended by numerous slaves, almost as sumptuously attired as their mistresses, they drove out in carriages, each of which, with its equipments, costs about 900,000 piastres (£8,000). Their apartments were constantly replenished with new furniture. In the space of two years the Seraglio was furnished about four times over.

Far from recompensing their master for his kindnesses by their fidelity, they were seen driving about, almost entirely unveiled, and conversing with the young men in the most lively manner. At night, sitting at their windows, they accosted the passers-by, and introduced them into the palace. Those who were without paramours formed quite the exception. Frequently the favours of one of the Sultan's wives, or odalisques, were attended with bounties and presents big enough to make the fortune of him who received it. In fact, these women were utterly regardless of the costliness of what they bestowed; it was a regular case of pillage.

The Sultan, who was of a kindliness of disposition carried to the very verge of weakness, refused to credit the reports that reached him, either against those whom he loved or any other lady. If he paid little attention to what was told him against his wives, he was so ready, on the other hand, to listen to the latter that he could deny them nothing. It was sufficient to be, or be acquainted with the favourite of one of the ladies of the Seraglio to arrive at wealth or one of the highest dignities. The Validé-Sultan, the mother of the sovereign, was the most powerful of all, and far surpassed all the other ladies of the palace by her libertinism and thirst for power. Judge what consequences such a system must produce throughout the whole range of administration.

The way Abdul-Medjid behaved to Besmé-Hanum, one of his wives, will show how far he pushed his weakness. Having gone one day to pay a visit to Missirli-Hanum, widow of the famous Ibrahim, Pasha of Egypt, he perceived a slave whose beauty made so lively an impression on his heart, that he had only one desire—to gain possession of her.

She, informed of the passion with which her charms had inspired him, refused to become the Sultan's concubine. She would not consent to hearken to his addresses unless he would take her to wife. At this reply the Padishah was greatly embarrassed. His power, great as it was, availed not to compel a slave to yield to his desires (the slaves are of much less consequence than might be supposed); on the other hand, a Sultan had never contracted marriage; in taking a wife, he was violating all established usages.

His passion and his character coming to his aid, Abdul-Medjid decided on the pleasant course; he consented to marry the object of his affections. Their nuptials were celebrated with dazzling magnificence, and—a rare thing with an Ottoman sovereign—he proved faithful. He not only loved his wife but esteemed her. He went so far as to confide to her his own son, a boy of about seven years old, whose mother was dead.

The Sultana, instead of responding to the passionate love which had been testified for her, preferred to engage in intrigues with the humblest servants in the palace—gardeners, porters, etc. Inspired with jealousy, she regarded with hatred the infant whose young age and rank she ought to have respected. She saw in him an insurmountable obstacle in this respect, that, if she gave birth to a son, her offspring could never reign. She incessantly maltreated the young prince; she went so far as to bite him severely in the arm. No one dared to inform his Majesty of what was taking place; enamoured as Abdul-Medjid was, he might refuse to believe what was told him, and then woe to the informer!

A faithful servant, however, found an opportunity of making known to his master the state of affairs, without compromising himself. Being occasionally employed to divert the Sultan with the entertainment called the Kara-Gheuz (theatre of Chinese shadows), he had the privilege of composing small pieces. He availed himself of this licence to represent before his sovereign a kind of comedy, in which the leading characters were an amorous Sultan who marries a slave, and a Sultana who prostitutes her favours to the lowest servants of her household, and ill-treats the heir to the throne, ending by killing him, and being forgiven by her weak and infatuated husband.

Abdul-Medjid understood the allusion. He sent for the young prince, questioned him, drew from him the avowal of his sufferings, and discovered on

x

his person the marks of the cruel treatment which he had undergone. The reader, perhaps, supposes that, infuriated with jealousy, and indignant at the conduct of Besmé towards his son, he had her sewn up in a sack, and thrown into the sea. Far from it. Temperate even in his rage, he sent for the Validé-Sultan, and, without giving any motive for his conduct, he ordered her to have Besmé-Hanum, together with all the riches he had heaped upon her, sent away on the morrow, in a pleasure-galley which he had presented to her.

Once outside the Seraglio, this woman continued, with revolting effrontery, the series of her misdeeds. Having openly formed intimate relations with a certain Tefik-Pasha, she succeeded in getting herself married to him, braving the displeasure of the Padishah. This is the first case recorded in Ottoman history where the wife of a Sultan has intermarried with an ordinary mortal.

The Pasha in question, notwithstanding his very limited salary, passed his life in the midst of amusements, contracted debts, and swindled all who had any dealings with him.

Tefik's rash conduct was naturally calculated to bring upon him the anger of Abdul-Medjid, and the scorn of his faithful subjects. It is true that the unhappy man was the victim of a violent passion, for he loved Besmé to distraction ; but the Turks are inexorable towards treasonable offences. To take a woman to wife who had been kept by the representative of Mohamed is to them a kind of religious and political sacrilege.

It was not long before Tefik-Pasha expiated his crime by a premature death. This capital penalty was exacted with all the ingenuity and circumspection of which Oriental diplomacy is capable.

At first Abdul-Medjid made a show of regarding with an indifferent eye the marriage of his former wife ; and he even carried the deception so far as to give up to Besmé one of the palaces belonging to the crown. Having thus succeeded in bringing about a change in public opinion, the Sultan, under an entirely futile pretext, exiled both Besmé and her husband to Brussa. There Tefik would, undoubtedly, have been made away with, but caution was necessary, and it was decided to make the unhappy Pasha return to Constantinople to drink hemlock. Tefik therefore received a pardon, and returned to Constantinople, where he died a few months afterwards. The former caresses and the latter pardon produced the desired effect, for no one ever suspected the cause of Tefik's death. Besmé was the object of the Imperial clemency, and her life was spared.

At the period of my marriage Riza-Pasha was Minister for War, and Mehemet-Ali-Pasha commander at Tophané; my husband served under the latter. These two came to an understanding with several other officials of high rank, and induced the Sultan to accept an invitation to the Seraskeriate, the residence of the Minister for War. Their object was to prejudice their sovereign against Mehemet-Pasha and his political friends. " You ought," said they to his Highness, in the course of the entertainment, "to purge the army of certain incompetent officers, who occupy important posts without doing any service. Mehemet-Pasha, for instance, gives himself up to culpable idleness; and, more than that, his arrogance is most overbearing, and his character rude and obstinate. He sets an example of failure of respect towards his superiors, and we think that his degradation, and that of others like him, would be a wholesome example to the army; it would afford an opportunity of replacing inefficient officers by men of more energy, and endued with the zeal and knowledge necessary for command."

As we have seen, the Ministers had habituated

their master to excess in drink. Whenever they wanted to get anything out of him, they took care to ply him with wine to such a degree that he was no longer in complete possession of his faculties. This plan they adopted at the banquet in question, so Abdul-Medjid replied that they had his entire confidence, and that he approved beforehand of the course they were going to take.

On the morrow, the degradation of twelve generals was proclaimed, my husband being of the number. Before we had learnt anything of what was going on, the Seraskier sent to demand from Mehemet-Pasha the surrender of his sword, and his decoration in diamonds, the distinctive marks of his dignity. This was a terrible blow, which our enemies dealt him to effect the ruin of both of us.

After some time we left the rented house which we had occupied, and purchased a new residence. One half of the price, about 20,000 francs (800*l.*), was paid through the sale of what little property we had left. This house contained twenty-seven apartments, but required many repairs, having been built more than one hundred and twenty years before. The reception-rooms were lighted by fourteen windows, arranged in two rows, one above the other, the upper being filled with small stained glass. In the centre

of the largest room was a handsome fountain, open
to the air, and entirely of white marble ; the spacious
and magnificent bath, of the same material, had cost
upwards of 40,000 francs (1,600*l.*).

Our furniture was barely sufficient to furnish
two chambers in the harem and one in the selamlik,
or men's quarters.

The garden, in which there was a pretty kiosque,
was planted with abundance of shrubs, flowers and
fruit trees, as various as they were rare.

The purchase of this house had exhausted all our
resources. Consequent on his degradation, Mehemet-
Pasha's salary was reduced to 300 francs (£12) a
month ; all the ordinary allowances of fuel, rice,
oats, bread, and other things which constitute the
wealth of an officer's household, were stopped. We
found ourselves exposed to the claims of workmen
whom we had employed on improvements absolutely
necessary to render some of the rooms habitable.
All this placed us in a situation of great embarrassment, notwithstanding that two black slaves formed
our entire domestic establishment.

Claims became more and more pressing. We
had no means of satisfying them, and they reached
such a point that my husband was obliged to conceal himself whenever creditors presented their

appearance at his door. As we lived in a somewhat remote quarter, they generally came mounted
on asses. As soon as the step of one of these
animals was heard, Mehemet-Pasha shut himself up .
in a closet. The creditor, having asked to see the
master of the house, and been told in reply that he
was not at home, proceeded to seek for him all over,
and to shout out demands for payment. We used
to hear of course their abuses and harsh words, but
we endured all these humiliations without a word.

My sole consolation, under these annoyances, ·
was in the society of the ladies of the neighbourhood, who often paid me visits to soothe my vexation. One of the most assiduous callers was the
daughter of old Rauf-Pasha, who had been nine
or ten times grand vezir. Barely three feet high,
she had extremely small eyes, and, to crown her
defects, her chin wagged incessantly. She told me
her history, and I think I shall entertain my readers
by relating it here :—

" My father married four wives in succession—
three Circassians and a Georgian ; and they presented him with a numerous family. But my
mother (wife No. 1), never had any child but
myself. She displayed great disappointment on
seeing me grow up to be what I am, since all the

rest of the Pasha's offspring were well-grown, and endowed with good looks. I have seen all my brothers and sisters united, one after another, to the families of ministers, generals and other high functionaries; it seemed impossible that I could ever find a husband.

" In the meantime, however, a certain old governor died, leaving an only son, a very good-looking youth, named Mustapha-Bey, to whom he left nothing but a dilapidated mansion. He, finding himself bereft of all resources, resolved to marry some one whose family was in a position to further his career in public life. He therefore engaged the services of an old woman, who suggested to him that he should take me for his wife. When my father heard of this extravagant project he was greatly astonished at it, and could not refrain from expressing the scorn which he felt for the young man, who, from motives of ambition, was willing to take such a woman as myself. He declared that he would give nothing for such a marriage.

" My mother, anxious to see me provided for, as were the daughters of her rivals, summoned her future son-in-law, and told him that her husband would grant no dowry to his daughter. As the suitor had not calculated on money, he agreed

without hesitation to take me to wife. Although
no mystery had been made with him about my
insignificant stature, he was far from suspecting
that I was of such singular plainness as he beheld
the moment he raised my veil.

" Driven to desperation, he left me at home, and
went off immediately to join the army. He had no
relation among the superior officers, but as they
were aware that he was the son of a governor,
and the son-in-law of a· Grand-vezir, they promoted him rapidly, thinking by that means to pay
their court to the father-in-law. This young man
had seen six months' service when the title of *bey*
(colonel) was conferred upon him ; shortly afterwards he received his nominations as *liwa* (general
of brigade) ; and scarcely three years had elapsed
when he was promoted, first to the rank of *ferik*
(general of division), and then to that of *mushir*
(field-marshal). To earn all these distinctions he
had nothing to do but to stay quietly at home,
drinking, smoking, and sleeping.

" Seeing that it was on account of his wife that
such great advantages were accorded him, he became reconciled to me ; we live on very good terms,
and I am now quite satisfied with my lot. You
see " (she added, to comfort me), " that after finding

myself most wretched when my husband had deserted me, I have now everything that I can wish for. Do not be discouraged; perhaps your present embarrassments will be succeeded by an unlooked-for turn of fortune."

While speaking to me in these terms, the poor lady little suspected that the husband with whom she was so well pleased, had taken a house, where he used to go on the sly, and divert himself with the society of two young slaves whom he had purchased.

In spite of the privations which our narrow circumstances imposed upon me, I was not so despondent as might be imagined; my attachment to my husband sufficed to make me forget both our debts and our penury.

As for Mehemet-Pasha, he was completely broken down; his evil fortune so affected him that he fell ill, and though he recovered by slow degrees, his health was never completely re-established.

Knowing what abrupt changes take place in Turkey, where the same caprice that has brought you low may replace you on the highest pinnacle of greatness, I endeavoured, but in vain, to console him. "One day the privileges of which you have been deprived will be restored to you," I said; "to-day our enemies triumph, but they will not be always in power. Take care of your health, and do not abandon yourself to these despairing thoughts, otherwise, when you are again received into favour, you will be suffering from the consequences which illnesses leave behind them, and then you will be unable to enjoy in peace the good things that fortune will offer you."

The master of the household was not the only one to disorder himself. The two black slaves, of one of whom I was extremely fond, and one of whom was an Abyssinian of great beauty, were so deeply touched at the sight of our sufferings that they contracted a fatal sickness which carried them off in the course of one and the same month. I remained alone with two young children whom I then had.

Whilst my husband was confined to his bed by rheumatism, my little boy, Moharem-Bey, fell sick and died. His father felt such grief at his loss that, in his despair, he beat his head against the wall. For my part, I assumed a delusive tranquillity, and, concealing the agony I endured, I strove, to the utmost of my power, to raise my husband's spirits.

CHAPTER VI.

WE continued for two whole years in the unhappy condition which the degradation of my husband had brought about. At the end of this period I resolved to call on Riza-Pasha. "Your Highness," said I, "I am the wife of Mehemet-Pasha. For three years past he has been oppressed by claims of every description; so great is his despair on seeing himself deprived of every resource, and rendered wholly incapable of supplying the wants of his family, that his life is in danger. I am come to demand from you the reason of such disgrace. If caprice has been the only motive, then a fresh exercise of good pleasure may restore to him the employment he has lost." "Madam," replied the Seraskier, " the recall of Mehemet-Pasha was caused by the insubordinate language, which he sometimes indulged in, regarding certain persons in high station, of whom he should have spoken with great reserve." "That," I replied, "would scarcely have called for a punishment of from fifteen to twenty days, and certainly does not merit so great an infliction as to be given up for two years to all the sufferings which poverty brings in its train. Your Excellency," I added, "it is in vain for you to conceal from me the true cause of my husband's disgrace. His enemies are enemies to me; filled with hatred, they wished to destroy us because they saw us happy. It is on my account that my husband is persecuted, and for no other reason. If my enemies thirst for my blood, let them attack me openly and frankly; but I must say that it is unworthy of the Imperial Government to refuse its protection to a woman who has sought refuge beneath the shadow of the throne. Pray, therefore, give my husband some situation which will allow him to meet his duties as father of a family: if, however, your Excellency is determined not to employ him, at least restore him to part of the salary which has been withdrawn. I am determined not to go hence until you have acceded to my demands."

He returned me no answer; I therefore remained at his house, in a chamber which his favourite wife, Seraïli-Hanum, had provided for me in the suite reserved for herself. Morning and night I went to renew my application to Riza-Pasha. In the meantime I had left with my husband a personal friend to take care of him. On the tenth day the Seraskier cried out, as soon as he saw me : "I see you are a determined woman, and it will·be impossible to escape from you. To satisfy you, I appoint Mehemet-Pasha governor of Akiah (St. Jean d'Acre) ; he will receive his nomination without delay" (1843).

The commission was sent us shortly afterwards, but we could not leave Constantinople without satisfying our creditors ; and, moreover, we wanted money for the journey. I went a second time to Riza-Pasha, who granted us funds for the expenses of our departure and the payment of our debts. Still the amount allowed was very moderate ; and, after converting all our furniture into money, and paying our creditors, my husband had barely enough left for his own expenses, and found it impossible to take me with him.

I remained, therefore, at Constantinople, at the house of one of his friends. At the end of eight months Mehemet-Pasha sent his cavasbaschi (chief of the cavas, or police) to escort me to his quarters, together with my daughter Aïsheh, then two years old. I purchased a slave ; we set out for Beyrout, and on our arrival took a sailing vessel, which landed us at Akiah. The Pasha was waiting for us with an escort.

The town, built entirely of mud (*pise*), presented a deplorable aspect. The houses, low and covered with mats, looked like the ruins of a conflagration. That which was called the palace—the governor's residence,—also of mud, contained two chambers ; that on the upper storey was reached by means of a staircase outside the building ; when it rained the water soaked through the roof. Two other rooms, situated in the garden, served as my husband's government offices.

The population was Arab. These creatures, naturally thieves and cheats, carried habits of uncleanliness to the most extreme degree. The only tolerable place in the whole town was the palace of Abdallah-Pasha, then away at Constantinople, the garden of which, planted with orange-trees, citron, olives, palms, and other Oriental trees, was the only promenade, and the most beautiful spot in the neighbourhood. As will readily be seen, the post, though defended by imposing fortifications, did not offer many advantages, nor many opportunities of enjoyment.

After we had been there three months a messenger, arriving at night, announced to my husband that he had been nominated to the command of Jerusalem, with the rank of *Wali*, or governor. We set off on our journey thither soon afterwards.

In going from Akiah to Jerusalem, we had to traverse an extremely poverty-stricken country. The sheiks of the several villages came on horseback, making profound bows as they raised themselves in the stirrups, but none of them ventured to cast their eyes on the litter in which I was seated. This modesty, real or assumed, is one of the characteristics of Oriental etiquette and manners.

While the sheiks were thus passing in review before us, their escorts received us with the sound of *tamburas*, amid various evolutions performed by the *dehlis*, or bravos of the troop. As for the lodging accommodation placed at our disposal, throughout our route, in the different villages, all I can say is that we were lodged in frightful hovels, infested with vermin. We were obliged to content ourselves with the food prepared for the inhabitants. It is impossible to mention what refinement of nastiness formed a leading feature in this horrible *cuisine*. The only place at all suitable that we met with on our route was Jaffa,· where we spent some days.

We stayed at the palace of the governor, Mustapha-Bey, who lodged us in his kiosque, which was surrounded by eight gardens planted with orange and other trees, that filled the air with their delicious perfume. I remained there while my husband turned his time to account by visiting the neighbourhood; for, in the capacity of *Wali* of Jerusalem, he held command over the whole province, or *vilayet*, and the *mudir* of Jaffa was under his control.

In the meantime, the neighbouring Arabs found out that the Pasha had gone from home, leaving his harem at Jaffa. My husband had given me for my protection two hundred *misracks*, or lancers of the irregular forces, commanded by a *Dehly-baschi*, literally "head of the mad-men." This officer, wearing red morocco boots, his loins enveloped in a large shawl, and a gigantic turban on his head, always placed himself, on the march, at the head of his troop of horse. These two hundred men were encamped around the kiosque where I was living with my daughter, four female slaves, and a eunuch. One night a stone, passing through

F

the opening in the roof (for the houses in this country were not closed in above), fell in the hall which surrounded our apartments. This was repeated twice; I then got up, and told the eunuch to go and inform the Dehly-baschi of what had taken place.

"Tell your mistress not to be alarmed," he replied; "there is, in this garden the tomb of a holy personage who has an antipathy to the people of Constantinople; every time they come into this kiosque he makes stones fall in this manner. This will continue all the time you are living here, but if you do not go into the hall these stones will not harm you."

The eunuch having returned with this reply, I wrapped myself in a *feradje*, veiled myself with my *yashmak*, went in quest of the Dehly-baschi, and told him that I certainly did not believe it was a dead man who threw the stones, and that he must go the round, and see whether he could not discover some thief concealed on the premises. He took with him several of his men, and accompanied by the eunuch, we went over the gardens in every direction, without finding anything suspicious. Scarcely had I re-entered my kiosque when I was roused by another missile. From the manner in which it was sent, it must have been a man armed with a sling who had hurled it over the roof.

In the morning I summoned the governor's wife, and told her that, being greatly afraid of dead men, I would stay there no longer. I wrote to my husband to inform him of what had taken place, and to ask him to come and take me away. He directed me to go and wait for him at Ramleh, and he would rejoin me there.

Before I left Jaffa the mudir's wife sent me a present of a pair of ear-rings of brilliants and emeralds, and upwards of 3,000 francs (£120) in gold. "If you refuse my trifling gifts," she said, "I shall think you are dissatisfied with us, and that you design to send another governor to Jaffa." I thereupon accepted her offerings.

Before we left Constantinople, Reshid-Pasha, my husband's patron, whose sentiments he shared, had spoken to me in the following terms:—"You are going to Arabia: do not, I beseech you, accept any present. We have promised upon oath that nothing more shall be received by the governors and other officials, on the part of their subordinates. I trust, therefore, that you will give no cause of complaint on that score."

"Surely not," I replied; "my husband shall not

receive any present, since you have forbidden him; but you cannot oblige me to refuse what the ladies may choose to offer me; that has nothing to do with politics or with the administration."

" Of course not," he rejoined, with a smile.

Mehemet-Pasha therefore refused all the presents that were offered to him; and when this was ascertained they were always sent to me.

Shortly after receiving the adieus of the family of the mudir of Jaffa, I left that place, and betook myself to Ramleh, where Mehemet-Pasha was awaiting me, with a numerous escort, formed of the authorities of various towns subject to his authority; and so we continued our journey to Jerusalem.

CHAPTER VII.

HALF a league from Jerusalem we were met by a regiment of infantry, headed by its band, and a crowd of inhabitants who had come to congratulate the new Pasha. We entered the city amid the roar of artillery, and proceeded to the palace, which contained only four or five chambers in the harem, and three for the selamlik, which was below the women's apartments.

Facing our residence was the mosque called Harem-Scherif, in which is preserved the stone whereon Mohamed is said to have set his foot when the angels had transported him to Jerusalem on the night of his ascension to heaven. This stone, about twelve feet high, was raised aloft at the moment that the prophet left the earth, and it has remained suspended ever since. I have indeed seen it; but as it is quite close to the wall, and it is im-

possible to get round it, it may very probably be
supported by some clever contrivance. At the back
of this mosque is a street where they show you a very
thick piece of marble, into which people assure you
that the Virgin Mary was consigned immediately
after her birth.

In that locality is also to be seen the Golden
Gate, through which, according to Moslem tradition,
all men are to pass on the Resurrection day.

The town of Jerusalem consists of narrow,
crooked, and dirty streets; it is only remarkable
for its antiquities. The climate is very agreeable;
neither too hot in summer nor too cold in winter.
It may be compared to that of Nice.

The inhabitants, for the most part Arabs, are very
troublesome to manage. They have no lack of intelligence, as is shown by their countenances, but
they are great cheats and robbers, and do not
scruple to commit murder. When they think they
have a favourable opportunity, they arrange their
plans together, sally forth from the city, to the
number of forty or fifty, and set to work, waylaying
and robbing travellers, sacking villages, and com-
mitting other depredations. They are objects of
abhorrence to the Turks, who regard them as
miscreants; instead of submitting quietly to the levy

of taxes, and contributing readily, they only pay '
under the stimulus of the bastinado.

As soon as they can secure a certain livelihood,
they take three or four wives; the very poorest
have at least two. They lead them wretched lives.
Besides being excessively jealous, they are such
violent characters that they are constantly beating
their wives. It is true that three or four rivals, with
their children, all living with one husband, in one
room, huddled together like beasts, cannot be expected
to exist on the best of terms with one another.

There were three principal convents in Jerusalem
at that period: the Franciscan, the Greek, and the
Armenian. No repairs, nor any change could be
effected in either of them without the permission of
the Pasha; and he, having pledged himself to
accept no presents, was never in a hurry to accede
to their demands; so the good fathers adopted the
expedient of applying to me, and endeavouring to
secure my favour in their interest. One or other of
these bodies would send me, sometimes a beautiful
watch, sometimes a diamond pin or a pearl necklace;
in fact they seemed to be rivalling each other in
their mania for making presents.

The Franciscans, though such a thing had never
been done before for any Turkish woman, invited

me to a collation. I went; sixty young girls were drawn up in line at the door of the monastery. The fathers of the convent of the Holy Land came out to meet me; they laid before me a magnificent banquet; afterwards one of the priests played the organ, whilst the others accompanied him with their chants.

The Jews, as natural, remained at the tail of the presents-offering multitude. The steward of our household, a man who knew the secret of extracting money from people's pockets, came one day to say that, if I pleased, he would find the means of getting me far more from the Jews than I had obtained from all the others. "Do whatever you think fit," I replied.

He went upon this and told the rabbis that he warned them, in their own interest, the governor intended to make them take away an enormous heap of rubbish that impeded the traffic in the neighbouring streets, and had been accumulating, for probably forty years, at the back of one of their synagogues. "I fear," added the crafty steward, "that you will only be allowed one day to effect its removal."

At this news the Jews were thrown into consternation.

"Alas!" they cried, "it is impossible to remove

such a mass in less than several months' labour, and without great expense; but, my friend," said they to their informant, " there is surely some means of appeasing your master."

" No," he replied; "he is inaccessible to every influence; but, if you will listen to a friend, I will tell you that the best intercessor with the Pasha is his wife."

" Ah! what good advice you give us!" they exclaimed; "we know now how to escape from the fatal difficulty, which, no doubt, some enemy of ours has suggested to the governor."

On the morrow they sent me a beautiful casket, containing several pearl necklaces, and 10,000 francs in gold: it need not be said that they never heard anything more about the nuisance, or its removal.

On another occasion the same steward informed me that one of the judges had been guilty of numerous exactions, and that, with my approbation, he would squeeze him a little and obtain from him a present.

" What will you do?" I asked.

" Very little. It will be sufficient," replied the steward, "to tell the judge that the governor desires to speak to him."

Accordingly he called on the magistrate, who,

feeling that his conscience was by no means clear, was greatly alarmed at such a summons.

" Oh," he cried, "those who administer justice are sorely exposed to the risk of displeasing folks. I am sure that some one has been making mischief about me with his Excellency. What can I do to appease him ? "

" You know," replied the smart steward, " that it is impossible to bend him; but, if you are willing to believe me, and to charm away the danger that menaces you, address yourself to his wife. She alone has any influence over him."

Next day the judge's wife hastened to pay her court to me, and laid at my feet a magnificent present, worth upwards of 40,000 francs.

" Pray," said she, with a submissive air, " do me the favour to accept what I offer you; if you refuse me, I shall see that you desire my ruin; if, on the contrary, you keep this little present, that will be as much as to say that you approve of my humble service. I shall have no longer anything to fear from anyone, if you once grant me your protection."

All this took place unknown to the governor. In a short time I amassed property to the value of upwards of four hundred thousand francs, partly in specie, partly in jewellery and trinkets of every

description. This course of action was suggested by
the remembrance of previous reverses. It appeared
to me that, at any moment, we might find ourselves
anew in the painful situation from which we had
emerged so suddenly. In a country where one '
has no recognised rights and no security, it is
necessary to take precautions against the reverses of
fortune.

Not wishing to remain shut up in the town, I
had a magnificent taktaravan, or palanquin, made for
me, of red velvet fringed with gold. Accompanied
by slaves and eunuchs, and escorted by a troop of
about two hundred misrachs, I used to go out
beyond the walls once a week, and pass the day on
some elevated spot in the suburbs, from which I
enjoyed a view of the country, while I occupied
my time in reading or in some feminine handiwork.
The muskets of the escort, piled like fascines in
order around me, formed a barrier against the
importunate attentions of the natives, who fre- '
quently came in great numbers to look at me.

I had formed a friendship with the wife of the
Greek consul at Jaffa, who had come to pass the
season at Jerusalem. She frequently visited me,
and I conversed familiarly with her on all subjects
in which I took an interest. Young, a native of

Athens, and of lively temperament, I found great pleasure in seeing her, and in talking with her in the Greek language. This lady feeling highly honoured by the friendship which I displayed for her, plumed herself greatly on it before her husband, and warmly eulogised my spirit, and my readiness in speaking the Greek, Italian, Turkish, and French languages.

The consul, a man of high spirit, like most Greeks, and, moreover, somewhat addicted to intemperance, took a fancy to me from his wife's account, and conceived a violent desire to see me. The lady told me the state of affairs : " My husband," said she " despairs of finding an opportunity of speaking to you ; he is sometimes so furious on that account that he breaks everything in the house." We both made merry and joked over this whim of the Consul, but the whim soon turned out a serious affair.

One day, when, having gone beyond the walls of Jerusalem, I was seated on a neighbouring eminence, surrounded by the arms of my escort, I saw a Greek approaching, dressed in his national costume : high cap, jacket of red cloth, embroidered with gold and elegant fustanelle. It was the consul in question.

Addressing the Dehly-baschi, he said that, the Pasha being away, he desired to hand me an important document, which it was urgently necessary that my husband should receive.

He was allowed to come within the barrier, and gave me the despatch. I at once replied that I would give it to my husband, and that he might withdraw. Seeing the numbers that were present, he did not dare to stay, and took his leave forthwith. I related to the Pasha all that had passed.

For some time afterwards I saw no more of the Greek lady, and thought nothing further of her or her husband, when, one morning, I saw Mehemet-Pasha coming in a furious passion, holding in his hand an open letter, which he laid before me. It was from the consul's wife, informing him that her husband had conceived such a violent inclination for me that he was resolved to carry me off with the assistance of two hundred of his fellow-country-men resident at Jerusalem, who would think they were doing a praiseworthy action in rescuing a Christian woman from the hands of a Turk. Persuaded that it was utterly impossible that such a project could be successful, and that it could not fail to bring great trouble upon its authors, and, above all, upon her husband, she had resolved, she said, to reveal the whole plot to the governor.

The perusal of this letter afforded me the utmost surprise, but, without showing the least concern, I remarked to Mehemet-Pasha:—"Well; you know all about it; it is this crazy Greek of whom I told you before."

"Let him be as crazy as you please, he and his worthy accomplices shall learn of what I am capable."

For several days the Pasha treated me with excessive coldness. I was afraid that, on my account, he would take some fatal resolution, and that jealousy would prompt him to suspect that, being a Christian, I had formed an intrigue with an infidel.

I reassured myself, however; for, shortly afterwards, I learnt that the governor's wrath was turned against the Greeks. He had committed to prison a great many of those resident in Jerusalem, and placed a seal upon their houses. Persons were sent to the country-house where the consul was staying, to keep watch over him. The charge was that of plotting against the Pasha. In his opinion, this scheme, set on foot by the Greek consul, was no other than a conspiracy, of which the principal authors were my enemies at Constantinople. It was natural that, finding I had become rich and powerful, they should be biting their nails with vexation, and should have attempted to cause my ruin.

The governor lodged a complaint in high quarters. It was only after the recall of the consul by the Court of Athens, and on the entreaty of the Greek Patriarch, that he consented to restore the prisoners to liberty.

Easter was then approaching; before this festival the Pasha was accustomed to send to all the Mussulmans in the neighbourhood, no matter whether they were highway robbers, assassins, or charged with other crimes, letters of safe-conduct to admit them into the city during the fête. He acted thus in order to make the number of Mussulmans present as large as possible, and to keep in subjection the Christians, who came in crowds to take part in the religious ceremonies pertaining to the season.

On Palm Sunday I saw through my window-lattice the inhabitants of various villages in the neighbourhood marching past. Each township formed a kind of procession; men playing on tamburas led the way, then followed the sheiks, clashing huge cymbals, and after them the populace, both Mussulmans and Christians, bearing palm branches in their hands.

It happened that year (1845) that the different religious communities celebrated Easter on the same day. The Turkish troops occupied the old church of the Holy Sepulchre, under the command-in-chief of the governor. From a gallery, protected by gratings, for the wives of the principal Mussulman authorities, we could see all that took place in the basilica. In a moment innumerable lamps illuminated with their dazzling lights every part of the edifice.

In the first place the Catholics celebrated the sacrifice of the Mass; then followed the Greeks. After the latter had terminated their religious chants, the priests made the circuit of the Holy Sepulchre. The moment the day broke, a fire shot up from beneath the tomb, and blazed for a while over it. The Greeks cried out that it was the Holy Spirit that caused those flames to appear; and they lighted their candles at them. Men and women alike applied these candles to various parts of their bodies afflicted with any complaint, in the belief that they would thus heal themselves. Several were seriously burnt, but such was their fanaticism, that those who suffered most cried out the loudest that the heavenly fire could cause no pain.

At this moment a violent quarrel arose between

the Greeks and the members of another communion, who pretended that the former ought to leave the church, their time having expired. Both parties, seizing large tapers, dealt each other violent blows with these novel weapons. The cavas and the military interfered, and arrested fifty of the ringleaders.

The Pasha, wishing to learn the real state of the case as to the apparition of the flames, threatened the priests that they should be excluded from the Holy Sepulchre, unless they would reveal to him the cause of this mysterious fire. They then showed him that a block of marble placed near the altar was raised, and that one of the priests, concealing himself in a cavity designed for the express purpose, lit up some vessels filled with spirits of wine, the flames from which passed through several fissures in the marble flooring. It was impossible to discover the mystery, as the priest only emerged from his hiding-place after everyone had gone.

It may easily be imagined to what an excess of enthusiasm and frenzy such a proceeding can excite a superstitious people.

A few days after the celebration, the Christians, both male and female, betake themselves to the Jordan, where they bathe, under the surveillance of the military.   The popular tradition avers that, every year, one of the bathers is drowned, and that he or she is the most saintly of all the persons who perform that devotional ceremony.   Those who have taken part in it preserve with care the garment that has been wetted in the waters of Jordan, and after death they are shrouded in it, and so laid in their coffins.

On the same day the Mussulmans go in crowds to the mountain on which Moses died.   Here they pay their devotions, while their food is cooking on the black and brilliant stones, which burn like coal.   Of these stones beautiful cups are made, on which are inscribed sentences in Arabic ; it is said that to drink out of such cups confers health and happiness.

During these fêtes I remained in the palace, where the ladies of the principal dignitaries of the city came to call on me ; it is usual in the East to do so at the time of the chief solemnities of the year.   My fair visitors belonged to the most diverse nationalities : Moors, with light hair and fair complexions ; Arabs, with their expression full of pride ; Georgians and Circassians, with regular and pleasing features.   All brought their narghilés or pipes ; they seated themselves in a circle round me, and we

passed our time agreeably, chatting together with
the utmost freedom; for all etiquette is banished
from conversations amongst women.

Sometimes they spoke to me about their protégés.
"Could you not contrive," said one, "to procure
my brother his exchange? he is *caïmakam* of a
sandjak (department), and I am very anxious to
have him appointed to a better post." "Perhaps,"
added another, "Madame will be able to get me the
place of this *caïmakam*, of whom such complaints
are made." "It rests with you," observed the first
speaker, "to do me this service; I assure you that
you won't find us ungrateful; if you succeed we
will give you a beautiful present."

To all this I gave no answer; but the next day
I would call the steward or the secretary,—"Such
a person," I would say, "has been recommended to
me, and I have a promise that my good offices shall
not go unrequited: do what you can to procure a
favourable exchange, and you shall have your share
of whatever I may receive."

The official whom I thus addressed, knowing that
his place depended upon me, would seize the first
opportunity to speak to his master. "Your Excellency," he would say, "the caïmakam of such and
such a sandjak is giving cause for much com-

plaint; he is said to be accessible to bribes, and to be careless in the discharge of his duties."

" I have heard some reports about him, but I did not think they were serious."

" These reports are, unhappily, too well founded; and, although they may be somewhat exaggerated, would it not be better to have, at so important a post, some person in whom you could place entire confidence ? I know, for example, some one of the greatest zeal in your Excellency's service; he is thoroughly competent, and, if you will allow him to wait upon you, I feel assured that you will be pleased with him."

The interview being held, and the Pasha satisfied, the exchange is effected, and I receive what has been promised me. In two years I disposed, in this manner, of more than fifteen important posts in favour of persons whom I had never even set eyes on.

Another means of procuring funds for myself was by engaging in commerce, a thing expressly forbidden to Pashas, but which I carried on in person, without the intervention of the governor in any respect.

The inhabitants are bound to furnish horses, mules, or camels for the public service, and this

without any remuneration. My agents demanded
of the peasants, on my behalf, their beasts of burden ;
and they fearing lest, by a refusal, they should draw
upon themselves the anger of the Pasha, lent the
animals, which were employed in conveying from
Jaffa the corn I had purchased there. This was
sold at Jerusalem at a considerable profit, although
it was offered at a somewhat lower price than that
asked by the merchants, who were obliged to defray
the heavy expenses of transport.

As may be seen, the promises which the ministers
make to the European powers, and the orders which
they give in consequence to the various authorities,
are eluded, and all the more readily since the Porte
has no real intention of making them respected. If
a European consul had lodged any complaint at
Constantinople about the trade in which I engaged,
what answer would be returned ?—" What you
complain of calls for no censure ; the merchants of
Jerusalem sell grain to the people at exorbitant
prices ; the governor's wife, in order to assuage the
misery of the inhabitants, finds means to sell wheat
at a reasonable rate, and the peasants associate
themselves in this good work by lending their
animals ; there is nothing to find fault with in
that."

CHAPTER VIII

Revolt of the Arabs of Khaïr-Ackman—Deplorable condition of the Ottoman troops.

IN the meantime my husband was obliged to place himself at the head of his troops, to go and put down the Arabs of Khaïr-Ackman, a place about three days' march from Jerusalem, who had risen in resistance to the military levy.

The rebels had taken refuge in a defile commanding the entrance into their part of the country. The route which had to be followed in order to get at them commenced, towards the plain, with an ascent, at first easy, and afterwards steep; it passed, finally, over a chain of hills, encumbered with rocks and broken ground, behind which the insurgents had taken up their quarters. Their infantry skirted the line of march, and from their ambush behind thickets, rocks, and earthworks hastily thrown up, occupying the slopes and crest of the mountain, they received the Turkish troops with well-sustained and murderous volleys of musketry.

Since morning, the repeated efforts and assaults of the Ottoman infantry had only succeeded in dislodging the enemy from their first line of entrenchments—that nearest to the plain. The heights were still defended by numerous sharpshooters, supported by great masses of half-naked Arabs, who offered a stubborn resistance. Night was drawing on, when the Pasha, taking counsel only of his courage, placed himself at the head of the half-discomfited infantry, which he formed in column. The soldiers, animated by the example of their general, vigorously attacked the enemy with the bayonet, and, in spite of their resistance, succeeded in attaining the summit of the range of hills on the right of the line of march. As soon as those who were still standing their ground saw the Ottoman standard floating on the height, they fled in disorder towards the villages. The Pasha's cavalry, launching themselves into the way that had been cleared for them, pursued the enemy, cutting them down with great carnage, to the gates of their principal hamlet, where they shut themselves up.

At day-break, the rest of the Turkish forces effected their passage, and proceeded to encamp on

the other side of the defile which had been carried
with so much difficulty. The artillery, drawn up
by batteries before the village, after firing all day
long, managed to throw down a great piece of the
wall. The assault was made at once, but vigorously
repulsed by the rebels. On the morrow the troops
were again pressed forward, and found the breach
abandoned ; on getting access into the principal
street, they discovered the adjacent streets blocked
by fallen timber, and the passages barred by gigantic
barriers ; moreover, being received with a terrible
fusillade from the roofs of the houses, they were
compelled to retire with severe loss.

The field-guns, for two days consecutively, were
directed against the mud houses situated between
the breach and the centre of the village ; when
they had been nearly demolished, and the entire
district presented the appearance of a heap of
ruins, the Turks advanced afresh, and, in spite of
the desperate efforts of the rebels, succeeded in
making themselves masters of the place. A frightful massacre commenced. The Pasha's troops, exas-
perated at the resistance they had encountered,
gave no quarter ; the houses, having first been
plundered, were given up to the flames, and their
spoils removed to the camp and divided.

While the hamlet was being sacked, the Arab women, shut up in a large mosque, witnessed the extermination of their fathers, husbands, brothers, and children, and the ruin of their homes; they alone were spared by the conqueror.

Eventually, fifteen days after the opening of the campaign, the revolted tribes sent to solicit *aman* (pardon), which was granted them; they furnished hostages, raised the required contingent, and paid the expenses caused by the expedition. As a reward for his important services, the Pasha received, through the *wali* of Beyrout, a sword of honour; he had also the rank of *ferik*, or general of division, conferred upon him.

We soon saw the army return to the city. Nothing was more dismal than the appearance of the Ottoman troops; preceded by monotonous music, their ragged garments barely covered frames of a leanness painful to behold. The officers themselves were as badly clothed as their men; most of them had their shoes in holes or soleless.

The uniform of the infantry consisted of trousers in the European mode, of white canvas in summer and blue cloth in winter; the jacket is also of blue cloth; the headdress is a red cap, or tarboosh,

ornamented with a blue tassel; the shoulder-belts
are white, worn cross-wise over the chest, supporting the cartridge-box, and a sabre; a musket and
bayonet complete the equipment.

The cavalry were attired in a like manner; their
arms consisted of a lance, and of a ridiculously short
clumsy sabre suspended from a waistbelt.

The causes of the deplorable state of the army
were numerous. In the first place, all the contractors made arrangements with the colonels and other
commanding officers for the supply of clothes and
materials of inferior quality. On the other hand, it
usually happened that deliveries were retarded owing
to the default of the treasury in payment of the
storekeepers charged with keeping up the supplies.
The funds were applied, in the first instance, to pay
the salaries of the chief commanders : as for the
soldiers, they seldom could touch their pay. It is not
surprising that, under such a system, the soldiers are
badly fed, badly clothed, and badly armed. It is a
common occurrence for winter clothes to be delivered
in the hottest of the summer months, and those
suitable for summer wear in the depth of winter.

The condition of the officers of inferior rank, up
to the captain and the *chef de bataillon* himself, is
if possible, more intolerable than that of the non-

*

commissioned officers and privates. They are all married, and have, for the most part, large families. Every month they have a right to an allowance of meat, rice, oil, and other matters. These rations are distributed with great irregularity, and the payment of salaries is still more in arrear than the delivery of provisions.

What, then, is the result? The officer who has an immediate right to demand the goods necessary for his subsistence, and which are left in arrear, sees himself deprived of every resource; and to save himself and his family from dying of hunger, he is obliged to negotiate advances with the money-lenders, and they buy for 150 francs the right to the delivery of goods to the value of 500 francs and upwards. This ruinous expedient naturally deprives the unhappy individuals who have recourse to it of two-thirds of their resources, already insufficient.

Salaries often remain unpaid for six months. It is only at the last extremity, and when their clothes have reached such a degree of old age as to fall to pieces, that the claimants resolve to sell to the Jews their precious goods, which afford a very clear representation of the liberality of the government.

These honest folks naturally take advantage of the urgent necessities of the borrowers to give them just the fourth of what they have to receive.

It is more especially when they are on garrison duty in some remote province that the officers experience the most severe privations; for then, not only are the payments indefinitely deferred, but the distributions of rations are made at such distant intervals, that they become quite illusory; at the same time there is no longer the means of finding some one to negotiate their claims on the treasury. The commanding officers avail themselves of these circumstances to buy up, on terms still more onerous than those of the money-lenders, and through the medium of their stewards, the claims of their unhappy subordinates.

It is not unusual to see officers going to seek the priest, and addressing him in the following lamentable terms: "I am married, and my wife and I are as well matched as possible, but I am in such a sad state of destitution that I cannot support her any longer. Separate us: she will be able to marry again, and find a husband who will preserve her from starvation."

It is evident that troops placed in such a predicament do not offer a very effectual safeguard. The greatest bravery gives no chance of promotion; it depends entirely on favour and intrigue.

However, if all the posts, all the dignities, as well in the army as everywhere else, are ·bestowed without any rule, on the other hand there is no hereditary aristocracy, keeping up its power from generation to generation, and closing every career to the multitude. It is a rare occurrence for a man in a high place to be the son of a father who has occupied a position even of moderate importance. The highest dignitaries are the sons of mere labourers, artisans, shopkeepers, or else they are Circassians, Poles, or Tartars, who have settled in Turkey.

The sons of the Pashas receive a very imperfect education, and their morals are generally of a most depraved sort. Early given to all kinds of excesses, they quickly destroy their health, both of mind and body; when their father dies they dissipate their wealth, and generally die in extreme poverty.

CHAPTER IX.

AVAILING myself of the governor's permission, I took with me my steward, and, escorted by a body of mounted Bashi-bazouks, I went on an expedition to visit the Druses of the mountains and the Bedouins of the plain.

The Druses (in the Turkish language *Durzú*) profess a particular sect of Mohamedanism; mounted on small but very active horses, they keep to the high mountain ranges, descending the steepest slopes, and re-ascending with extraordinary rapidity. As soon as they perceived my cortége they bounded down from the heights like flocks of goats. Armed with long muskets, they are clad only in a small piece of canvas, wrapped round their loins; they dwell in mud huts covered with thatch, and secured by keys and bolts of wood. They eat with their fingers, without employing either knives,

forks, or spoons. Their only furniture consists of a
carpet spread on the ground, and cushions here and
there. The cocks and hens are kept indoors, which
makes it anything but pleasant, both on account of
the dirt and the noise they keep up during the
night, disturbing one's slumbers perpetually.

The women, although the heat is very great,
are remarkably fair-complexioned; those who are
married wear as a headdress a long coronet of cloth-
of-silver, and all wear collars of the same material;
their heads are enveloped in a loose handkerchief of
flowered muslin, falling over the shoulders; they
have chemisettes, with short sleeves, reaching very
little below the shoulder, and leaving their bare
arms covered with bracelets. Above these garments
they have a small vest, tight-fitting and without
sleeves; their wide trousers are covered with a
short petticoat, coming down just below the knee.

On the day of my arrival I was invited to supper
at the house of one of the great men of the country.
A young lamb was served up, so underdone that its
flesh was quite red; it was stuffed with rice, and
covered with a kind of cream. It was impossible
to eat of this dish, so I was offered rice, which
my host kneaded in his hands into a ball; to
refuse his politeness was a delicate matter, so I

reluctantly resigned myself to my fate. The next course was of cakes made of flour, sugar, and butter. The bread is baked in an oven of burnt clay, hollowed out of the ground in a circular form to the depth of two feet, and of double that width. This oven is called *tandour*. As soon as the embers have been taken out the dough is put in, and gets baked instantly: this bread, which is extremely crisp, is as thin as a sheet of paper. Unhappily the oven is commonly used as a bath. I one day saw a woman draw out of it the water from which five or six children, of from five to eight years old, had just emerged, and pour it over the dough she was engaged in kneading.

After supper I was shown at the window the horses belonging to my host, who invited me to choose whichever I preferred. As I knew nothing of horse-flesh, my steward pointed out to me the one I ought to select. At the different visits which I paid during this journey I was presented, in succession, with forty-five horses, that followed in my train.

The dwellings of the people are constructed so as to leave in the centre a large square court. When night came, and I and the ladies of the house were sitting at the window of the harem, the mountaineers brought torches of resin, which they planted here and there to illumine the vast enclosure. The men, both of the neighbouring houses and those in the country round about, came, bearing cushions, on which they sat while they smoked their narghilés. Then came the musicians, followed by youths of from sixteen to eighteen years old, attired like women, who proceeded to dance in an entertaining manner to the sound of the music. These amusements were prolonged well into the night. At every place I came to I took part each night in a similar demonstration.

From the country of the Druses I descended into the plain inhabited by the Bedouins (*Bedewya*). They are in the habit of tattooing themselves in blue, on the edges of the lips, the neck, and the arms, from the wrists to the elbow, which produces a most unsightly effect upon their swarthy, and often black skins.

They live in hovels underground, formed like gigantic hives, subsist on the produce of their flock, and are in a wretched condition. The sheiks alone wear the burnous, the rest of the people have no other clothing than wide linen drawers; a few, however, wear a kind of shirt. The women go covered with a long wrapper of blue linen, falling from the shoulders, and secured by pins. On their head is a loose handkerchief, with which they veil themselves whenever they perceive a stranger. The greater part have black eyes, and eyebrows of remarkable beauty; nearly all have teeth of brilliant whiteness. The richer persons attire· themselves, over their blue *habbara*, in a kind of white petticoat, fastened round the loins and open on three sides.

All these peoples, both Druses and Bedouins, like the Arabs in general, are greatly addicted to theft and rapine. No traveller would dare to penetrate as far as I did without being well attended, otherwise he would run a great risk of being plundered, and even killed if he made a show of resistance.

The Turkish government requires from these tribes no other mark of submission than the payment of an impost arranged with each of them : amongst such a people the conscription is of course a dead letter. As the Arabs possess nothing that can easily be taken—the flocks belonging only to a small number amongst them—they oppose the most active resistance to the payment of the capitulation.

When a village has not paid up the whole of the tax the inhabitants are arrested, and beaten severely on the soles of the feet with a scourge of elephant's hide,

called *courbash*. Seeing how wretched these people
are, it would be thought impossible that they could
pay anything; but after receiving, at times, some
hundreds of blows without uttering any complaint,
except the word *Allah!* (God), repeated with every
stroke, it is astonishing to see them bring out gold,
hidden, perhaps, in their mouths, perhaps in a little
purse concealed under their arm-pits, or elsewhere
about their persons.

Since very few people, especially ladies, venture
to come amongst these people, I was the object of
lively curiosity on their part. As soon as I arrived
at any place, all the women, eager to see the governor's wife, came out of their *gourbis* (hovels),
and offered me little presents—eggs, fruit, and other
things of the kind,—while others flourished huge
fans of plaited straw, endeavouring to keep the air
cool around me ; all were attentive, and solicitous
of the honour of showing me hospitality. I was
surprised, on entering on one occasion the residence
of one of the principal sheiks, to see a European
bedstead of iron, painted green, the fruit of some
pillaging exploit.

Finally, having visited a great number of villages
and towns, I returned on my way to Jerusalem.
In the course of my journey my cortége was aug-

mented by numerous *mudirs* and sheiks, who, in so honouring me, sought to dispose me favourably in their behalf.

On my return I found the Pasha was absent, having gone to put down an armed dispute that had arisen between two Arab villages.

One day, when I was quietly resting in the harem after the fatigue of my journey, I heard a great tumult in the court-yard of the palace, where the Pasha's court of justice and other offices were situated. My apartments communicated with this court-yard by a large staircase outside. I saw through the window a furious crowd of Arabs, raising terrible shouts. I inquired for the steward, the cavas-baschi, and the other officers, in order to ask them the cause of such a disturbance. They, fearing for their lives if they showed themselves to these people, had done their best to conceal themselves.

Seeing that, if the Arabs were allowed their own way they might proceed to extremities, I quickly made up my mind, and, half-covering my face with a shawl, presented myself at the head of the staircase :—

"What is the matter, my friends, that you raise such an outcry? Tell me what you want, and although the Pasha is absent, I will do what I can to oblige you."

"The matter!" said one of them, who appeared to be one of the ringleaders. "They have lately established, at the gates of the city, a duty upon all the merchandise we bring in, in such a manner that we are obliged to pay before we have sold anything; moreover, the licence to collect this tax has been conferred upon a Frenchman; so that we are toiling to enrich an infidel. We wish the duty to be removed."

"I am on your side," I answered; "I had pledged the Pasha not to impose this tax, but an order from the Sultan compelled him to do so, and he was forced to obey; the Frenchman of whom you complain is not responsible. Moreover, we have written to Constantinople to ask for the suppression of this levy; in two or three days we shall receive a reply; there is every reason to believe that the Padishah, who is a father to his subjects, will grant the abolition which we have solicited."

At these words they all cried out, "God bless the wife of our governor! Allah protect our Pasha! Long live our Sultan! Amin! Amin!"

"In praying for your master, you do well," I replied; "always continue to act thus, and you

will obtain whatever is just. Return to your
homes, and as soon as the answer arrives it shall
be proclaimed."

They withdrew, satisfied at the result of their
proceeding. As for me, I was better pleased to see
them depart than I cared to show. I returned
to my apartments attended by their clamorous
blessings.

The next morning I summoned the cavas-baschi,
and asked him the names of the principal authors
of the disturbances of the day before. He named
fifteen. I immediately directed him, as usual in such
cases, to seize them ; an order which was executed
before they left their homes. They were forthwith
sent into exile, and were not permitted to return
until their spirit had been completely subdued. It
may be that some among them were innocent, but
in such affairs it seems preferable to run the risk
of inflicting some slight suffering both on the innocent and the guilty rather than to excite popular
passions by proceeding in the regular course of
justice, in order to apportion the blame attaching
to each. In the East these nice distinctions are not
attended to ; guilty and innocent are arrested, and
chastisement inflicted upon them.

For five or six years past, a young Circassian, whom

I had bought, had been growing up in my house.
I had given her a certain education, and, at the age
of fourteen, she acted as governess to my daughter
Aïsheh, who was scarcely five years old.

Although my husband was extremely good, and
very affectionate towards me, there grew up in my
mind a jealous thought; I feared lest the Pasha,
charmed with this young person, whose pleasing
expression of countenance was relieved by a certain
air of distinction, might wish to associate her with
me in the capacity of a second wife, the Mussulman
law allowing as many as four lawful wives.

I determined to take advantage of the governor's
absence, to rid myself of every ground of fear by
removing this girl; but I reflected in vain; I could
find no means of satisfying this desire without
disclosing the feelings that influenced my conduct.
One morning my attention was drawn to sundry
groans and lamentations coming from the streets;
I perceived some hired mourners accompanying the
funeral of the wife of a *caïmakam* (lieutenant-
colonel). This sight distressed me, for I had known
and loved the deceased; but the circumstance suggested to me a sudden idea; I resolved to give my
Circassian maid in marriage to the officer who now
found himself a widower.

This project was quite capable of being realised; the deceased, a Turkish lady of about forty-five, had her face pock-marked all over, and was consequently very plain; her husband, of the same age, was still vigorous and well-preserved. As the men are not in the habit of remaining a long time deprived of a wife, and frequently remarry within the very week of their late wife's burial, I resolved to make short work of the matter; moreover the near return of the Pasha prompted me to haste.

I sent my housekeeper to that of the colonel; she talked with this woman about the match which I offered her master. It was accepted with enthusiasm, for the officer could not find at Jerusalem any but Arab women, as ugly as they were dirty; on the other hand, he was not ignorant that she who was proposed as his bride was beautiful, and, further, he thought himself highly honoured in having for a wife one brought up in the house of the Pasha, and through whom he might hope for advancement. He therefore showed himself quite favourable to the prompt conclusion of a marriage which I desired as ardently as he.

Three days before that fixed for the ceremony, I sent the trousseau, which was my gift. The trunks containing the clothing, the beds, and every thing

needful were placed on camels, magnificently capari-
soned, and bearing collars with large bells. Scarves,
presents for the camel-drivers, were tied to the
necks of their animals. They were preceded by
numerous servants, uniformly clad, bearing in their
hands pieces of silver plate, and each with a scarf
worn cross-wise. Thus they proceeded to the house
of the future husband; the people, attracted by the
sound of the bells, formed in line along the route of
the procession, and wondered at the magnificence of
the bride's dowry. That was all sent on the part of
the young lady; the only present that I was deemed
to have made was a gold snuff-box on a silver stand.
The porters were rewarded with trifling presents;
these are generally small pieces of gold wrapped in
flowered handkerchiefs.

I next busied myself in getting ready the apartment where the ceremony was to take place, for the
betrothed, out of respect for the memory of her
whom he had recently lost, did not wish the marriage to be celebrated at his own house. I had the
walls of one of the largest rooms in the palace hung
with pieces of white silk, embroidered with gold;
over these were disposed cashmere shawls, relieved
by rich scarves, and forming tapestry. In the
centre of the room was placed a kind of throne,

covered with velvet, on which the bride was to be
seated.   When the day arrived I had her magnificently attired in the best that my store could afford,
which I lent her for the occasion; this was an
Arab costume.

She wore large trousers of red silk, embroidered
with gold; over them a robe of white gauze, striped
with silk of the same colour; then came a vest of
green velvet, embroidered with gold, with a trian-
gular opening in front, so as to expose the bosom;
the sleeves were narrow, cut open from the wrists
to the middle of the forearm, and furnished with a
great many small buttons.   On her hair, which was
cut square on the forehead, and arranged behind in
long, hanging tresses, and adorned with golden
sequins, was placed a rich tarboosh of red velvet,
also garnished with sequins, and embroidered and
adorned with pearls.   On the forehead, the cheeks,
and the chin, were written verses in praise of the
husband, by means of spangles of gold, pasted on
the face.

The head was covered with a thick veil of gauze,
worked in gold, formed of one piece, of which half
fell in front, the other half behind.

I had sent my *Kjaja-Kadun* (housekeeper) to
invite the ladies of the principal authorities of the

country; for that purpose she left a little candle at the house of each. On the morning of the appointed day they came in great numbers, and seemed charmed to find that the nuptials were to be celebrated after the fashion of their country. I allowed them to act, as they understood the matter. All, taking their seats in the chamber that had been prepared, began to smoke their narghilés, which they had brought for that purpose. The bride, throwing back her veil, went and kissed the hand of each, after which she placed herself on the raised throne assigned to her.

Such an assemblage was an enchanting spectacle. There were about one hundred ladies, the greater part very dark-complexioned, young and pretty, and all were clad in their finest costumes. Some were distinguished by their large tresses, adorned with sequins; others wore on their shoulders a kind of belt, formed of eight or ten large pieces of gold; some had tassels of large pearls, placed on each side of their faces; with them the principal extravagance was in gold and pearls, just as in Turkey diamonds constitute the most valued article of ornament. The singular noise that was heard at every movement they made; the gold they carried on their persons; the variety and brilliancy of the colours

displayed in their costumes; the different shapes
and sizes of their narghilés, some green, others red
or blue, all contributed to the remarkable character
of this assembly.

One of the party commenced a song, accompanied
by the *Koudoum* (an instrument composed of two
small tambourines placed together on the ground,
and beaten with two drumsticks), and the *tar*, or
large tambourine. Two of the principal assistants
began to dance; they stood facing each other at a
certain distance, then they swayed themselves forwards and backwards successively, following the
time marked by the music. This dance allows no
movement of the legs; the feet scarcely stir. The
performers balance themselves on their haunches,
inclining their heads right or left, make graceful
gestures with their arms, and assume attitudes
most charming and most impassioned; everything
breathes in them, while dancing, an ardent yet
restrained voluptuousness.

The dancing was kept up until all, old and young,
the wives of the *cadi* (judge), the *nakib* (first inter-
preter of the law), the *imam* (priest), and of other
officers, civil and military, of every rank, had
successively taken part in it.

After the ball, supper was served up. The

attendants brought *sofras* (round thin planks or plates of wood, inlaid with mother of pearl, bronze, marble, and other materials), each of which was placed on a stool about a foot high. Round each of these tables ten guests seated on cushions were accommodated. All the dishes were served at the same time; soup, meat, rice, dessert; everyone washed her hands before taking her seat, and helped herself with her fingers to whatever she fancied; there were neither plates, nor spoons, nor forks. ·

The supper over, all rise from table, and again seat themselves to take coffee and smoke narghilés. At sunset, all the ladies present wrap themselves in a long piece of white stuff, which conceals their costume, and with which they cover their faces, excepting the eyes. The bride does likewise; then they all issue forth to escort her to the house of her husband. Four of the guests bear over her head, by means of staves, a canopy of red cloth, shaped like a tent and open in front. The bridegroom, standing at the door of his house, welcomes the cortége, and scatters small pieces of money, whilst all the women cry *lou, lou, lou!* recite verses in honour of the bride, and loudly declare their good wishes in her favour. The bridegroom then goes out, whilst the whole assemblage enters the house; the bride takes her seat on the divan, and kisses the hands of the assistants as they severally withdraw. Two old female slaves then raise her veil, and give her some refreshment.

At eight o'clock, at the time when the night's prayer is offered, the husband, leaving the mosque where the nuptial prayers have been said, comes accompanied by a numerous suite of acquaintances, carrying lighted candles or torches, and chanting prayers ; the priest pushes the newly-married man into his house by the shoulders, and, after drinking a glass of sherbet, they all retire.

Then the husband goes up-stairs, and seats himself on a chair, while his wife, accompanied by two old female slaves, each carrying a candle, presents herself before him, and all three dance ; they withdraw, change the bride's dress, and return to renew the dance. This performance is repeated until all the robes in the trousseau have been put on. The husband then takes his wife by the hand and enters the bedchamber with her.

The next morning the newly-married husband, as was the custom, came to thank me. I made him a present of a beautiful Arab horse.

Five or six days afterwards I was informed of the arrival of the governor. The caïmakam went to meet him, and kissed the hem of his robe, as soon as he accosted him.

" What new thing has happened, that you should pay me this mark of deference ?"

" I am the husband of the young lady who was brought up in your house."

" Oh !" cried the Pasha ; " then you are my son-in-law." And they continued to converse familiarly until they reached the city.

When the Pasha entered the house I felt very uneasy as to the manner in which he would take the affair.

" It appears that you have been celebrating certain nuptials during my absence. . . . Well, you have amused yourself, and you have done well."

Seeing him in this frame of mind I was satisfied, both because my arbitrary conduct met with no reproach, and because I saw myself freed from all disturbing causes of jealousy.

CHAPTER X.

ONE Friday that I received, as I did every week, the wives of certain subordinate officials, the eunuch in attendance came to tell me that an old lady, accompanied by a slave and a eunuch, had arrived, bringing a letter for me. I directed that she should be admitted into one of our finest apartments, until my reception was at an end. As soon as I was at liberty, I went to see what this person wanted. She was lady-in-waiting to the Princess Nazly-Hanum, daughter of Mehemet-Ali-Pasha, Viceroy of Egypt. She brought a letter from her mistress, in which the writer informed me that having heard me spoken of as a person of ability, and highly energetic, I should be conferring on her a great pleasure if I would spend a few days in Egypt with her. I was naturally obliged to offer hospitality to the messenger of her Highness, and to those who accompanied her.

I acquainted my husband with this invitation, and asked permission to comply with the request of the Princess. "You are obliged to go to her," said he, "for an invitation coming from a person of such rank is a command."

Taking with me my daughter Aïsheh, two slaves and a eunuch, and accompanied by the messenger of the Princess, I went to Jaffa, and embarked for Alexandria, where I found the equipages and servants of her Highness in readiness. The carriages were all fitted with red embroidered velvet; instead of windows the two sides were furnished with gilt trellis work, to admit the air. We immediately went to take up our residence with the Princess, at her palace of Mahmudieh, which situated near the Nile, in the centre of a magnificent garden, had quite the appearance of a European structure. The mosaics which were set in the floors of the inner apartments were remarkably fine.

After getting out of the carriage in one of the courts, I entered a spacious vestibule, beyond which was a magnificent staircase leading to the upper rooms. On each side of the passages were drawn up lines of female slaves, dressed in silks of brilliant

ɪ

hues, and wearing necklaces, ear-rings, and bracelets of great value. To do me honour, other slaves, took me under the arms, as though to assist me up-stairs, while others again, and some eunuchs, supported the skirts of my *feradje* (a large mantle), sweeping the ground, closed in front, garnished with immense pagoda sleeves, and a tippet. I was received at the head of the stairs by the Princess's treasurer, who introduced me into a large hall, where she made me sit down and rest before being presented to her mistress.

Shortly afterwards the treasurer came to inform me that her Highness was waiting to receive me. I found her seated on a magnificent divan, and calmly smoking a long chibouk. On seeing me she rose, and, with a firm step, approached and bid me welcome. The Princess was of the middle height, and of a somewhat dark complexion ; her face bore the impress of a degree of energy and passion not commonly met with; her eye, penetrating and bold, denoted intelligence. I prostrated myself to the ground ; she graciously bowed in acknowledgment of my salutation, inviting me, by a motion of her hand, to take my seat on a divan placed opposite to her own.

Around the apartment stood sundry old women,

who were employed to entertain the Princess by relating stories. As soon as I had taken my place, a chibouk was brought me, and I began to smoke. The Princess then commenced the conversation, complimenting me at considerable length on the good reports she had heard of me. We then talked on various subjects. Nazly-Hanum gave proofs of a shrewd intellect, and an extensive knowledge of Eastern affairs. During our conversation glasses of sherbet were brought in, variously perfumed, and lastly coffee. After we had conversed for about half an hour, I took leave of the Princess, and retired to the apartments prepared for me. Like the rest of the rooms in the palace, they were magnificently furnished ; divans, cushions, hangings of embroidered velvet, were in every chamber. When the dinner-hour arrived, Nazly-Hanum dined alone with me. The table, covered with embroidered silk, was garnished with numerous dishes, served on silver plate of rare workmanship ; even the spoons were ornamented with precious stones.

During the repast we talked very little. Presently we rose, and went to sit in the garden, where we all sat round a table smoking and taking coffee. Towards ten o'clock fruit was brought, and sherbet in golden cups, adorned, together with their covers, with diamonds. The Princess began to drink both brandy and wine, and to talk familiarly with me ; then she permitted several of the oldest of her slaves to sit near us.   One of them acted the part of her lover ; they both began talking about affairs of gallantry, and exciting themselves. Nazly, in fact, had formed in her youth many amorous intrigues ; but as she could only see her lovers by stealth, and for brief moments, she had adopted the plan of having all sorts of fun in the harem. I was present at this scene, which became more animated in proportion as the two principal actresses got more intoxicated. In the meantime, some young slaves danced, accompanying themselves with *zaganets* (castanets of copper), while others sang. Those whose duty constrained them to remain standing round the room fell down with fatigue ; it could be seen from their appearance, that they were accustomed to pass the night without sleep. They were forced to endure this weariness without a sign of impatience, for if their mistress observed it, she would have had them beaten unmercifully ; many had even died from the ill-treatment they had suffered under such circumstances.

Eventually, being weary of such revolting scenes

of debauchery and selfishness, towards midnight I •
requested permission to retire.

I was reconducted to my apartments by the person who had called on me at Jerusalem. Out of
compliment, I asked her to be seated for a short
time near me. She began talking to me about Nazly.

"You have seen our mistress: she passes all her •
nights as she has commenced this. She rises at
noon, and spends her days in visiting, driving,
drinking, and amusing herself.

"Formerly, although the Egyptian ladies are far ￢
more strictly confined than the Turks, she found
means, thanks to the fear with which she inspired
us, and the frequent absences of her husband, to
introduce, with impunity, her lovers into the
harem. She usually ensured their reticence by
having them put to death; but these murders
having made some noise, she has given up that
kind of pastime.

"We are all very unhappy under her. She is
excessively capricious and cruel. During her husband's lifetime, he having one day said to a slave who
was pouring out water for him, 'Enough, my lamb;'
this word, reported to his wife, put her into a fury.
Forthwith she ordered the poor girl to be killed; then
she had the head stuffed with rice, cooked in an oven,

and placed on a large dish surrounded with rice.
When the *Defterdar* came to his dinner, his wife had
this strange dish served up to him, saying, ' Help
yourself to a piece of your lamb.'   At this word he
threw his napkin on the table, went away, never
reappeared for a long time after, and had no longer
any affection for his wife. If he did not separate
from her, it was because he was bent upon keeping
her riches, and remaining the son-in-law of Mehemet-Ali. This jealousy extends to those of her
slaves who minister to her passions; at the least
suspicion of infidelity she dooms them to die under
the lash."

She related many more instances of the violent
character of her cruel and imperious mistress. " If
she has induced you to come here," said this good
old lady, " it is because she has heard you spoken
of as one who has travelled in Europe and in Arabia,
and who knows many things calculated to entertain
her.   However, her Highness is very generous, and
you will have no cause to complain of her."   This
conversation was prolonged to a late hour.

It was about ten o'clock next morning, and I had
not yet risen, when the Princess entered my room,
attended by two slaves. She had evidently got up
earlier than usual. " What !" cried she, " you still

in bed, my dear?" Then coming up to me, she embraced me, and began to pay me a thousand compliments. Finally she withdrew, saying that she was going to wait for me.

I was soon dressed, and found the Princess inspecting some designs for jewelry which she wished to have prepared. "Come," she exclaimed, "you shall give me your advice." We together proceeded to examine the designs. When we had made our selection, she sent for two caskets, each upwards of three feet long, and wide and deep in proportion. "Now," said she, "let us choose the stones." These caskets were filled with an infinite number of diamonds, emeralds, and other precious stones, the greater part very large, and altogether of incalculable value. She was on the point of locking them up again when she remarked all of a sudden, "I am going to make you a little present: here are two diamonds; get one made into a ring for yourself and the other for your husband." Each of these gems was worth upwards of five thousand francs.

She then asked for a large casket. This was full of long bars of gold.

"I intend," said Nazly, "to have these ingots made into plate. What is your opinion?"

"I think," replied I, "that vessels of massive gold

would be extremely heavy; those of silver are much lighter."

"You are right. I will apply the contents of this box to another purpose." Then taking two or three of the bars, she cast them at the feet of a slave. "See, they are for thee," she said.

At the invitation of her Highness, I went down into the garden. This was remarkably beautiful. The date-palms, orange-trees, flowers, and shrubs were arranged with a degree of art not often seen, especially in the East. The very walls were covered with verdure. Here and there elegant kiosques, in the midst of which graceful jets of water refreshed and cooled the air, contributed to the charm of the scene. I walked about for some time, accompanied by women, each of whom wore on her neck a white handkerchief, adorned with embroidered verses, the distinguishing mark of those who were in the good graces of their mistress. The latter presently made her appearance.

"What do you think of my garden?" said she. "Are you pleased with the climate of Egypt?"

"The garden and the climate are both very fine, and in every respect agreeable; but how could I enlarge upon their praises, when it is to you that such praises are due?"

She smiled at this compliment, and testified her
satisfaction by gently pinching my cheek. "If
you would like to see something of the country, let
us go out," she said. We then each took a *feradje*,
and over it a *bourko*, a kind of hood which completely covers the head and neck, and admits the
light through holes made in front of the eyes. The
features of the women are nowhere concealed with
so much care as in Egypt; everywhere else they
have their faces covered with a *yashmak*, a slight
veil of silk gauze. We got into our carriage, the
trellis of which was not so thick as to hinder us
from seeing anything, and went to the palace of
Ibrahim-Pasha, brother of Nazly-Hanum. We were
both received with the same ceremony that had
attended my arrival at the residence of the Princess.
She introduced me to Ibrahim's wives, and praised
me highly to them. I went over the palace, which
was as richly furnished as that of my amiable
hostess. The women who lived in it were all young,
and far more beautiful than those of Nazly's establishment. They all bore on their countenances the
impress of fear and of *ennui*. An old slave, with a
cheerful expression (for the old slaves are generally
more gay than the young), conducted me all over.
She told me that the Pasha was of a terribly jealous

disposition. "A black eunuch," said she, "becoming enamoured of a Circassian of rare beauty, of whom our master was passionately fond, was naturally rejected by her, and resolved to effect her ruin. One day he placed, as though it had been forgotten, a man's cloak near the Circassian girl's door. When the Pasha, preceded by two eunuchs carrying torches, arrived at the door, and saw this garment, he was transported with rage.

"'What is this?' he cried.

"'My lord,' answered the wicked eunuch, 'no doubt it belongs to some one who has been with the Circassian, and has fled at your approach.'

"Ibrahim-Pasha knocked rudely; the poor girl came to open the door; at that instant our master, drawing his *handjer* (a short curved dagger), struck her dead. You may readily understand that with a master so suspicious, and so ready to believe calumnies, we cannot be happy."

I returned to Nazly, and we were served with a superb cold collation, after which we went into the garden, which was still more magnificent than that of the Princess. All the Pasha's wives accompanied us. They were Circassians and Greeks, of a gentle disposition, and generally beautiful, but badly educated. Then we went to the warm bath, while

slaves sought to entertain us by dancing, and singing to the *derbouka*—a kind of mandoline. When
night came we returned to her Highness's palace. •

One of the tale-tellers then gave us one of the
stories which they are accustomed to recite. There
are about ten. Each woman knows one or two of
them, which she repeats; when there is any poetry,
she sings it. Those who go through recitations of
this kind have no other employment.

Next we were given a representation of *Kara-
gheuz*, or Chinese shadows. Those who directed
the movements of the marionettes introduced
imaginary characters, whose dialogue was full of
allusions to the acts of the Princess and of the various
members of her establishment. In a general way,
pantomimes, or tales revealed in the acting, are
produced on this limited stage; it is the theatre of
the Orientals. In Turkey it is often employed as
the means of communicating to the Sultan or some
other great personage what no one would dare to
tell them openly.

On the morrow, taking with me Fatmah, the lady
who was sent on the mission to me, we dressed
ourselves like merchants' wives, and went to see
the town. What most struck me was the horrible
filth that prevailed everywhere. In the bazaar the

female fellahs were covered from head to foot with
a long surtout of blue linen. These women do not
generally conceal their face. Their garments were in
rags and threadbare. The fruit, the bread, the vegetables, were literally covered with myriads of black
or bluish flies, because the vendors did not give
themselves the trouble of covering their wares.
It surprised me that anyone could purchase such
articles, offered by such filthy saleswomen.
Swarms of squalid children, barely covered with
miserable rags, infested the environs of the market;
the streets leading to it were, so to speak, impassible, on account of the heaps of filth that had
accumulated. We went into several shops; it was
just as bad. I could not possibly understand how
these people could live amid such an atmosphere of
stench. The merchants, dressed in long *jubbehs*
(mantles with long sleeves), their heads covered
with large turbans, and their feet bare, stood at the
doors of their shops, which were left open to show
what was sold, as they had neither sign nor stall.
The streets, very narrow, and generally unpaved,
were continually cut up, sometimes by carriages,
before which ran a person clad only in a blouse of
blue linen, reaching to the knee, and bandaged
round the loins, sometimes by hired asses, preceded

or followed by young boys, and mounted by men or women.

These asses, very handsome,—for Egypt is celebrated in that respect,—are extremely convenient.
For about two or three pence you can go all over
the town on one, and two young conductors are at
your service. If you stop anywhere, you fix the
time when they are to return for you, and you pay
only as for one taking up.

Now and then we visited the cafés, which were
distinguished by benches placed out in the street
where men sat, gravely occupied in smoking and
drinking. Here and there we met Arab women
singing *maonâls* (couplets) to the sound of the *tar*,
or tambourine.

Finally we arrived at a quarter called the Course,
where are to be seen houses built in the European
style, and shops with glazed fronts, showing the
goods tastefully arranged. The trees planted before
the houses make this square resemble that of a
town in the south of France.

Shortly afterwards, taking with me Fatmah and
several more of the Princess's women, I left for
Cairo, in carriages belonging to her Highness. As
soon as we got beyond the walls of Alexandria, it
seemed as if we had entered a vast furnace. After

suffering greatly from this excessive heat, we put up at the palace of Halim-Pasha, at Shoubrah. I went to visit the town of Cairo, which comprises a great number of palaces, surrounded by magnificent gardens and squares. The bazaars are numerous, and a different kind of merchandise is sold in each. Amongst the merchants, dealers in trinkets, jewellers, and others, are many Europeans. This town did not please me as much as Alexandria, which, refreshed by the sea-breezes, and the flowing waters of the Nile, was a most agreeable place to live in; whereas Cairo, on the contrary, only separated from the desert by the river, has an excessively hot climate. Many of the inhabitants suffer from ophthalmia. Another inconvenience is that there is no other water than that of the Nile, which is exceedingly brackish and unpleasant to drink, even when filtered. The scorpions, the serpents, and the mosquitos add to t. discomforts of the country.

After spending some time at Cairo I returned to Alexandria, where I stayed about a fortnight longer. I then took leave of the Princess, and embarked on a steam-vessel which conveyed me to Beyrout. This town is built in the form of an amphitheatre, on a hill, the base of which forms the port. It serves as the residence of the *Wali*, or governor-general of

Palestine. The houses are surrounded by immense gardens, planted with mulberry-trees. Water is very scarce, and is brought from a great distance. The population is largely employed in the management of silkworm nurseries. There are also extensive silk manufactories, and the dealers in satin damask are numerous. After resting two days in the palace of the *Wali*, I resumed, by road, my journey to Jerusalem.

CHAPTER XI.

ABOUT three months after my return, there arrived from Constantinople an order recalling my husband, and appointing a new governor.

In the East, when an official is recalled, he is accounted of less consideration than the lowest of the inhabitants. From all parts signs of discontent were displayed. The chief complaints lodged against us were that Mehemet-Pasha proceeded with too great severity against the Arabs, both those who had rebelled, and those accused of crimes, and that I was too greedy for money and presents.

The Pasha resolved that I should take my departure first, with our principal effects and our servants, before the arrival of his successor, and thus, being still in the possession of authority, he could be on his guard against the malevolent. He furnished me with an escort of Bashi-bozouks, and told me to go and wait for him at Akiah, where he would meet me and take me to Constantinople.

I followed a different route to that which we took on our former journey. On the second day, the commander of the escort was informed that a dispute had arisen between the inhabitants of a neighbouring village and those of the town through which we were going to pass, and they had come to blows that self-same day. Indeed, we heard the distant sound of the firing. What complicated the matter was the circumstance that both parties were equally hostile to my husband, who had severely chastised them for their repeated and sanguinary outbreaks. The Dehly-baschi was sorely embarrassed as to what he should do.

" Believe me," I said, " there is only one way of avoiding the danger that threatens us and continuing our journey in peace. Instead of going straightforward, we must make the circuit of the village which we have to pass, enter it by the gate which looks upon the road from Akiah, and you say to the inhabitants that I am the wife of the new governor, just arrived from Constantinople, and whom you are escorting to Jerusalem."

This stratagem, carried into effect, succeeded

K

beyond all expectation. As soon as they learnt that the new governor's harem was approaching the combat ceased. The Arabs and their sheiks came to meet me, raising shouts in my honour. They conducted me, with great pomp, to the house of the wealthiest inhabitant in the place. The women received me with all the respect and all the good-will possible. They served up an excellent supper, and did their very best to make me comfortable.

"We are happy," said they, "to see you take the place of our late Pasha. He was so cruel that he punished by exile or imprisonment the least appearance of rebellion. . One could never obtain any benefit from him, save by robbing oneself for the benefit of his wife."

"We have heard that spoken of in Constantinople," I replied, "and for that reason it has been determined to send a new governor to Jerusalem, to repair the evils you have hitherto endured ; you will find the new Pasha as humane as the former showed himself rigorous, and I trust you will be satisfied with him."

I tranquilly passed the night amongst these good folks. In the morning, the sheik's wife came to offer me a ring, richly chased, which I was obliged to accept for fear of exciting the displeasure or distrust of my entertainers.

My escort having assembled, we again set out on our march, the Dehly-baschi and his men rejoicing greatly at the success of our trick. As they had given themselves out as Bashi-bozouks sent to Jerusalem in charge of the harem of the new Pasha, they had been very well treated; the greater part of the night had been spent in festivities on their account. We repeated, at the last halting-place, the performance that had proved so successful the day before, and so arrived without inconvenience at Akiah on the fourth day after setting out from Jerusalem.

The governor of the town, formerly steward to the Wali of Beyrout, who had procured his nomination to our post at Jerusalem, received me with great demonstrations of respect. Knowing that my husband had been sent for to Constantinople, and presuming that he might be nominated to a high post, he wished to secure his good graces by treating me to the best of his ability. On the night of my arrival he had me serenaded, and commanded a superb exhibition of fireworks in my honour.

This worthy governor was about fifty years old,

pock-marked, and extremely plain. Introduced to
his wife, she received me very graciously. She was
a person of about twenty-three, very pretty, the
daughter of a merchant at Broussa. As soon as
we had conversed for a moment, we discovered
such mutual sympathy, that we soon became like
two friends of ten years' standing.

Next morning I was with her when her husband,
going to the bath, sent to ask for some linen he
required.

"Carefully observe," said she to the slave charged
with this commission, "with whom the Pasha is
going to the bath, and with whom he con-
verses."

"My dear friend," said I, as soon as the slave
had gone, "it seems to me that you have a very
singular idea, in allowing yourself to be jealous of
such a husband."

"Ah!" she cried, "you don't know what a man
he is. He has made me the mother of two children,
aged respectively three and two years. I procured,
to take charge of them, a woman of Chios, about
forty years old, and pock-marked. I had full confidence in her, and was far from supposing that she
could attract the attentions of my husband. A
fortnight passed, and one morning I awoke early,

and did not find the Pasha by my side. In great
distress, I put on my pelisse, and went to see what
had become of him. I found him in the servant's
bedroom with gold in his hand, which he was
endeavouring to induce her to accept. At this
sight I swooned away. Hearing me fall, my faith-
less husband was greatly alarmed on seeing me
there, and hurried away into the selamlik, leaving
the partner of his guilt to reconduct me to my
chamber. Indignant at such deceit, and resolved
not to survive my shame and sorrow, for I dearly
loved my husband, I swallowed a ball of opium
which I had in the house. I soon began to manifest
all the symptoms of poisoning. A doctor was
called in, and he succeeded in counteracting the
effects of the poison. In ten days I was beginning
to get well again. As the Pasha and I have not yet
made peace with one another, I fear he will make
another attempt to have a talk with his Greek
favourite. You see it is not without reason that I
charge my slave to watch him."

Such was the story told by this poor woman. I
did my best to console her, telling her that, while
becoming reconciled to her husband, she should
insist on his slave being sold, and thereby she
would have no further anxiety.

Mehemet-Pasha arrived soon after, and we remained two days at Akiah, and then went on to Beyrout. On our way we had to pass through an extremely mountainous district. Several times I was obliged to leave the *taktaravan*, or palanquin, and mount on horseback; for the road, flanked by precipices, was so narrow that it was dangerous to remain in the palanquin. One of the horses might make a false step, and precipitate me down some ravine, whilst the size of the vehicle still further increased the danger. After resting one night at Beyrout, we took the steamer for Constantinople. As was customary, my husband had engaged the saloon for his harem. When a lady wishes to go on deck, she must put on the *yashmak* and the *feradje*, as when she goes out in a town. A pavilion of canvas is, moreover, arranged on the different packet-boats, to conceal the ladies from the eyes of Europeans who embark in the same vessel with them.

We stayed at the same house where we had suffered so much before our appointment to Akiah. Thinking that we should not have to wait long before we got a new post, we only furnished two apartments, leaving the remainder of our effects packed up. As soon as we arrived we had a visit from my husband's *capu-djohadar*, the name given to a kind of agent, who goes to the Porte for dispatches on account of some two or three functionaries whom he represents, and solicits for them vacant offices superior to those which they are then enjoying. He came to tell us that there was a report abroad that the governorship of Belgrad was about to be conferred on Mehemet-Pasha, although he was only a mirimiran, or general of division, whereas this command is not generally given to anyone under the rank of a *mushir*, or field-marshal.

This favour was owing to Reshid-Pasha, the grand-vezir, the political friend and supporter of my husband.

A fortnight had hardly elapsed when we heard several couriers hurrying to our house, and uttering shouts of joy. Thirty *mekters*, or couriers, people who hang about the Porte to learn the news, came in fact to announce the nomination of Mehemet-Pasha as governor of Belgrad.

After receiving numerous visits of congratulation, we left Constantinople to proceed to our new post. A packet-boat brought us to Varna, in abominable weather and over a frightfully rough sea. There we landed, and, after a short journey, embarked again on a steam-boat. As we were passing *Widin*, the governor invited us to stay. As it was night, he sent to meet us a great number of torchbearers, and also his carriages, and thus we were conducted to the palace. We were very kindly received, and I passed the night with the four wives of the Pasha, Turkish women, as ignorant and as old as wives of the time of the Sultan Mahmud could possibly be. Aga-Hussein-Pasha had formerly been an aga of the Janissaries. He had participated in the massacre of that body by setting fire to one of their principal barracks, and so was promoted to the grade of *mushir*. A beautiful and sumptuous supper was placed before us. In the morning we re-embarked at four o'clock, but were soon obliged to leave the steam-boat, a dam preventing our passage higher up the river. We then had to avail ourselves of horrible flat boats, drawn by oxen, to clear that part of the Danube where the shallowness presented an obstacle to the passage of steamers. I preferred to go ashore, and follow on foot the barges in which the baggage and the slaves were stowed. I thus enjoyed the prospect of the beautiful defile bordering on the river. We afterwards took a small steamer at the point where the stream again became navigable, and by that means arrived off Belgrad. Instead of landing on the

Turkish bank, the Pasha stopped at Semlin, on the Austrian side, to pay his compliments to the commander, who gave us a favourable reception, placed a house at our disposal, and sent a military band to play under my windows while he conferred with my husband.

CHAPTER XII.

THE following morning we crossed the Danube, and found the Turkish troops drawn up to receive us. They escorted us to the fortress, which stands on an elevation overlooking the town, which is built on an amphitheatre, stretching upwards along the river Sava. The palace is situated in the centre of the fort; casemates are placed under the batteries to serve as a refuge in case of siege, and these gates must be passed before you reach the principal court-yard, on which the palace abuts.

Residence at this place was not very agreeable. We had no garden, and I attempted to obtain some recreation by walks in the surrounding country, but it was utterly barren; there was no verdure, and only a tree here and there at long intervals. The only herds or flocks I ever came across were composed exclusively of swine. The Serbian population being hostile to the Turks, I had no acquaintance except amongst the old wives of officials who were superannuated, and compelled by the government to reside on the spot.

The Princess, wife of the reigning Prince Alexander, came to call upon me, and I received her at the foot of the staircase,—a mark of attention which produced a great effect upon her, since none of the Turkish ladies who had preceded me had ever taken the trouble so to receive a Christian. They would remain sitting on their divans, and would never return the calls made on them. On the contrary, with the governor's permission, I went in a carriage, escorted by cavasses, to see the Princess. Her husband met me in the court-yard of his palace, and, by his orders, his guard was drawn up in a double line, through which I passed, while the band played the national Ottoman march. He took me by the hand and conducted me to his wife, who received me, attended by her two daughters, lovely girls of sixteen and fourteen respectively. All three were in the national Serbian costume : red cap, worn on the side of the head, with a tassel hanging over the shoulder ; plaited hair, the plaits being turned back on the forehead ; embroidered jacket, with large sleeves, inside which were other and falling sleeves of muslin; and a short skirt reaching to the ankle. After exchanging a few words, I took my leave of their highnesses, and was reconducted to my carriage in the same ceremonious manner as that in which I had been received.

Belgrad was then an ill-built town; its streets were narrow, dirty, and ill-paved. The shops were numerous, but they offered no attractions. The Belgrad of that period, therefore, was a very different place from what we see it now-a-days. At that time it contained about five hundred families of Turkish origin, supported solely by pensions, given them by the Ottoman Government in consideration of the prosperity they had formerly enjoyed, and which the Serbians had monopolised. The customs of this little colony differ, in some points, from those of Constantinople. Most of the girls have light hair, but when they marry they stain their hair, eyelashes, and eyebrows. They also paint themselves in an extraordinary manner: you may tell a married woman by this. Their dress is somewhat different from that of other Ottoman women. They wear a tarboosh, over a loose flowing handkerchief, an embroidered jacket, with pendent sleeves, and wide trousers, embroidered at the sides.

The climate of Serbia is extremely hot in summer,

and fevers are prevalent ; in winter the cold is very severe, and there are heavy falls of snow. Every year the Danube freezes, which causes numerous accidents. At a day's notice, the boats are shut in by the ice; whilst the break-up comes with equal suddenness, and they are shattered to pieces without the least chance of avoiding the catastrophe.

Deprived of the amusement of walking, and having intercourse with only a very limited number of people, I endeavoured to occupy myself in various ways.

During the winter, the town is absolutely deprived of water, the river being frozen over. The ice is brought into the house in wooden buckets, and water procured by melting it. This mode of supply came very dear, so I purchased ten carts, and the requisite number of horses, and engaged men to take charge of them, and my steward employed them in carrying ice from house to house. This little speculation brought me in more than a thousand francs a month, a thing not to be despised in a post where we had no other income than the salary paid us by the Porte. One day the Pasha saw one of these carts. " Whoever took up that idea ought to realize a famous profit," said he to me. I took good care not to let him know that the idea was my own.

The want of a garden distressed me so much that I resolved to have one. I ordered my steward to procure fifty convicts, to whom I gave a small gratuity. Every morning, while the Pasha was absent on the duties of his office, the galley-slaves were employed in clearing a waste piece of land by the side of our palace. Afterwards they went for shrubs and plants, which I had demanded from the Turkish inhabitants, and brought them, together with the earth that surrounded them. In about three weeks' time I had a beautiful garden, embellished with an arbour covered with climbing plants.

The labour over, I invited the Pasha to take a turn in the garden.

" A turn in the garden ?" he cried. " Why we have none ! "

" Very well; then let us walk on the plot of ground there, close by the side."

" As you please," said he; " but I don't know what fancy you have for walking in that barren place."

I leave my readers to conjecture his astonishment when he arrived at the place and saw the ground covered with shrubs, and with flowers already full-blown. He could scarcely believe that all this had been done in twenty days.

After this I set about the realisation of a new project. I summoned twenty young native girls to come to my house, and proceeded to teach them to spin and weave silk, to embroider, and do other light work of the kind. I gave them suitable remuneration, whilst teaching them to work; I gave them their meals also. It afforded me great diversion to see myself surrounded by these young folks, and so I passed all my days among them.

An unlooked-for event suddenly forced us into quite another occupation. One night a Turk and a Serbian took to quarrelling. The dispute rose to such a height that the Christian was killed by the Mussulman. The latter, without awaiting the discovery of the crime, took refuge in the citadel. As a vessel was leaving for Constantinople next morning, the governor made him embark in it, fearing that, if he kept him at Belgrad, he would be obliged to deliver up to the Serbians a man who had acted as a true believer in taking the life of an infidel.

When the corpse was discovered the whole town rose in indignation on learning that a member of the orthodox religion had been the victim of a

Mohamedan. The Turks resident in the town rushed
in to ask our protection, bringing the most valuable
of their effects, and pouring forth the terror of their
souls in describing the excitement that prevailed.
Soon we saw the populace in arms rushing towards
the citadel, raising infuriated cries and demanding
the culprit. They threatened to take the place by
storm and massacre the whole garrison. The
Pasha, having nearly two thousand men under
his command, could not resist a prolonged siege,
while he would infallibly have succumbed to the
attack of an enemy ten times superior in numbers.
For seven days we remained shut up in the fort,
dreading every instant to see the attack commenced.
A state of anxiety so prolonged became all the more
unendurable as we had the prospect of famine,
should the situation continue unaltered. No one,
not even the governor himself, dared to venture
beyond the entrenchments.

Weary of seeing ourselves deprived of all communication with the outer world, I resolved to make
an effort to change the posture of affairs, to go out
of the citadel and call on the Prince. Without informing anyone of my intention, I had my carriage
prepared, and ordered the cavasses to accompany me.
This command struck them with amazement. They

thought they were marching to certain death. For my own part, I thought that the insurgents would respect me as a woman. It was not, however, without a certain feeling of apprehension, that I heard the vociferations which arose on all sides when the outer gate was opened. My carriage, meanwhile, advanced, surrounded by the reluctant cavasses. As soon as the Serbians perceived me they ceased their hostile demonstrations, ranged themselves respectfully along the road, and escorted me as far as the Prince's palace. His Highness received me with perfect courtesy. The guards formed in lines on either side, and the military band struck up.

"You are courageous," said the Prince, as he conducted me to his apartments, "but the Pasha has been, in some degree, the cause of what has occurred, in giving protection to a murderer. I could not repress the public indignation, without exposing my authority to misconstruction."

"Your Highness," I replied, "we are here to protect the Turks; it was our duty to receive the man of whom you complain."

"However," said the Prince, "it seems to me an unwarrantable thing that a crime like that should remain unpunished. It is necessary that a public offender should be surrendered to justice."

L

"We are not invested with unlimited authority," I rejoined in my turn, "we are bound to execute the commands of the Sultan, so we have written to Constantinople, to ask for instructions."

"Well," cried Prince Alexander, "how do you propose that I should calm the populace, when I have no satisfaction to offer them?"

"That is your affair," I answered. "It appears to me that we cannot do better than await the orders of the Imperial government. Your Highness must try in the meantime to appease the excitement of the population." The Prince having given me an assurance to that effect, I left and went back to the fortress accompanied by an escort.

Soon afterwards the Prince issued a proclamation to the effect that the Pasha had demanded authority from the Porte to deliver the criminal up to justice; that an answer would be received ere long, which, it was to be hoped, would be a favourable one.

The Serbians beginning to tire of their hostile attitude, and the body having been buried, they calmed down gradually and returned to their homes. In the course of a week or so after my visit to the prince, communication was re-established between the fort and the town. The governor then invited the Prince to come and look for the accused. It was impossible, he said, to give him up, inasmuch as, the very night on which the crime was committed, he had escaped on board a vessel just putting out to sea. It was therefore useless to spend any more time over an affair the settlement of which was impracticable. "If," he added, "I have not sooner informed you how the matter stands, it is because I was unwilling to let you suppose that I feared the threats that were levelled against me when your subjects demanded the surrender of the Mussulman who has been the cause of these disturbances." The Prince pretended to believe what was told him, but remained convinced that the escape was the work of the governor.

To confirm, however, the reconciliation, he asked the Pasha to accept, in my name, an invitation to a banquet which the Princess offered me. She would invite a certain number of Serbian ladies, and they, proud of the honour I did them, would forget, and make their husbands forget, the late dissensions.

To put an end to all further agitation on the subject, the Prince gave out that the delinquent had been sent to Constantinople, there to expiate his crime.

Desirous of responding to the polite attention shown me, I ordered some of the Turkish ladies resident in the town to accompany me to the residence of the Princess of Serbia. They went with reluctance, having a horror of the pork and the wine that would certainly be found on the table of a Christian. Most of them being, as I said before, the wives or daughters of ex-officials, formerly in the service of the Sultan Mahmud, were very zealous followers of Mohamed. One was upwards of eighty years old.

All the Turkish ladies placed themselves on the same side of an immense table with myself. Her highness and the Serbian ladies faced us. The banquet was on a truly princely scale. In order not to hurt the feelings of her Highness, I partook with indifference of the various dishes on the table. The other ladies imitated my example, thinking that I would never eat pork. Presently champagne was poured out for every one. I proposed a toast to the health of the Sultan, and another to that of Iskender-Bey (Prince Alexander of Serbia). The Turkish ladies, who had never before seen champagne, were not at all sure whether what they were drinking was wine or lemonade ; the sparkling of it seems to have puzzled them a bit.

The Prince, to show how much he was pleased with me, sent me next morning a very handsome ring and a pair of magnificent ear-rings. Thus terminated an affray, the beginning of which was as threatening as the issue was pacific.

During my sojourn at Belgrad our home was rejoiced by the birth of an heir to the Pasha, whom his father named Mustapha Djehad Bey. Mustapha was the name of the Pasha's father, while the surname Djehad, which signifies " war," was given because the infant came into the world in time of war—the Hungarian war of 1847.

The birth of an heir was for the Pasha an event which filled his heart with so much joy, that he celebrated it by means of festivals and fireworks.

CHAPTER XIII.

Recall of Mehemet-Pasha—He is appointed Mushir—Invitation from the
Kadin-Effendi—Her History—Condition of Slaves in Turkey.

AFTER remaining about a year at Belgrad, we
were recalled home. As we expected, this time, to
reside there for a lengthened period, we furnished
our house suitably. Scarcely had we got fairly
settled when a *mahbendji,* or chamberlain of the
Sultan, came, attended by a military band, bringing
my husband the *firman* which appointed him to the
rank of *mushir,* or field-marshal. The imperial
warrant was enclosed in a cover of green silk,
adorned with gold tassels. After placing it on the
table, the chamberlain kissed the firman, raised it
respectfully to his forehead, and read it in a distinct
tone; the band struck up a triumphal air, and all
then retired.

During the next few days, my husband received
numerous congratulatory visits, while the ladies, on
their part, came to pay their respects to me. The
Kadin-effendi (second wife) of Mahmud, and
mother of Mcrimah-Sultan, sister of Abdul-Medjid,

sent her *Kjaja-kadin* to invite me to go and spend two or three days in her palace, situated at Tarla-Baschi, facing Dolma-Bagtchè, a residence of the Sultan.

Dressing myself in my best attire, I took with me a beautiful white slave, and a eunuch of good height, both designed as presents to my hostess. Another eunuch attended me as my servant. I drove to the palace, and on arriving at the garden entrance was received by more than a hundred slaves drawn up on each side of my carriage, and lining the way to a magnificent marble stair-case, leading to the harem. Several of them, taking me under the arms, assisted me to ascend. The *Hasnadar-Housta*, or grand mistress, here met me, and conducted me to my apartments. These consisted of three rooms—drawing-room, bed-room, and dining-room. Roses, white and red, adorned the walls; the curtains were of beautiful striped cashmere; costly carpets covered the floors; splendid mirrors were arranged at intervals; golden cups, en-riched with precious stones, and filled with sweet-meats, were placed here and there, in case I should need any refreshment. Besides comfortable divans, there were arm-chairs of European manufacture, and lamps were disposed together with large massive silver candlesticks in the Oriental style, resembling those used for tapers in the churches in France. All the other rooms were furnished pretty much in the same fashion.

I gave my yashmak, or veil, and my feradje, or mantle, to a servant, who placed them in the proper receptacle. After resting for about an hour, I was told that the Sultana awaited me.

I found her seated on a *tandur* (above described), of red velvet embroidered with spangles. The curtains of her room were of flowered cashmere, and slaves stood round about. As soon as I entered, she congratulated me on the good taste of my toilet, and invited me to sit at her feet on a velvet cushion embroidered with gold. This was a great honour. We began to converse, and the Sultana displayed a vivacity of spirits, and a degree of intelligence which I have rarely met with in a Turkish woman. She was tall and fair-haired; and her skin, extremely white, set off the freshness of her complexion.

Knowing that I had been in Europe, she interrogated me as to the manners and customs of the Christians, the way the towns were built, the balls, theatres, systems of lighting by gas, architecture of the palaces, and a thousand other matters unknown to Oriental women. I answered all these questions,

and she seemed well pleased, and testified her satisfaction by recounting to me her troubles.

"I was the adopted daughter," said she, "of
Behiyé-Sultan, sister of the Sultan Mahmud. The
latter rarely visited her sister, but dreading lest
I should take his fancy, knowing, as I did, how
short would be the duration of his attachment, I
hid myself every time he called. I would rather
have preserved my liberty by marrying some Pasha
than become the Sultan's wife. In the meantime,
Mahmud had learnt that his sister had adopted me,
and he was often surprised that he did not see me.

"One day, Behiyé-Sultan gave a grand banquet
to her brother. I barricaded myself in my room,
by placing a chest of drawers against the door, but
the Sultan, who had a strong predilection for the
fair sex, conceived a stratagem in order to get at
me. 'Before supper,' said he to my mistress, 'I am
going to pay a visit to your harem.' He entered,
in succession, all the rooms. Seeing my door shut,
he pushed against it so vigorously as to displace the
chest of drawers, and discovered me concealed
behind a divan. Offering me his hand, he conducted me to his sister, and presenting me to her,
said, 'You see I have done well to visit your palace,
for I have discovered a treasure.'

" 'It is my adopted daughter,' replied Behiyé-Sultan.

" 'I am so greatly enamoured of her,' rejoined Mahmud, 'that I cannot rest until you have given her to me.'

" 'I can refuse you nothing,' she responded, 'because you are my master; but, as I have adopted this young lady, I will treat her as my daughter—I will give her a dowry and send her to you as a lady of good birth.'

" My mistress some days after, sent me to the seraglio, with great ceremony, and with magnificent presents, which she gave me as my dower. For ten days the Sultan was most assiduous in his attentions; after that period he showed himself no more. I had separate and sumptuous apartments, numerous slaves, as many ornaments as I wished for, but I endured with impatience the monotony of my existence. I concealed my grief, and strove to make myself as agreeable as I possibly could to those who attended on me. I never left the palace; I never received a visit from anyone; every morning I took my bath, said my prayers, and then shut myself up in my solitude.

" The few days I had passed in the society of the Sultan resulted in my eventually giving birth to a daughter, Merimah-Sultan. When the time came to get her a husband, I resolved that she should make her choice. I showed her the portraits of several young men, each worthy of her hand. She fixed upon Saïd-Pasha.

"Very few months had elapsed, when my poor daughter, already enceinte, died, and with her my last solace disappeared.

"The mother of Sultan Abdul-Medjid always regards me with a jealous eye. She will scarcely allow me to receive, once a month, a visit from Saïd-Pasha when he is at Constantinople. Moreover, I am never allowed to hear my daughter spoken of."

While uttering these words I saw the big tears start from her eyes. The spectacle of so lively a sorrow touched me, and I felt myself overwhelmed with sympathy for her.

"Judge," continued this poor woman, "whether The Valideh-Sultan, the Sultan's mother, can regard me favourably. Whereas *I* was the adopted daughter of a Sultana, *she* served in the harem, and was engaged in the most menial occupations. One day when, her hair in disorder, she was carrying fuel to the bath, the Sultan saw her through a window, and took a sudden fancy for her. He bid her imme-

diately to lay down the bundle of firewood, and
come with him to the bath. It is in this way
that she became the mother of the present Sultan.
This woman always shows herself my enemy. She
sees with envy that her son, desirous of showing
respect to his father, comes to see me sometimes."

After conversing some time longer with the Sultana, I retired to my apartments, where an abundant
supper was presently served. I stayed three days
at the palace, and spent my time very agreeably.
Sometimes I talked with the Sultana, at other times
some of her principal slaves came to keep me company, and told me the story of their flirtations.

"We like," said one of them, "to drive out alone,
now and then, in a hired carriage, to tease the
young men, who amuse themselves by following us.
One day, when four of us were in the same carriage,
we saw two Pashas, still in their youth, approach us.
They distinguished our features through our yash-
maks" (these veils are of very thin silk gauze),
"and drew near to the door of our conveyance.

"They asked us, by signs, whether we would
accept some fruit, to which we answered in the
affirmative. After offering refreshment, they gave
us a serenade, and then presented us with small
purses full of gold, which we accepted. Em-

boldened on seeing that their gifts were welcome, they followed us to learn where we lived, and to know who we were. What was their surprise when they saw our carriage direct its course towards the palace, and observed that we stopped before the great gate of the harem! The poor fellows seemed overwhelmed with chagrin and wrath. To mock them, we waved our hands as a farewell salutation."

It was thus these poor girls sought at times to entertain themselves. There is no doubt that the position of the slaves is not a very happy one. As the opportunity presents itself here, we will avail ourselves of it to say a few words on the condition of these victims of misfortune and jealousy.

The greater number are poor Circassians; the remainder comprise Arabs, Persians, and others. They are sold to the slave-merchants, either by agents, who have brought them up, or by the parents themselves. The latter look upon their daughters as a means of raising money; they also think that by selling them they are contributing to their happiness. It is a fact that the women in Circassia spend anything but an agreeable existence, being employed in the most laborious field work, and looked upon as mere beasts of burden by their fathers and husbands. All the household duties also devolve upon them. The men would scorn to abase themselves by doing anything useful : they are warriors, and that is all.

In Constantinople, the slave-merchants generally inhabit the district of Top-hanè. When anyone wishes to buy a slave, he applies to these gentry, and they exhibit, for his selection, a band of young peasant-girls, scantily clad, who have only left their mountain homes a few months previously, and speak none other than the barbaric language of their tribes. They sell for various prices, according to the degree of beauty qualifying them for engagements as dancers, musicians, bath-women, *femmes-de-chambre*, or odalisques. The amount ranges from about four thousand up to twenty thousand francs, or thereabouts (£160 to £800). They must be of extraordinary beauty to come up to the last-mentioned figure. If they are not good-looking, they are only employed in duties that do not necessitate their appearance in the presence of their masters, in which case their value does not exceed from fifteen hundred to two thousand francs. They are sold usually at about twelve or thirteen years of age, but there are cases of sales at the early age of six or seven. This happens, however, only where a lady wishes to bring them up as her slaves, either

to accustom them to her service, or to re-sell them
at a profit when they are older. Their mistress
makes them dress becomingly, teaches them to conduct themselves properly, and to speak the Turkish
language. Their attention is bestowed on the cul-
tivation of the particular talent by which they are
to distinguish themselves; such as music, dancing,
hairdressing, etc. If their charms seem to justify
their aspiring to the dignity of odalisques, they
learn to deck themselves gracefully; to observe the
usages recognised in Mussulman society; to offer
sherbet or coffee; to salute with greater or less
formality, or to seat themselves higher or lower,
according to the rank of the person paying or
receiving a visit; to accompany their mistresses, etc.

When they have received this primary education, their value is proportionately augmented, and
it is at this period that they are re-sold. The
singers, the performers on the guitar, flute, tabour,
or tambourine, the dancers and castanet-players,
then enter the harems of great ladies, whom they
are required to entertain. These are held in the
highest estimation. They cost from six to eight
thousand francs.

If any lady possesses a pretty-looking slave, the
fact soon gets known. The gentlemen who wish to

buy an odalisque or a wife, make their offers. Many
Turks, indeed, prefer to take a slave as a wife, as,
in such case, there is no need to dread fathers,
mothers, or brothers-in-law, and other undesirable
relations.

A girl can never be sold for a wife or an odalisque
without her own consent.

The purchase of a slave is transacted in the
following manner :—After having examined her
from head to foot, the intending purchaser, male
or female, agrees on the price. The bargain concluded, next day the girl is sent to his or her house,
accompanied by an old woman, who never lets her
out of her sight. She remains several days, in order
that it may be ascertained whether or not she has
any material defect. A mid-wife is called in to
make sure that the newcomer has never previously
had intercourse with anyone. It is after this examination that the purchase-money is paid, and the
sale legalised by a formal receipt, called *petcheh*.

In every house which a slave enters she is nearly
equally miserable. Wives and odalisques comprise
the superior class. If their master is rich, they
enjoy all the refinements of luxury : carriages,
excursions, banquets, servants of all kinds. But it
frequently happens that, after being for some time

the only wife, the husband introduces another, as her associate in his affections.

Whatever may be her condition, slave or free, the new wife reduces the first to the second rank. If she be equally a slave, the only result is jealousy ; but if she be wealthy, and of a family which the husband holds in respect, then the poor slave-wife has to put up with all the annoyances, all the humiliations that a jealous and all-powerful rival can invent. Her life is one long martyrdom, which frequently reaches a tragical termination.

When a slave enters the harem of a lady of high rank, her situation is truly deplorable. As has been described in the establishment of Nazly-Hanum, she is usually compelled to spend her nights standing, attendant on the riotous excesses of her mistress. From sheer caprice, they often find themselves condemned to be scourged by eunuchs, armed with *curbatches* or whips of elephant's skin.

On the other hand, these unhappy creatures are often subjected at once to the desires of their master and the terrible jealousy of their mistress. Threatened with perpetual celibacy, excited by the idea of being chosen either as odalisques or as wives of the second grade, frequently taken advantage of by force,—everything contributes to their downfall. As soon as their mistress has an inkling of any intrigue, all the vials of her fury are poured out. Her husband, his patience being at length exhausted, abandons his victim to the resentment of his wife, who proceeds to get rid of her rival forthwith, by selling her.

If the unhappy girl finds herself *enceinte*, she cannot be sold while in that condition. Moreover, she cannot be sold if she gives birth to a son. Her mistress, therefore, takes her to a mid-wife, in order to procure abortion.

Slaves, however, have occasionally a dismal kind of solace. They may please their mistress without attracting the attentions of their master. If they are in the Seraglio, or in some great house, they may become *Kjaja-kadin* (first lady), or *Haznadar-ousta* (treasurer), in which case they have separate apartments, with carriages and servants at their disposal. These are great ladies. The treasurer to the Valideh-Sultan had more than two hundred slaves or eunuchs under her orders.

I began to get tired of my residence in the palace. Accustomed to a quiet way of living, I was obliged, for fear of vexing those who attended on me, to partake of all the dishes placed on my table; which seriously inconvenienced me. In the meantime I could not take my leave; such a proceeding

would have been a breach against the etiquette of
the Seraglio. I had to wait therefore till my feradjé
and my yashmak were restored to me, and it was
with real satisfaction that, on the fourth day, I saw
the ladies in waiting bringing these articles. I sent
the Sultana the eunuch and the young slave-girl,
whom I had brought for her acceptance, and she
sent me, in return, a present of a beautiful gold
watch, green-enamelled, and set with brilliants, as
was also the chain. She sent my daughter a piece
of striped cachmere.

As the Sultana had made presents of money to
my eunuch, my coachman, and my other servants, I
was obliged to return the compliment with respect
to her household. I wrapped small gold coins in
embroidered handkerchiefs corresponding in number
to her servants, and remitted the whole to the
treasurer, one of whose privileges it is to undertake
distributions of this kind. If by accident, in making
up my packets, I had overlooked any slave, it would
not have been good manners on my part to go
before repairing the omission, and, if I had not
sufficient money left for the purpose, I should have
been obliged to send and procure a fresh supply,
before taking my departure. After satisfying everybody, I got into my carriage, and drove off.

THE invitation which the Kadin-Effendi had sent me was not altogether disinterested. Knowing that my husband was in favour with Reshid-Pasha, the then all-powerful Grand-vezir, she wished to secure my services in behalf of Saïd-Pasha, husband of her deceased daughter, then in exile at Castambolu.

Saïd-Pasha, like all the partisans of the ancient Ottoman institutions, saw with jealousy the elevation of a minister imbued with European ideas. As soon as any official whatsoever shows himself to be animated with ideas of progress; decides, without respect of persons, all matters that come in question before him; or gives proof of intelligence and education, the title of *ghiaur* (infidel) is conferred upon him. All things straightway conspire to bring about his fall. If he cannot be entrapped into some fault sufficiently grave to ensure his complete disgrace, attempts are made to get him banished to a command in some semi-barbarous, frontier province, destitute of every resource, and where the most brilliant talents and the best intentions become unproductive of advancement; exercised, as they are, in countries far removed from the eye of the master, by whom whatever takes place, good or bad, is regarded with equal indifference.

At the period of which we are speaking, the policy of Russia with regard to the Porte was becoming more and more menacing, and war was imminent. The Grand-vezir saw that all was lost if he could not contrive to counterbalance the power of Russia by means of an alliance with the Western Powers. The Sultan viewed with repugnance the formation of alliances which, in case of war, would bring foreign troops to Constantinople. " Who knows," said he, " whether, when they have once gained admission, the Allies will consent to withdraw from a place which all European nations covet with about equal ardour ? "

Riza-Pasha, Saïd-Pasha, Mehemet-Ali-Pasha, and all the other ministers attached to the old Turkish party, resolved to take advantage of the repugnance of Abdul-Medjid to European preponderancy. They spread a report that the *Sadr-azam* (Grand-vezir), only spoke of the intervention of the European Powers in order to realise the bargain which he had concluded with them. "He is about to sell to the Europeans," said they, "Constantinople, and all our possessions in Europe. Now he wishes to deliver up to them all they have bought of him, for its price in gold."

Saïd-Pasha then addressed a memorandum to the Sultan, in which he called his Majesty's attention to the designs of Reshid ; warning him that, if he was not on his guard, the French and English would be taking possession of his fairest provinces ; that the Russians had an understanding with the other Powers as to their partition ; that the Muscovite threats and the French and English offers were in furtherance of an adroit manœuvre, designed to trick the Porte through the concerted action of the several cabinets.

The other ministers were to affix their seals to this document, which it was intended to present to the Padishah as the expression of the fears entertained by all. At the decisive moment, they induced Saïd-Pasha to make, in the first instance, a verbal communication to their master. "You are his brother-in-law ; what have you to fear ? If you find that you have a favourable hearing, you may

reckon beforehand on our approval." The too-con-
fiding minister listened to their counsels, went to
the Sultan, skilfully turned to account the suspicions with which the prospect of a Western alliance
had possessed him, and thought to convince him
of the Grand-vezir's treason.

Abdul-Medjid was naturally little addicted to
forming violent resolves, and a reaction was at work
in his mind.

"All you tell me appears true," he cried, "but,
up to the present time, Reshid-Pasha has served me
faithfully. He has always given proof of great
zeal, and I have never known him betray the interests
of his country. You are bringing against him an
accusation of the gravest possible character, and
you stand alone in mentioning it to me. I hesitate
to believe you, and to ruin, on mere suspicion,
the most intelligent man in the empire."

"I am not alone in my warnings," replied Saïd-
Pasha. "All the other ministers are in accord with
me, and I am ready to give your Majesty a written
proof to that effect."

"If it is so, I yield," said the Sultan. "Furnish me
with this document, and I am resolved to take action
on it," he added, as he dismissed his interlocutor.

The latter hastened to his colleagues to announce

the successful result of his undertaking, but he strove in vain to persuade them to sign the required document. They thought, and with reason, that their adversary would not fail to defend himself vigorously before his master. He would challenge his accusers to supply proofs of which they were devoid. They saw themselves, in prospect, exposed to the hatred of a vindictive and all-powerful minister.

Reshid-Pasha got to know of the steps taken before the Sultan, and of the insuperable difficulty which Saïd-Pasha had found in the way of his again presenting himself with the confirmatory evidence demanded of him. He decided, therefore, of ridding himself of Saïd and driving him into exile.

It was under these circumstances that the Kadin-Effendi invited me. She entreated me to speak to my husband, and get him to intercede with the Grand-vezir, in order to obtain the recall of the disgraced Pasha. I promised to exert all my zeal in his favour.

Reshid-Pasha made a pretence of pardoning. He recalled Saïd, and gave him the governorship of Damascus. This was a clever scheme to effect his utter ruin. Damascus was one of the most troublesome commands in the empire, on account of its mixed population. Arabs, Greeks, Turks, Mussulmans, Christians, Jews, found themselves side by side. Hence arose perpetual difficulties.

The success of my husband's intervention made me none the less friends with Saïd-Pasha and his mother-in-law.

That which the spiteful Reshid foresaw came to pass. A Jew having committed a theft, the governor had him severely bastinadoed to make him confess his crime. The accused died next day. The Israelites were in rebellion, they despatched a deputation to Constantinople, and brought to bear upon the Porte the whole weight of the *Société Israelite Universelle*, and of Sir Moses Montefiore's diplomatic ability. The Grand-vezir, content with the power of charging his enemy with murder, lost no time in degrading him, and sending him into exile at Koniah. His vengeance was satiated.

Reshid-Pasha, was a man endowed with superior intelligence, and who possessed, in addition, great strength of character. His expressive countenance indicated, at the same time, great determination and great subtlety. He could not, however, quite conceal an air of vindictiveness, which displayed itself especially when he fixed his glance on an adversary whom he had just received with exquisite courtesy, and who was withdrawing, convinced of the minister's favourable intentions in his behalf. He was rather below the middle height; dark complexioned, with black beard and very thick eyebrows; while his broad shoulders and massive neck betokened the man of vigorous energy.

CHAPTER XV.

LEAVING the palace of the Kadin-Effendi at an early hour, as it was a Thursday, and as, at Constantinople, each day has its particular promenade, I directed my steps to the Sweet Waters.

This is a spot to which people resort either on foot, in carriages, or in boats. The women keep on one side of a long alley winding along the bank of the stream; the men on the other, but the intervening space is small, and readily available for purposes of flirtation. The gentlemen throw flowers, or little complimentary notes, to the ladies; and the latter, if respectable, content themselves with acknowledging the attention by the gift of a flower, or a note of thanks, and the matter goes no further; for no one would dare to follow a woman of decorum. It thus happens that young gentlemen and ladies meet one another every day for years without becoming acquainted; but, on the other hand, it is through

these interviews that women of indifferent character
find opportunities of contracting intimacies with
their admirers. They reply to the notes thrown to
them, appointing a place of meeting, or giving their
name and address, so that the suitor may employ
an old woman, as a go-between, to arrange the
affair.

These promenades offer a very attractive scene at
the times when they·are frequented. The 'ladies
descend from their carriages, have a carpet spread
on the grass, and seat themselves, with their slaves,
to partake of a collation. They vie with each other
in the luxuries of the table which are set forth on
these occasions. Everywhere may be seen the
glitter of gold and silver plate. Bands of music
perform, sometimes on the ladies' side, sometimes
on the opposite. Numberless skiffs are wafted along
over the surface of the water. You may frequently
see some lady of quality, seated with coquetry on
a crimson cloth, fringed with gold, while her slaves
sit opposite to her. The various colours of the
feradjés, red, green, or blue ; the magnificence of
the equipages ; the animation called forth by the
strains of music, and the banquets enjoyed on the
grass ; the arrivals and departures of carriages and
pleasure-seekers on horseback and on foot ; the dif-

ferent costumes of the servants, eunuchs, and couriers ; the picturesque costumes of the coster-mongers ; all these afford a lively and agreeable spectacle.

The Turkish ladies of rank never go out, on ordinary occasions, except in daytime. During the Ramazan, however, as before mentioned, they go out only in the evening, and seldom come home before midnight. Throughout that month it is customary for the men and the eunuchs to take part in a prayer called *Téravi*, which is offered at the close of each day, and lasts for about an hour and a half. Many ladies take advantage of this period to go out and have an interview with their sweet-hearts, under the pretext of visiting a female friend. No husband would dare, at the risk of making him-self an object of ridicule, to refuse his wife permis-sion to go out with an old woman slave, to a mosque, or to a female friend.

Indeed one of the great sources of entertainment among the ladies, apart from the promenade, is the interchange of calls. It is not unusual to see at the house of a lady of some rank, as many as twenty or thirty visitors. They pass the time in gossiping, watching the slaves dance, listening to songs, drink-ing coffee or sherbet, and smoking. The ordinary townspeople often stay till after supper, and light themselves home with lanterns.

The women are generally the first to learn and circulate news. The men often visit one another, but they are always reserved. They speak with less restraint to their wives, and tell them, for their entertainment, what they have heard, and what they think of doing. The wives of the high functionaries are on terms of close intimacy with other great ladies, and repeat to them what their husbands have said; in this way the news is spread abroad with unheard-of rapidity.

The Baïram now arrived,—a three days' feast succeeding the Ramazan. This is the most memorable epoch of the Mussulman year. It comprises, in importance, both the Easter and Christmas of the Christians.

On the first morning, every husband embraces his wife, the children come to kiss the hands of their parents, and friends and relatives exchange congratulations and embrace each other in the streets. Every Mussulman, from the poorest to the richest, dresses himself in his best. The ladies go to pay their compliments to those of higher rank than their own. The great ladies do not make their calls until eight days after the termination of the festival. The great drum that, every night during the Ramazan, gave the signal to arise from slumber, now makes its appearance to offer the compliments of the season. The watchman who beats it, marches through the streets, followed by a crowd of children of both sexes. The ladies, looking out through the wickets in their lattices, give him pieces of money wrapped in muslin handkerchiefs. At the same time, the poor come round, offering oranges and sweetmeats, and generally receive in exchange clothes and small pieces of money. The men also pay visits to one another; those of inferior degree bringing presents of bonbons or fruit to their superiors.

On the first day of the Baïram, the Sultan goes, on horseback, in great state, to the Mosque, accompanied by all the ministers, and high state officials, the ladies of the Seraglio, the wives of the ministers and other dignitaries. On his return, the Sultan places himself under the cupola of the throne, and there receives the homage of his subjects. Everyone, on approaching his Majesty, kisses the edge of a scarf carried by the first chamberlain of the Court. The Grand-vezir is the first to perform this ceremony; then his *musteshar* (lieutenant), after kissing the scarf, salutes him, by raising his hand to his forehead, and then takes his place at his side.

Every high functionary, in the order of his degree, follows the example.

The people celebrate the Baïram by tumultuous rejoicings. They go in crowds to the principal squares, where are to be seen itinerant musicians, mountebanks, fencers, exhibitors of magic lanterns, vendors of sweetmeats and pastry, in fact, all the tribe one is accustomed to meet with at the public fêtes in Europe.

Three months after the Baïram, following the Ramazan, comes the Kourban Baïram, which also lasts three days. Every man, no matter how poor, has two sheep allotted to him. Having uttered a prayer, he kills both the animals,—one for himself, the other for his wife, as, according to the Mussulman creed, the sheep that anyone kills in the year of his death will serve as a steed on which he may cross the bridge of Siraht that leads to the gate of paradise. The rich, instead of performing the sacrifice themselves, employ a butcher, and have not one only, but often as many as ten or fifteen sheep killed, according to their means. The animal is cut into a great number of pieces, and the owner sends a portion to each of his neighbours, and to all to whom he is desirous of paying a compliment.

The three days of this festival is passed in entertainments, of which the poor have their full share, so that they avail themselves of the presents that have been made them, to provide for the present, and to put on one side whatever food they wish to keep during the winter. During these days the slaves and domestics are hard at work in the kitchen. Their chief occupation is that of preparing the meat preserves. The method they employ is to fry and salt the meat; this once done, they put it inside some big jar which is covered up to the top with an air-proof coating of grease.

CHAPTER XVI.

IT was in the month of Ramazan, in the year 1848, that my husband was appointed ambassador to the English Court. This appointment was occasioned by the threatening attitude assumed by Russia by her intervention in the Austro-Hungarian difficulty. The Porte, alarmed at the progress made by this Power, thought it necessary to form an alliance with the West, and particularly with Great Britain. This delicate mission was entrusted to Kibrizli-Mehemet-Pasha, who was intimately associated with Reshid-Pasha, the promoter of this new policy.

Independently of the political reasons which influenced this nomination, Reshid had certain entirely private motives for the selection of my husband; he wished to secure the friendship and support of the Palmerston Cabinet, and to bring financial operations to bear upon the London market. In other words, he offered England commercial and financial advantages in exchange for the support which that Power would undertake to give to his own policy and personal control. The negotiations which preceded this appointment did not take place altogether unknown to me. On the contrary, my share in the transaction materially assisted its prosperous issue. With this view I used my personal influence with the Grand-vezir, to induce him to nominate my husband to the post, in preference to any other candidate. Kibrizli-Pasha used immense exertions to achieve his object, but he thought it prudent to send me alone, in advance, as a negociator, for he feared lest he should compromise himself in vain. Experience had taught him that nothing was impossible to a woman.

Indeed, some days before the Baïram, Reshid-Pasha's wife sent to inform me that my husband's nomination had been laid before his Majesty, and that, before long, the Imperial rescript would be forwarded to us. The publication of the firman of investiture having taken place shortly afterwards, the Pasha received the congratulations of the *corps diplomatique*, and the high dignitaries of the Porte.

These ceremonies concluded he made his preparations for the voyage.

Since religious prejudices and custom forbid Mussulman wives to accompany their husbands into a Christian country, I was, of course, unable to go with my husband to his embassy. He, consequently, took all the steps necessary to the maintenance of his house. To this end he spared neither trouble nor expense, and left everything at my disposal, that I, my children, my slaves, and my domestics could possibly desire.

Our farewell greetings were most affectionate and affecting. With tears in his eyes, the poor Pasha could scarcely tear himself away from me and his children. So strong was his grief that his voice was choked with convulsive sobs. This emotion was natural; for it was the first time since we had become man and wife that we were to be separated.

But these adieus were the last that we should ever exchange, little as we suspected it. A fatal destiny was soon to put an end to our happiness and that of our children. If a prophetic voice could have disclosed the future, the poor Pasha would not have hesitated an instant in turning with disdain from grandeur and ambition; never would he have consented to obtain them at the cost of what he valued more than all the world beside. Destiny, however, whether cruel or pleasant, works its way in spite of our wishes or fears, and these adieus, as I said, were our last.

It was long before I could find any solace for the grief that my husband's departure had occasioned me. Moreover, the solitary and monotonous life I led in my residence at Yuksek Caldirim could not but aggravate my sorrow, by rendering my very existence insupportable. I was principally occupied in silent contemplation of the beautiful view afforded from my window of the seven hills of Stambul, crowned with mosques, and surrounded by houses and gardens. The visitors who, from time to time, came to see me did something towards enlivening the dreary sameness of my everyday life. Among these, the ladies of the palace and the eunuchs of the Seraglio afforded me most entertainment, and for this reason,—that persons of this class are far more sprightly and unconstrained than the towns-people. Their manners are less affected, and consequently more sincere, and thus it is that their society is so agreeable, and brings such a charm to the spirit oppressed with the tedious routine of harem life.

Amongst the eunuchs, moreover, I found friends

whose company gave me pleasure, in that some of
them were accomplished poets and musicians.
Ferhad-Agha, for example, combined both these
qualities. He was a genuine troubadour, whose
chivalrous sentiments and gaiety of heart repelled
everything that was ignoble or that savoured of
spleen. His besetting weakness, however, was a
love of *raki;* but this was only natural: from all
time, Bacchus and the Muses have dwelt together
in harmony. Whenever, therefore, I could have my
palace friends, I never failed to welcome them. As
to the outdoor amusements offered in the public
promenades, they were things for which I had little
predilection; besides, in Turkey, it is not etiquette
for a lady to go much abroad in the absence of her
husband. In proof of this, instances may be cited
where ladies have refrained, for many years, from
setting foot outside their houses, in order to testify
thereby their love for their absent husbands. My
horses, therefore, confined to their stables, had
plenty of leisure to enjoy their good fare, and grow
fat in their sloth. Whole months often passed and
I cared not to cross my threshhold.

It is clear that so retired and uneventful an
existence could not but react upon my spirits, and
afflict me with a sense of uneasiness which I should

find it difficult to describe. But, while thus tormented with enforced idleness and *ennui*, an unexpected and most serious event occurred to rouse me from my lethargy, and irrevocably to affect my future.

My boy, Djehad-Bey, was naturally of a sickly and feeble constitution, so that he had always been a subject of great anxiety both to me and to his father. Soon after the Pasha left for London, Djehad's health grew worse from day to day, so that the physicians at length lost all hope of his recovery. This crowned my despair, for I knew that nothing could console his father for such a loss. The Pasha dearly loved this child, whom he regarded as his future heir. The death of his elder son, Moharem-Bey, had already caused him lively sorrow, and now, if Djehad died, he would be inconsolable. The moment, then, seemed to me to have arrived to carry out a plan agreed to between my husband and myself, before he quitted Constantinople, and which the delicate health of the boy had suggested. It was to replace him, in the event of his death, by another child, to be obtained secretly. Now, unless this scheme could be executed within a given number of weeks, so as to bring the factitious birth within a natural period since the Pasha's departure, I knew it would be impossible to attempt it. I kept him informed of the critical condition of Djehad, and received the Pasha's replies and consent to the prosecution of our plan, without delay, should the necessity become imperative. But how to carry our plan into effect was a most perplexing question.

The state of feverish excitability into which I was thrown could not be concealed from the eyes of my acquaintances, nor of those members of my household who frequented my presence. My housekeeper was one Fatmah, a native of Syria, to whom my husband had entrusted the management of the harem, and the supervision of the slaves. This person enjoyed a certain degree of importance, in consequence of the authority my husband had conferred upon her. Her position, and the attentions she lavished upon me, insured her free access to me, and warranted a certain familiarity which no one else would have dared to indulge in. She had observed the change that had come over me since the sickness of my son, and in no doubt as to its cause, sought to pry deeper into the secrets of my heart. Possessed of ability and tact, she was not slow in bringing them to bear upon the subject of the thoughts which were agitating my mind. No sooner had she succeeded to her heart's content, than this vile woman conceived the diabolical scheme of taking advantage of my confidence, by contriving a plot which would make me her victim and place me in her power. She had come to Constantinople to push her fortune as an adventuress, and all means of achieving her object were good in her eyes.

Skilfully feigning to share my uneasiness and to take to heart my interests, while discussing the probabilities that might arise out of the death of my poor boy, this woman, far from striving to tranquillize my spirits, sought to incite me to jealousy by the suggestion of suspicions regarding my husband's future course towards me, asserting that she, herself, knew, on good authority, that the Pasha had resolved to marry again, in case his son died. Such an event, she remarked, would inevitably bring about my destruction. I need scarcely say I never told her my husband and I were agreed.

Having succeeded, by fair words and promises, in convincing me of her devotion and exciting in my breast the most violent emotions, Fatmah then proceeded to give me advice, and to tell me that it was needless to give way to despair, for that, in this world, a remedy could be found for every ill. Pressed to explain herself more particularly, Fatmah

added, as though she had read my thoughts :—
"Well, madam, you have only to buy a child of
some unhappy creature, and to put him in the place
of your own. The Pasha's absence affords a golden
opportunity, which should not be lost."

This counsel, harmonizing with my own plan,
seemed to afford me the very opportunity I sought
of executing it; and although my acceptance of it
involved me in a false position towards the Pasha,
in the eyes of my accomplice, I was blind to the
danger, so intense was my desire to contribute to
my husband's happiness. Even now, when I reflect
on the imprudence of which I was guilty, I cannot
believe it amounted to crime, as the party principally
concerned was privy to the deceit.

To have recourse to a feigned confinement, in
order to put forth as my own an infant that was
the offspring of another, was a simple impossibility,
for the very agents whom I should have to employ
to execute such a piece of jugglery, would be the
first to reveal the secret and compromise me before
the world.

But the phantom of that child's death that seemed
to be pursuing me, and the dread I entertained of a
catastrophe, so utterly blinded me, that I believed
everything to be possible. And so, with incon-

ceivable simplicity, it appeared to me that nothing could be easier than to give oneself out to be *enceinte*, and to borrow an infant, just as one may borrow a costume, or set of jewels, or anything else. As for the agents whom it was necessary to employ in the performance of this precious trick, it never entered into my head that they would take the earliest opportunity of betraying me.

And, in the meantime, I was the woman whose intellect was vaunted and admired by every one ; she whom all were ready to consult as if she were an oracle ! But such is the weakness of the human mind, which from the loftiest height may fall into the abyss of insanity and blind infatuation ! It is an acknowledged truth that the more brains one has, the more follies one commits. , That my folly was morally inexcusable I admit, and this conviction has led me to endure with resignation the twenty years of suffering to which I have been condemned. But this fault, which had its source in a feeling of love, very natural in a devoted wife, attained, thanks to the spite of my enemies, the proportions of an infamous crime. They who • thirsted for my blood, transformed, I say, a simple fault into a crime, and punished me by social degradation, by exile, by the confiscation of every-

thing I possessed, and by condemning me to a life
of misery and shame. It is time, however, to take
up the thread of my story at the point from which I
have digressed. Fatmah succeeded in obtaining my
consent, and all the needful measures were taken to
prepare for the birth of the pretended infant. The
critical period having arrived, Fatmah went in search
of a child, and bought one from a poor woman,
who was glad to get rid of what she found too
heavy a burden.

It must here be mentioned that Fatmah was not
alone in the enterprise, for it would have been impossible for her to accomplish her work without
previously securing the aid of another agent. With
this view, she thought fit to take into her confidence
one of the eunuchs, named Beshir, in order that he
might have a hand in the clandestine introduction
of the infant. However, all the pains they took were
absolutely useless, inasmuch as the sickness of my
son Djehad, all of a sudden, took a favourable turn,
and his recovery was not long delayed. And so,
after all, the only result of this affair was that I
found myself charged with an additional burden,
and became the victim of those of whom I had
been the accomplice.

The blow once struck, its consequences were not

slow in making their appearance. Fatmah and her confederate, elated by their success, assumed, all at once, the air of masters, and imposed their commands alike upon their fellow-servants and upon me. Seeing that my connivance in this sad affair rendered me mute and powerless, these two fiends threw the house into utter confusion.

The slaves and servants, unable any longer to endure the insolence of these two tyrants, loudly called for my intervention ; but as their appeals were ineffectual, a revolt ensued. My impassible demeanour was, not unreasonably, interpreted as a proof of my connivance with the excesses committed by Fatmah and Beshir. In vain I attempted to promote tranquillity by liberally bestowing kindnesses, now on one, now on another. Such treatment only served to light anew the fire of discord with redoubled force, for these sacrifices had no other result than to excite the cupidity of the disaffected.

My patience quite worn out, and feeling justly alarmed at the menacing proportions that the spirit of sedition had assumed, I thought it necessary to call to my assistance the authority of our man of business, Reshid-Effendi, to endeavour to re-establish order in my household. As Fatmah and Beshir from associates had become sworn enemies to such a degree as to long to kill each other, I insisted that they should both be expelled from the house, as the only way of preventing a catastrophe; for the two rivals made no mystery of their determination to take each other's life. Reshid, however, treated the matter with an air of incredulity, and refused to interfere, saying that "it was only an affair between a woman and a eunuch."

This reply and the indifference displayed by Reshid-Effendi on this occasion did not contribute to my tranquillity, for I was in a better position than himself to judge of what passed before my eyes. Abandoned, then, to my own resources, I found no other alternative than to attempt one last experiment : that is to say, to separate the two rivals by dint of a pecuniary sacrifice. With this object, I entered into negociations with Fatmah, in order to induce her to leave the house. She consented to take her departure, but only after extorting from me a considerable sum.

Delighted to have got rid of this wicked woman, I set to work to appease Beshir, who, seeing himself fawned upon, and satisfied with gaining a triumph over his rival, promised to conduct himself in a becoming manner. As to the matter of the adopted child, it was agreed that it should remain in abeyance, until the return of the Pasha, who would make such arrangements as he thought fit.

A month had elapsed since the departure of Fatmah, when I had to give a reception to celebrate the first reading of the Koran, which was to be performed this year by my daughter Aïsheh. It is customary among Mussulmans to celebrate this event with an *éclat* corresponding to the position and means of the parents of the pupil. Invitations were accordingly sent to all our acquaintances, and no expense was spared to make the reception a sumptuous one.

In the meantime Fatmah had opened a correspondence with my enemies in the palace, and had been instigated by them to revenge herself both on me, who had discarded her, and on her mortal enemy Beshir, by every means in her power, not even excepting murder. She thought the best means of introducing herself into the house, and perpetrating the crime that she meditated, was to mingle with the crowd of guests, and make her entrance, unobserved in the confusion. Being informed that Fatmah was in the house I sent for her, and inquired her motives for making her appearance in a place where her presence was by no means desired. Her reply was dry and curt.

"Madam," she said, "am I to understand that I was expelled from your house?—have I no right to come to assist in the celebration of a fête?"

As I saw clearly, by the tone of this response, that Fatmah would have no hesitation in creating a scene in the midst of the guests, I thought it prudent to retire ; not forgetting, however, to summon Beshir, and caution him to say nothing to the woman, for I did not wish to have a disturbance in the house. I gave him to understand that Fatmah would only stay a very short time, and consequently he need not think anything at all about her.

Counting on the efficacy of the measures I had taken, I entered the room where my guests were assembled, and gave myself up to the duties of hospitality.

But, while the company were regaling themselves with the charms of music and of song, Fatmah was engaged in the prosecution of her sanguinary designs. Skilfully evading observation, she proceeded gently to open the door that separated the selamlik from the harem, and admitted one of the servants, named Omer, who, as her lover, was to bear a hand in the contemplated assassination. Fatmah then succeeded, by a *ruse*, in inveigling Beshir into the bath-room ; there the two assassins sprang upon the unfortunate Arab, hurled him to the ground and suffocated him. Such was Fatmah's rage against her victim, that she resolutely took his life herself, by sitting on his face, while Omer contented himself by throwing him down, and holding his hands.

CHAPTER XVII.

SCARCELY had Beshir heaved his last sigh when
the doors of the harem were broken open, and an infuriated crowd invaded the apartment, with cries of
"Murder! murder! Vengeance! vengeance!" Terror seized on every one. The guests took flight
from the fury of the mob. The insurgents made
their way to the room whither I had retired, with
three or four of my slaves who had remained faithful to my cause. The wretches, on entering, did not
scruple to bespatter me with the blood of Beshir,
and to menace me with sabres, sticks, and other
weapons which they brandished in the air.

I must here pause to remark that amongst this
swarm of invaders, there were not more than five or
six members of my household; the remainder,
numbering, perhaps, thirty or thereabouts, were

strangers, whose presence at this moment is quite incomprehensible. It would appear as though they had been collected together in order to give a theatrical effect to the tragedy.

Order could only be restored through the intervention of the police, who lost no time in appearing on the scene of the disaster. The police agents hastened to make out their official report, by submitting the assassins to examination. When they came to inquire into the motives for the commission of the crime, a scene of violence ensued. On the one hand, those who sought my destruction boisterously called upon Fatmah and Omer to inculpate me alone; on the other, these preserved an obstinate silence. This strife was carried on for some time without inducing the culprits to depose that it was solely by my orders that they had killed the eunuch. It was only through a hint that by this means alone' could they hope to escape capital punishment, that the two murderers were induced to avow I had ordered them to put Beshir to death. As soon as the depositions were taken, the prisoners were conducted, under escort, to the office of the Minister of Police, to take their trial.

During the course of these tragic events, my enemies, and those of my husband, tried their

o 2

utmost to achieve our ruin. My enemies were
delighted to have, at last, found the means of
crushing me for ever, and putting it out of my
power to injure them. The political enemies of my
husband, on their part, hastened to take advantage
of the opportunity afforded them of separating us,
and so destroying our combined action. Without
me, Mehemet-Pasha was a half-disabled foe, for it
was well known what a part I had had in his promotion. It was through me that an understanding
had been established between him and the Grand-
vezir, and it was by my efforts that his nomination
to the post of Minister for Foreign Affairs had been
spoken of with favour. Such an event, his opponents
well knew, would be a death-blow to them. These
said enemies were the Valideh, the Sultan's mother;
Mehemet-Ali-Pasha; Mehemet-Pasha, Minister of
Police; Rifaat, and a host of other Pashas more
or less influential.

Impelled by such motives, these people made as
great an uproar as possible, and spread false reports
of my alleged crimes and atrocities. The journals,
native and foreign, were filled with stories designed
to gratify public credulity, and to exhibit my character under the most revolting aspect. This was
an easy task, for I had no one to take my part.

Finding that, by such means, they had produced the desired effèct, my enemies had recourse to legal proceedings, and procured my arrest. Four days, indeed, after Beshir's death, I received a summons to appear before the Minister of Police to answer the charges that had been brought against me. Tearing myself from my children, and from those about me who had remained faithful, I got into my carriage, and was driven to the office. I was then confined in a house which the Government had prepared and furnished for the occasion. My keepers were two female servants and a domestic, in the confidence of the minister, and upon whom he could rely. As to the treatment I had to undergo from them during my imprisonment, I may say that while, on the one hand, they affected to lavish on me those attentions which were due to a woman in my position, on the other hand they resorted to every means of intimidation.

It was thought advisable, in order to overcome my obstinacy, to threaten me with the most exquisite tortures ; and, to show that they were not jesting, the police-agents busied themselves in recounting all the horrible cruelties of which their master was capable. They told me, amongst other things, that when the old Pasha was Governor of Cyprus he had

a number of people impaled and burnt, in the most
cold-blooded manner imaginable.   These threats and
anecdotes could not but produce a painful impression upon me, and the rather because I knew that
the   Valideh-Sultan   and my   other   enemies   were
eagerly thirsting for my blood.

There were moments, especially during the silent
watches of the night, when my spirit succumbed,
beneath the pressure of the moral torments I was
condemned to suffer.   At such a time, despair had
full dominion over me, for I knew I could look for
no mercy at the hands of enemies who had sworn to
push their schemes of vengeance to the utmost limits.
After subjecting me to threats and terrorism, the
Minister of Police finally summoned me to his
presence.   A kind of sitting was held, in which the
Minister himself, Rifaat-Pasha, and a secretary took
part.   This court was a regular *hole-and-corner*
concern.   The two Pashas proceeded there to give
a cursory *résumé* of the affair, after which they put
questions to me, the object of which was to make me
confess my participation in the murder of Beshir.
My answer, from which I never swerved, was as
follows :—

" I never gave any order of the kind, nor have I,
in any way, been a party to the crime.   Indeed," I

said to the two Pashas, who were gazing at me in astonishment, " do you think that if I had wished to rid myself of Beshir, I should have been so stupid as to have him strangled in so public a manner, while with a few pennyworths of poison I could have made away with him quietly enough ? Moreover, if I had made any choice between the two, I should have striven to get rid of Fatmah rather than of Beshir, for it is she to whom I owe all my sorrow."

Seeing that their questioning was fruitless, the two Pashas did not repeat their sittings more than twice.

In speaking of what happened to me while I was in prison, I ought to mention how the confiscation of my jewellery took place. Some days after my incarceration three police-officers made their appearance, and desired me to give up to them the casket containing my jewels. These consisted of a quantity of necklaces, girdles, chains, &c., all set with brilliants, and their value would amount to about six or seven thousand pounds sterling. All these articles were counted over, one by one, after which the minister's seal was affixed to the casket. When this was done, the officers informed me that these jewels would remain in their custody until such time as I was set at liberty, and then they would be restored to me untouched. When I ventured to ask for a receipt for the jewels I had entrusted to them, the only answer I could obtain was that their instructions forbid them to comply with my request.

It is needless to remark that from that moment my jewels were taken away from me altogether. On the arrival of my husband from London, the Government hastened to place them in his hands. This arbitrary act was a flagrant violation of the Mussulman laws, which maintains respect for the property of a wife.

While these things were going on in the office of the Minister of Police, intrigues outside were running their free course. The enemies of Reshid-Pasha's cabinet were making superhuman efforts to crush, at one blow, myself and my husband. Taking advantage of the prevalent public feeling, they endeavoured to make my affair a ministerial question, and impeached Reshid-Pasha for shielding me.

The Grand-vezir, indeed, saw that it was impossible to save me from the hands of my enemies, for such a course would have been fatal to his administration.

Compelled to yield before such a coalition, Reshid found himself under the necessity of abandoning me to my fate.

However, he did his best to save Kibrizli-Pasha from being involved in my ruin ; for, by so doing, he neutralised the efforts of those who were seeking to disable one of his colleagues. With this object, therefore, he forthwith summoned my husband to Constantinople, held sundry long conferences with him, and succeeded in persuading him of the necessity of appeasing the clamours of the opposition by repudiating me.

This sacrifice, as I learnt afterwards, cost the poor Pasha many tears, but political exigences prevailed over sentimental and all other considerations, and my husband was forced to bow to the will of his chief. My divorce was immediately notified to me by the emissaries of the Minister of Police, who handed me back my dowry, a mere trifle, and made me sign a receipt. My enemies, meanwhile, were not satisfied with this concession on the part of Kibrizli and Reshid, inasmuch as they suspected them of entertaining the idea* of restoring me to my former position, so soon as the temporary excitement should have calmed down. Under the influence of this suspicion they continued to clamour against me and to denounce Reshid.

The latter then formed the opinion that the best means of putting an end to these denunciations was to get another wife for Kibrizli-Pasha, and thereby to separate him irrevocably from me. In fact no other guarantee could have satisfied those who wished to take advantage of existing circumstances to effect my irremediable ruin.

This necessity, then, obliged Reshid to seek a wife for his colleague, and the choice of the Grand-vezir fell on a lady named Ferideh, the sister of one of his favourites. Thus Kibrizli-Pasha was compelled to marry a wife whom he had never set eyes on, and for whom he entertained no predilection.

After remaining four months in prison, it was high time that I should be informed of the decision that had been come to with regard to the question of my guilt. One of the Minister's secretaries brought me the intelligence that Fatmah and Omer had been condemned to the galleys, and that I was to be banished to Asia Minor, whence, at the expiration of some months, they would allow me to return. This measure, he informed me, had been prompted by the necessity under which the administration found themselves of calming the mind and closing the mouth of the public. When the Minister of Police himself notified to me this decision of the Government, I made him the following reply :—

" You have taken from me my husband, my
children, all that I had in the world ; why not take
my life also ?   I have no longer anything that can
lead me to desire to live ; kill me, and all will be
over !"✳

In speaking these words, I had no doubt whatever but that the cup of my sufferings was already
full to overflowing.   But I was to be subjected to
yet another trial.   Some days before I went into
exile, the Minister of Police sent for me, and spoke
as follows :—

" There is one question, madam, as to which we
pray you to have the goodness to give an explanation before your departure, for neither the Pasha nor
we can permit any doubt to remain on the matter.
The infant whom you borrowed naturally throws
some suspicion on the birth of Mustapha-Djehad-
Bey ; for all the world will say that if one child has
been borrowed, so, in all likelihood, has the other.
As to your husband, he does not believe the boy
belongs to him ; nevertheless, he wishes to have a
deposition on your part, that he may know what to
think and what to do."

It did not require a very acute perception to see
through the manœuvre cloaked beneath these words.
But, at the moment, I failed to account for it, and

to divine the true nature of the snare thus laid for me. From the circuitous language employed by the Minister, I could see that there was mischief in the case, but what it was I could not make out. To escape from this embarrassment without falling into the snare, I thought it necessary to reply in an evasive manner, which, while dispelling the intrigues of my foes, would secure me liberty of action.

Moreover, it appeared to me that an answer of this kind would be the best means of revenging myself on a man who had abandoned me without a word, for the sole reason that he feared to compromise his political interests. Clearly, for him, an evasive response would be equivalent to a disavowal or denial of the parentage of his son, for a simple doubt as to his birth would compel the Pasha to separate himself from him. But what above all induced me to follow such an unnatural course as that of denying my own child was the fear I entertained with respect to Djehad's safety. I could not consent to leave in the hands of my rival Ferideh a child who was her natural enemy, inasmuch as only by his death could she hope to lay hands on the whole inheritance. My reply, therefore, was couched in the following terms :—

"Is it possible that a man should not know his own child ? If the Pasha says that Djehad is not his child, that is a proof that he must have been borrowed also."

This answer puzzled the Minister of Police, and he did his best to extract a straightforward reply from me. For my part, I persisted in reiterating what I had already said, as though they were the last words I had to utter.

My conduct actually produced the desired result. Kibrizli-Pasha having been informed that I had refused to proclaim distinctly the legitimacy of his son Djehad, found himself constrained to separate from him.

After my return from exile, the question of Djehad's legitimacy was several times raised by Kibrizli-Pasha, who made me many advances and offers in order to induce me to make an explicit declaration on the subject. However, as he, on his part, refused to accord me the satisfaction I demanded, the matter remained in suspense.

The penalty of exile decreed against me by virtue of an Imperial rescript was the finishing blow by which the Valideh-Sultan endeavoured to crush me. Abdul-Medjid, with that generosity for which he was distinguished, at first refused to affix his signature to any such document. I have heard it said that the Sultan observed to his mother that, my participation in the murder of the Arab not having been substantiated, there were no grounds for punishing me. As to the affair of the borrowed infant, the Sultan was of opinion that it concerned no one except my husband. Seeing that her son refused to lend himself as the facile instrument of her will, the Sultana had recourse to a theatrical demonstration in order to extort the much-desired signature. She called the chief of the eunuchs, and told him that the only means of getting me punished was for him to throw himself at the feet of his Majesty, and entreat him to execute justice on the guilty. That very night, the chief of the eunuchs awaited the Sultan near the door of the harem, and, on his entering, threw himself at his Majesty's feet, crying with a loud voice, ."Your Majesty, take pity on us unhappy creatures, otherwise the women will murder us all!" Next day the Sultan signed the decree, banishing me for an indefinite period.

On the day fixed for my departure, the Minister of Police sent for me, and communicated to me the order banishing me to Asia Minor. He made a hypocritical pretence of feeling deeply touched at my fate, and entrusted me, with a show of the warmest interest, to the charge of an officer who was to escort me. With an excess of courtesy, he . placed at my service his own carriage, to convey me to the steam-packet about to start for Ismid (Nicomedia).

I may add that, for some reason or other, it was thought advisable to conceal from me the place of my destination, which proved to be Koniah, in Cappadocia. On leaving, I never dreamt of taking anything that might be of use to me. I got into the carriage, accompanied by a single slave, and with no means beyond about one hundred francs in small change, which I usually carried with me for trifling current expenses.

On arriving at Ismid, I was courteously received by the governor, who came to meet me, and conducted me to the presence of his wives, in whose apartments a room had been prepared for my accommodation. After a brief repose, I took some refreshment offered me by my host. While conversing with him, I noticed, every time he looked at me, that his face assumed a look of sadness and commiseration. I questioned him as to the cause.

" I am grieved to think of the orders I have to comply with, as regards you, madam."

" Indeed ! and what are those orders ? " I asked.

" They are of such a character that I dare not inform you."

" Don't be afraid. I am prepared for whatever may be my lot. You can tell me of nothing worse than death, and that I am ready to undergo."

" I am commanded," said he, " to prepare an escort, and to send you to Koniah, a town distant from here a fortnight's journey."

" Do your duty. As for me, I will go wherever they please to send me. Whether to this place or to that, it matters not."

" Then to-morrow morning a palanquin shall be got ready for you, and I will make the necessary arrangement for your journey."

" I do not require a palanquin. A horse will suffice for me."

Next day, before setting out, I freed the slave who had attended me thus far, as I was unwilling to involve her in my misfortunes. I then commenced my journey, in bitterly cold weather, escorted by some ten or twelve cavasses. The indifference I manifested produced a greater impression upon them than the most violent demonstrations of despair could have done. I saw big

tears rolling down their cheeks when I mounted my
horse. "Is it possible," they remarked to each
other, "that, on account of a wretched negro, they
should thus persecute a woman. Why make such
a fuss about a negro who was bought for a few
piastres? He was her property, and our law lays •
down no punishment for those who take the lives of
their own slaves."

"What you say, my good friends, is of no use.
I must obey without a word, since complaint would
be vain."

Everywhere I passed, the governors of the towns
and the sheiks of the villages endeavoured, by every
means in their power, to alleviate the fatigues I had
to endure. They welcomed me with their utmost
hospitality; gave me their best rooms; and spread
before me most beautiful repasts. The *mudirs*, or
commanders of the small towns, would pass the
night under a canopy, in order to give up to me
their only bed. The further I advanced, the more
severe became the cold. I had to cross lofty mountain ranges covered with snow, in which our horses
frequently sank up to the girths. I was sometimes
obliged to rein in my horse to prevent him from
being suffocated by the thick masses of snow that
lay in the path we had to follow. My conductors

P

themselves were astonished at the vigour I displayed. The fact is, every depressing thought had been banished from my mind. I had so resolutely fixed my determination, that I would bear, without impatience, whatever happened to me.

CHAPTER XVIII.

At length we reached Koniah, and I was left in a house without casements to the windows, and falling into ruins. The sorrows I had experienced, the fatigues of so long a journey, as well as the cold, to which I had not been habituated, seriously affected my health. I fell ill on the very day of my arrival. The woman in charge of the house and a Greek doctor she called in took care of me, and succeeded in effecting my recovery.

I was especially anxious to learn whether the Government had given the necessary orders to provide me with the means of subsistence. In the meantime, the mushir invited me to call on him. I found him to be animated by the most kindly feelings towards me, and asked him whether he had received any authority to supply me with the funds necessary to meet my expenses.

"I have received no instructions in the matter," he answered; "but your situation moves my compassion. I see that you are persecuted. If you like, you shall come and live with my wives; you will have no expenses; and I will give you five hundred piastres a month, which is just what I allow them for their little amusements."

As I was not acquainted with the governor, I was afraid to go and reside in his house, but I accepted his offer of money, and received it without trouble for a whole year. At the end of this period, Hafiz-Pasha came to take the place of the preceding mushir in the command of the garrison of Koniah. The new governor was a worthy old man of nearly sixty, who had known me at my uncle's house when I was quite a child. Some days after his arrival I went to pay my compliments, when he received me with truly paternal affection.

"How happy I am, my daughter, to meet you here. I am told that you live in a house by yourself. You are thereby incurring the risk of being carried off by brigands, or other lawless characters. Come and stay with me. You will be well received by my wives; you will not have to dream of any expense; and I will give you whatever I afford them."

I eagerly accepted so benevolent an offer, and
took up my residence in his harem, which was well
provided, for he had four wives who cherished him
as though he were a spoilt child. These were not
the only wives he had taken in the course of his
matrimonial career. It was said that Hafiz was a
regular Bluebeard, who had had at least a dozen.
But, for all these rumours, he was a virtuous man,
who did nothing beyond what the Koran sanctioned :
he had never had more than four wives at a time ;
but as soon as a vacancy occurred, Hafiz-Pasha
hastened to fill up the gap by taking a new wife. In
presenting me to his wives, the Pasha sought to
interest them in my favour by language which
showed the purity of his thoughts, and the generosity
of his heart.

" Whichever of you loves me the best," said he,
" will prove her affection by the care she takes of
this bird that has come to seek shelter beneath our
roof."

These poor women, though simple and ill-educated,
did not the less endeavour to make themselves agreeable to me in every particular. They discharged all the
duties of hospitality in a most praiseworthy manner ;
they gave up to me the best room in the harem ;
one took charge of my clothing ; another conducted

me to the bath ; a third assisted me in my toilette ;
a fourth put my room to-rights ; one would say, on
seeing how they conducted themselves, that my
power over them was that of a mistress over her
slaves.   These noble women, accustomed to humble
themselves to give pleasure, could conceive of no
other means of testifying their friendship than by
the performance of almost servile duties, whilst
they proved their true affection by banishing every
thought of jealousy on my account.   Although they
were all jealous of one another, yet they had full
confidence in me ; I was the confidante of their
troubles and their desires, and we became inse-
parable companions.   What they wished for beyond
everything else was to please their husband ; but
they knew of no artifice by which they could effect
this object.   "You are so good and so clever," said
one of them to me one day, "that I am sure you
will consent to make me a charm (talisman) to
inspire the Pasha with love for me."

"Oh," I replied, "you think me a great deal
wiser than I am.   How should I know how to
compose so powerful a charm ?"

"If you choose," she insisted, "you certainly will
be able."

I saw that if I continued to refuse I should only

succeed in alienating her affection, without convincing her of the folly of her request.

"Very well, my dear," said I ; " I will endeavour to comply with your wishes."

Accordingly, next day, I took some powdered sugar, mixed with it some salt, and put the whole into a small bag of silk, fastened with string tied into sundry very complicated knots. "Here," said I, handing her the bag, "this is the charm you asked me for. To-night, when the Pasha is sitting smoking in the midst of you, do you silently unfasten the string, and suddenly throw the contents into the chafing-dish." She did as I recommended.

"What is the meaning of this noise and this smoke?" cried the Pasha, hearing the crackling of the salt in the fire, and seeing the smoke of the burnt sugar.

"It is doubtless the slave who has put some bad coals into the brazier," said the poor wife, all in a tremble.

The Pasha, observing her demeanour, guessed what she had been about, but made no sign. He resolved to fulfil her desire, and to keep her with him all that night. I leave to conjecture whether or not she remained convinced of the efficacy of my witchcraft. When I had once gained the reputation of being a skilled sorceress, each wife, in her turn, came to ask me for some magic means of increasing the love of her husband. One of them, more ambitious, implored me persistently for a long time to teach her some charm by which she might become a mother, promising me, in return, a very considerable sum. I gave her a large bag of ground potash, recommending her to go frequently to the bath, and every time put into it a spoonful of this compound, which was of singular potency for effecting the desired result. As luck would have it, she became *enceinte* shortly afterwards. To tell what caresses she lavished upon me would be an impossibility. All these women were thus thoroughly convinced of my profound knowledge of the occult sciences, to my great amusement.

All Eastern women are persuaded of the efficacy of talismans, charms, philtres, and all the ridiculous tricks of sorcery. A great number of women and men (for the latter engage in it also) live by this means on the credulity of their fellow-creatures. But it is not so amusing to learn that through the ignorance, or occasionally the malevolence of sorcerers and sorceresses, serious consequences ensue; frequently even death, through swallowing, under the advice of these wretches, some most incongruous mixture or other.

During my stay at the house of Hafiz-Pasha I was invited by Tchelebi-Effendi to spend some days at his palace. He was chief of the Mevlevih Dervishes, and the last descendant of the Abassides, who would be heirs to the Ottoman throne if the race of the now reigning Sultans should become extinct. This personage enjoys the privilege of girding on the Sultan's sword on the day of his proclamation. At Koniah and elsewhere, he is held in boundless consideration; the mushir, the cadi, the nakib, and all the other dignitaries of the town, although completely independent of his authority, nevertheless show him such respect that their power appears insignificant compared to that which he exercises over people's consciences. No one would presume to sit down in his presence. All throughout the East, the dervishes maintain a great number of religious houses, where they receive, without distinction, all travellers, poor and rich. The latter by no means consider it beneath them to avail themselves of the simple and cordial hospitality of these holy men, who afford food and lodging for three days, without ever accepting the slightest remuneration.

The Mevlevih Dervishes go through a singular exercise in the mosques, consisting of a peculiar dance. They join hands in a circle, facing outwards, and whirl rapidly round, raising at intervals a guttural cry, very like a bark. They sometimes keep it up for several hours with surprising velocity, and without showing any sign of fatigue or giddiness.

Tchelebi-Effendi received me with marked kindness, and made me take a place on the divan beside him. He seemed greatly touched at my fate; offered to intercede for me at Constantinople, and confided to me the troubles he had with his wives. I remained several days in his palace, and did my best to reconcile the ladies to one another; an attempt in which I succeeded; after which I returned to Hafiz-Pasha.

As Tchelebi-Effendi had said, he addressed a petition to the Divan in my favour, which was supported by the dignitaries residing at Koniah. Several times was this application renewed, but always without effect. I subsequently found that all these petitions had been suppressed on their arrival by the ministers who had been the cause of my troubles.

Months, years passed away without any change in my situation, which would have been sad and

wearisome in the extreme, but for the generous hospitality of the worthy governor.

I need scarcely say that during my stay at
Koniah, the mental depression which weighed upon
me as an exile could not be alleviated, either by the
sympathy or generous kindness which the good
Hafiz-Pasha and his family bestowed on me. I can
say that, though exiled in body, my spirit was at
Constantinople with the objects of my affection, my
children and my husband. Day and night my
thoughts carried me to my native land, and I felt
almost inconsolable ; frequently, in a fit of despair,
I turned my eyes to heaven, and cried, " My God,
when will my afflictions cease ?—when shall I find
peace ? The fervency of my prayers brought about
my deliverance in an almost miraculous way, for the
Almighty sent me a protector in my son Frederick,
who came unexpectedly to my assistance, comforting
me in my sorrow, and reviving me in the midst of
my enemies.

The reader will remember my stating at the beginning how I had left at Rome my daughter Eve-
lyn and Frederick, my eldest son. Since my marriage with Kibrizli-Pasha I had entirely lost sight
of these dear children, who had been placed in convents, and brought up under the care of their aunt.

It happened, however, that Frederick on his return to Constantinople, hearing of my persecution and exile, determined on joining his fate to mine. Driven almost to madness by the love of a mother he had scarcely seen, he threw himself at the feet of Mehemet-Ali-Pasha, the then Minister of War, 1854, and implored him to allow him to join his mother, she to whom he owed his existence.

The Pasha, touched by this proof of filial affection, acceded to his prayer, and immediately issued the orders necessary to enable him to proceed to Koniah. Mehemet-Ali also gave him out of his private purse the sum of thirty pounds to provide him with the funds for the journey.

I had gone one day to visit one of my friends, who lived near to the tomb of the patron saint of Koniah, and was resting myself near a window, when we heard a knock at the door. My friend hastened to ascertain who it was, but, instead of coming back to me, she remained talking in a low voice with the stranger, whoever it might be.

Animated by a feeling of curiosity, I looked towards the door, and all at once saw an elegant looking young man, dressed in uniform, who suddenly walked into the room and up to the place where I was sitting.

This strange apparition, and the boldness shown
by the youth alarmed me, and involuntarily I re-
coiled and was about to rise from my seat, when
the stranger threw his arms round my neck, crying
out,—

"Don't you know me, mother? I am Frederick."

These words quite overcame me, for at that
moment of supreme excitement I could scarcely
believe my eyes, or trust my ears. Frederick, whom
I had left almost an infant, and whom I considered
as lost to me for ever, could it possibly be the
handsome young fellow before me? Was it a
dream, the past thirteen years, or was it reality?

My poor boy, enraptured by the sight of a mother
upon whom he could at last gaze, kissed me over
and over again, holding me in his arms, and seemed
never tired of looking at me. He took out his
purse, containing his whole wealth, and placed it in
my hands, saying,—

"Take it, mother; you are poor, but I love you."

From that moment the fairest prospects seemed
opening before me; I was no longer a desolate and
deserted woman without a defender or helper. The
news of my dear son's arrival produced a great sensation at Koniah, all my friends sharing in my joy.

Frederick, who had assumed the name of Osman-

Bey, remained with me a month, and on his return to Constantinople did his best in order to have me recalled from exile. It was owing to intelligence I received from him that decided me on endeavouring to make my escape, so as to join him at Constantinople, or wheresoever else he might be, and this without delay.

Before my departure from Koniah, an incident occurred which brought great trouble on the town, and was the cause of much dissension. A married man had gone as a soldier, leaving his wife at home. While engaged on a certain expedition, he disappeared, and was believed to be dead. As often happened in these provinces, the towns of which are encircled by desert plains, on which the inhabitants pasture immense flocks, the wife was carried off by a miscreant, who took her with him to a remote part, and when she informed him of the disappearance of her husband, he married her.

Presently the husband returned, discovered his wife, and wished to take her back, but her paramour refused to restore her, pretending that, according to his version of the Mussulman law, the former had been absent a sufficient time to permit of his wife's re-marrying. The complainant answered that she might perhaps have been able, of her own accord, to contract a second marriage, but she had not, in this case, been a free agent. The Pasha was disposed to order the restoration of the wife to her former husband, but the other magistrates, holding to the text of the law, maintained the validity of the second marriage. Of a most determined character, the governor, instead of yielding in a matter that had so little interest for him, envenomed the dispute to such a degree that he soon came to an open rupture with the ulemas and other authorities. His position became insupportable, and one morning he set off, incognito, for Constantinople, leaving his wives behind him. Very soon after his arrival in the capital he obtained the government of Trebizond, and then sent for his harem; nevertheless, he continued the pension he had allowed me while I was living under his roof.

CHAPTER XIX.

About four years had now elapsed since I went into exile, and no answer had ever been returned to the various applications addressed on my behalf to Constantinople. I had every reason to believe that I was to remain, for an indefinite period, in a country where, since the departure of Hafiz-Pasha, I felt myself in anything but a safe position. I therefore presented myself before the authorities who were in charge, pending the arrival of a successor to the late governor, and asked for a passport to enable me to return to the capital.

"I am not under the burden of any condemnation; I was ordered to be transported hither, and here I have been for four years. As you have not been forbidden to let me go, I am come to demand the necessary documents to afford me a free and safe passage."

"If you were a person of ordinary condition, we would comply with your request," they replied; "but you are the wife of a minister, and we might compromise ourselves by giving you leave to go."

"I have done my duty in warning you of my intention, and I have nothing more to add." So saying, I withdrew.

Taking what little I had saved out of the liberality of Hafiz-Pasha, I came to terms with two of the inhabitants, who engaged, for four thousand piastres (about £40), to conduct me, by devious paths, to the vicinity of Constantinople. In order not to arouse suspicion, I went one night, accompanied by a single servant, to a farm situate beyond the walls, to which I often used to go, the proprietor being one of the richest persons in the country, who had always shown me the greatest kindness.

I had given my guides notice of the rendezvous, and they were waiting for me, with horses for themselves, for me, and my servant. We set out at once to traverse the immense plains of Caramania, travelling night and day, through the most deserted places, carefully avoiding the towns and villages, and taking only such rest as was absolutely necessary to prevent ourselves and our horses from breaking down with fatigue. We had to cross steep and dangerous mountains; and finally, after a journey of four days, and without meeting with any mishap, we reached Kutayeh, on leaving which the country became more inhabited and safer. We could not go on from thence to Constantinople without an authority from the governor of the place.

Not well knowing how I should manage to get the requisite authority, I, with my companions, put up at the house of a lady, named Aïsh-Bey, a sort of muscular woman who used to carry on mercantile pursuits between Constantinople and Kutayeh. On alighting I represented myself to her as the wife of a colonel who had died in the Crimea. I had not been long in bed when my hostess, knocking at the door, came to inform me that the Pasha's secretary wanted to speak to me. The visit of this official at such an hour foreboded no good, and it was not without considerable trepidation that I saw him presently enter the room. His face, however, wore an expression of courtesy that augured favourably.

"His Excellency the Pasha," said he, "takes it very much amiss that you have not thrown yourself on his hospitality instead of taking up your quarters here. He has sent me, therefore, to express his regret on this account, and to request your kind permission to call and pay his respects to you to-morrow."

I answered, as in duty bound, that I should be most happy to be honoured by such a visit, and I thanked the governor for his kind attention in giving me notice of the proposed compliment.

The secretary then withdrew, leaving me several boxes of sweetmeats and other delicacies, sent by • the Pasha's wives.

My attendants had been so imprudent as to let out that I had come from Koniah, and, as my escape had been talked of on all sides, the governor at once knew perfectly well who I was ; but, since he had been acquainted with me for a long time, he was unwilling, by arresting me, to lend himself to the evil designs of my persecutors. For this reason he had the delicacy to notify his good feelings towards me, fearing lest I should be led to commit some imprudence through uncertainty as to his intentions.

On the morrow he made his appearance magnificently attired, and respectfully saluted me by kissing the hem of my robe. He consented, after a polite show of resistance, to seat himself on the same divan with myself. After conversing on various

unimportant subjects, he questioned me about myself, and the motives for my journey. I told him
that I was returning to Constantinople, and requested
him to furnish me with the necessary pass, to
enable me to proceed on my way. Satisfied with
the result of our conversation, in which he had
displayed the most courteous and obliging disposition, he promised to give me the authority I
required, and withdrew, giving me an invitation,
which I accepted, to pass the remainder of the day
at his house.

This delay caused me some uneasiness, for I
dreaded every moment lest I should see the arrival
of messengers from Koniah sent in pursuit of me ;
an event that would have seriously complicated the
situation. My two guides, filled with alarm, secreted
themselves in the stable when they saw the governor
approaching. " It is all over with us," they said
to each other. " In return for the pay we have
received, we shall be prevented from ever returning to our wives and children. The lady whom
we have conducted thus far is the wife of
a great personage, and it is certain that they
have come to arrest us forthwith and carry us off
to prison." Fearing to excite suspicion, they dare
not leave by daylight, for their strange appearance

could not fail to attract attention. I boldly went to the Pasha's house, and he welcomed me at the head of the stairs, introduced me to his wives, who received me very kindly, and gave me quite a banquet by way of supper.

Desirous of fulfilling his promise in a manner altogether noble and generous, he sent for his secretary, and instructed him to make out the pass in whatever terms I should dictate.

"Write," said I, "that all commanders of troops and way-wardens are commanded to pass and to give protection and assistance to Fatmah-Hanum, of Kutayeh, returning to Constantinople on business, and intending to stay there about two months."

The passport was made out accordingly, and the governor, in order to arrange everything with still greater munificence, gave me a purse full of gold, to help to defray the expenses of the journey, and moreover granted me an escort of four cavasses.

When I returned to my hostess, I found my guides more dead than alive : they were expecting every moment to be taken bodily and dragged before the Pasha. Summoning them forthwith, I made them read the paper that had been drawn up for me, and they could not believe their eyes. Next morning I set off at daybreak, and after three days' good riding I reached the Gulf of Nicomedia at a point called Dil-bash; from there a sort of barge conveyed me straight to Constantinople, by the side of the custom-house. I then rewarded the cavasses and guides who had attended me thus far, and intrusted them with a letter of thanks to their master.

On approaching the town I was accosted by an official, who demanded my papers. "If we are so unusually exacting," said he, "it is because the wife of a Minister of State has escaped from Koniah, and we have received very strict orders as regards ladies returning to Constantinople. Fatmah-Hanum of Kutayeh," he added, reading my passport; "she is a merchant of my acquaintance" (here he looked fixedly at me). "I have heard her spoken of frequently. She is not travelling on business to-day for the first time." Whereas the beginning of his speech filled me with terror, the conclusion strongly tempted me to laugh, but I restrained myself.

Instead of seeking the hospitality of some person of high position, in which case my arrival would have created a sensation, I went to the dwelling of an old woman, whom, in the days of my pro-

sperity, I was accustomed to employ to amuse me
with her stories. I gave her what was necessary to
furnish me a room, and then wrote to Fety-Pasha,
who, as ambassador in Paris, had received me so
kindly in time past, to ask if any harm could come
to me in case of my retreat being discovered. He
hastened to send me his secretary Yusuf with
assurances that I had absolutely nothing to fear.
Yusuf was at the same time bearer of a stock of
linen and dresses besides a round sum of money,
which his Highness put at my disposal.

I sent the woman at whose house I was lodging
to find out the state of public affairs, for I knew
not to whom I could apply for protection with any
certainty. She could not obtain any positive information, and I then intrusted her with a letter to
Fehim-Effendi, one of my husband's relatives,
who had always shown himself animated by bad
feelings towards me, begging him to come and see
me, without letting him know who I was.

He came accordingly, and was profoundly astonished when he saw me.

" How came you here ? " he cried. " It is impossible that you can have found your way from
Koniah, without meeting anyone to stop you. The
roads were all carefully watched."

As I was anxious not to compromise anyone by disclosing how I had come, I replied—

"Nothing was easier. My husband sent me a passport."

"I dare say," he answered; "for when I told him, recently, that you had escaped from Koniah, he smiled maliciously; but," he added, "what do you intend to do here?"

"I intend," said I, "to apply to Reshid-Pasha, and beg him to request Mehemet-Pasha to restore my property."

"Don't do that," he cried with alarm; "he is now your husband's deadliest enemy."

"Oh, very well," I rejoined, "since they are at variance, there can be no question of writing to him."

He then told me that if I would only remain quiet, Mehemet-Pasha would like nothing better than to give me, from time to time, a small sum, to assist me in supporting myself, and that, he said, was the best thing I could do. I pretended to enter into his views, and dismissed him, delighted to have learnt from him that I should have in Reshid-Pasha a protector as energetic as he was influential, and well-disposed towards me.

Desirous of finding out what had taken place

during my absence, and what was the present state of affairs, I applied for information to everyone with whom I came in contact, and the result of my investigations shall be mentioned in the ensuing chapter.

SINCE my departure for Koniah, Kibrizli-Pasha had been appointed Governor of Aleppo, a place rendered extremely dangerous by the perpetual dissensions that existed between the Mussulmans and the Christians. In sending him to Arabia, it was hoped that he would perish ; but, contrary to expectation, he succeeded in repressing both factions with such rigour, — imprisoning, executing, and refusing all presents,—that tranquillity was soon re-established. Seeing this, the Sultan appointed him to the command at Damascus.

He did not remain long in Syria, for he was soon afterwards appointed Grand-vezir. The circumstances that led to this appointment were as follows :—

Abdul-Medjid's daughter was of a marriageable age, and the sons of some of the most exalted personages aspired to the hands of the young princess. Reshid-Pasha, and more especially his wife, who was excessively proud, were particularly anxious that their son, Ali-Galyb-Pasha, should become the Sultan's son-in-law. The other Ministers wished to please the Grand-vezir, and tried to induce their master to give the hand of the princess to the son of their colleague.

After much pressing, the Sultan consented to the proposed union. However, Reshid-Pasha feared that if this marriage took place while he was Grand-vezir, the people would murmur. Indeed, there were not wanting remarks to the effect that the Padishah did everything his vezir wished, and had so little will of his own, that he could refuse him nothing,—not even his daughter. He, therefore, sent in his resignation, and had Kibrizli-Pasha nominated in his stead.

The latter exerted his utmost efforts to promote the match that his predecessor had so greatly at heart, and the nuptials were accordingly celebrated with great pomp. The person best pleased was the mother of the youthful bridegroom. The widow of a certain Ali-Pasha, one of the cruellest and bravest of the Turks who so greatly distinguished themselves in the war with Greece ; the wife of an illustrious vezir, and now become the mother-in-law of a princess, she saw herself one of the greatest ladies in the Empire.

But the marriage so eagerly desired had not those favourable results that were anticipated by its most ardent promoters.

The husbands of Sultanas are almost the slaves of their wives. They cannot enter their presence un-invited. If the wife does not send for her husband, he must remain in the selamlik and not venture into the harem. He may spend the night, for a whole fortnight or more, sleeping on a divan in the men's apartments.

Now the young Pasha, although very intelli-gent and fondly attached to the Princess, failed to win her good graces. In the course of a month, he scarcely passed two nights in the harem, — a state of things that was a source of bitter grief to him.

A most unwelcome discovery crowned his trou-bles,—he found that his wife had a liking for the son of an old Minister. The two corresponded toge-ther, and the poor husband had his suspicions on the subject, but knew nothing for certain. One day, when he was supposed to be out, an eunuch arrived with a letter, but seeing the master of the house, retreated hastily, without delivering it. The young man at once went off to his father, and told him what proof he now had of the reality of his unhappy condition, of which hitherto he had been willing to doubt. Guess what the grief of his parents must have been. The father hastened, without a moment's delay, to the palace, presented himself before the Sultan, and disclosed to him the manner in which his daughter was making her husband miserable.

Abdul-Medjid, instead of blaming his daughter, inveighed against Reshid-Pasha. "How is this?" he cried. "You beset me with entreaties in order to bring about this marriage, and now you come with complaints, and you invent I know not what accusations against the Sultana. Begone, if you do not wish to expose yourself to the full weight of my resentment."

The poor father, overcome by a reception that he had not anticipated, returned home in a state of utter consternation. The way his sovereign had treated him and the disappointment of his son plunged him into despair, and conduced, with other causes we shall speak of presently, to hasten his end.

His wife displayed a lively sense of indignation. All her affection was lavished on her son. She strove to console him by every means in her power.

He came to pass several hours of each day in her company, endeavouring to forget the troubles that his wife had brought upon him.

Nearly three months had elapsed since his father died, and for nearly three weeks the Sultana had not sent for him. In order to seek some recreation, the young man determined to go and pass the evening at the country-house of a wealthy Jew, named Camondo. He accordingly went on board a boat, and spent his time agreeably in the company of the banker and his other guests.

When night came he re-embarked, and was making his way homewards, when a steam-boat, suddenly appearing, bore down upon and shattered to pieces the frail vessel in which he was; two slaves endeavoured to save their master, and perished with him.

On the morrow, his mother not seeing her son as usual, waited anxiously for his arrival. Noticing an unusual excitement in the house, the slaves and eunuchs talking together in a low voice and keeping silence when she drew near, she suspected the fatal intelligence and fainted away. When she opened her eyes again it was found that she had gone mad. She spent the remainder of her existence confined to her room, and bound hand and foot.

The Sultana, when she heard of her husband's death, displayed real grief. She fell ill, and her recovery was but slow. Although she had never shown any love for the Pasha, she had, nevertheless, a certain friendly feeling towards him. Abdul-Medjid, always kind, came several times to console her. The young man who was the prime cause of all these sorrows, asked the Sultan for the hand of his daughter, but he never would accede to this union. He married the princess to another suitor, and her conduct was thenceforth irreproachable. Seeing the consequences of her former intrigue, she had no desire to engage in any fresh ones.

In order not to interrupt the recital of the fatal consequences of the marriage of Ali-Galyb-Pasha, we have neglected to speak of other events that occurred since the celebration of that alliance, and previous to the death of Reshid-Pasha.

After the appointment of Mehemet-Pasha as Grand-vezir, at the recommendation of Reshid, his friend and protector, his new wife began to entertain a dislike for the wife of the old Minister. The latter, who was extremely proud, was much hurt at the proceedings of a *parvenue* who owed her elevation to her. Hence arose a coldness between them, which developed soon into open hostility. The two wives having quarrelled, the intimacy between their husbands was affected. Mehemet-Pasha began to follow with less docility the counsels of his predecessor, and presently told the latter that he intended to exercise his functions according to his own ideas, and not in conformity with the instructions of a patron, who exacted, as the price of his support, an obedience incompatible with the dignity of the chief Minister of the Empire.

From this moment, Reshid-Pasha, without manifesting open dislike, desired nothing more than the ruin of his former *protégé*. An opportunity shortly offered itself for the execution of his designs.

The Sultan's brother-in-law, Mehemet-Ali-Pasha, had borrowed, at different times, very large sums from his banker, Djezaïrli-oghlu. The Orientals, by way of a signature, instead of writing their names, merely affix their seals. Each time the Pasha received a sum he put his seal on the receipt. The banker, wishing to be repaid, presented to Mehemet-Ali-Pasha a certain number of receipts for which he demanded payment. The Pasha objected that the seal which appeared on the greater part of them was not his own, and that he had no intention of paying any but those that bore the right impression. The banker then pretended that his debtor had sometimes em-

ployed a different seal to that which he generally
used, and claimed the protection of Reshid-Pasha,
who was the avowed enemy of Mehemet-Ali-Pasha,
with whom the Grand-vezir had become intimately
associated since he had refused to conform any
longer to the orders of his too exacting predecessor.

The old Minister determined to take advantage
of the occasion to strike down at one blow, both his
former *protégé*, and the latter's new friend. He
went to Kibrizli-Pasha and handed him the receipts
in question.

" By virtue of your office," said he, " you are
obliged to make justice prevail amongst the subjects
of the Sultan. Here are documents which show
that Mehemet-Ali-Pasha has received from a *seraf*
(banker) very considerable sums of money. This
day he denies his own seal—an abuse which you
ought to put a stop to."

" This seal," replied the Grand-vezir, " was never
that of Mehemet-Ali. The banker has committed a
fraud by affixing to the receipts you show me, the
seal that you pretend is that of his debtor. Besides,
I know Mehemet-Ali-Pasha to be incapable of doing
an injury to anyone, above all to a man who has laid
him under obligations."

R

Reshid-Pasha could not have wished for a better answer. He at once went to the Sultan.

"Mehemet-Ali-Pasha, your Majesty's brother-in-law," said he, "has been borrowing money of a merchant. Knowing that it would probably be difficult to refund the large sums he has received, he has affixed to the receipts sometimes his ordinary seal, sometimes another which he now ignores. Mehemet-Pasha, your Grand-vezir and his friend, refuses to do justice to the lender, alleging as an excuse that the prince is incapable of denying his own seal, and still more of using a false one. He adds that the documents in dispute have been forged by the merchant. This, in my opinion, shows a degree of partiality much to be regretted. It would be an evil example to allow persons of rank to abuse their position by cheating private individuals. Since Mehemet-Ali-Pasha is allied to the Imperial family, he ought not to be a judge in his own cause. If a man of his rank is to be permitted to refuse to answer in a court of justice the demand of a merchant, others will imitate his example, and we shall soon see all state officials pleading their high position as an excuse for appropriating to their own use the goods of merchants. If you will be influenced by me, you will summon Mehemet-Ali-Pasha to appear before the Divan, to make good his plea.   If he refuses to obey this order, you will know what steps to take to vindicate your sovereign authority."

The Sultan, moved by the reasons advanced in support of this measure of policy, immediately signed a firman summoning Mehemet-Ali-Pasha to appear before the Porte, to defend his cause against the banker.

As soon as Kibrizli-Pasha learnt what had occurred, and knew of the firman addressed to his friend, he returned the official seals, the insignia of his dignity, and the Sultan at once conferred them on Reshid-Pasha.

SUCH was the state of affairs when I returned from Koniah. I called on the new Grand-vezir, and begged him to have justice done me at the hands of Mehemet-Pasha. This was a fresh opportunity for harassing his rival, so he gave me a favourable reception. He asked whether I wished to return to my husband, or to demand the restitution of my property. I replied that, as Mehemet-Pasha had taken a new wife, no reconciliation between us was possible; I therefore demanded the return of my fortune.

"Very well," said the Minister: "cite him to appear before the Porte. If he refuses to go, do you come back to me." With these words he handed me a purse full of gold, to support me pending the decision of my cause.

Several times did I send the messengers of the

court. They were brutally repulsed by the servants of Mehemet-Pasha. I was thereupon obliged once more to go to the Minister, to whom the citations also were sent. The Grand-vezir informed the Sultan of what had happened, and got him to sign a firman, ordering my former husband to reply to the demand which I had presented against him before the Porte. The Imperial rescript was conveyed to the defendant by one of his Highness's chamberlains.

It would be impossible to say what trouble reigned in the house of Mehemet-Pasha on the reception of the royal mandate. The Pasha's new wife, the Pasha himself, Bessim-Bey, his brother-in-law, who had flattered himself that he had appeased me by his delusive promises, all were thrown into consternation, and thought themselves lost. Next day, Fehim-Effendi, one of my husband's relatives, came to me, and, in a most obsequious tone, offered to give me all I was pleased to demand. I had only to present my statement of claims, when he would immediately discharge them.

"As soon as you are satisfied," said he, "you shall give me a declaration to the effect that you have no further claim. He can present it to the Divan when he makes his appearance there."

After the zeal that Reshid-Pasha had displayed in my favour, I could not do him so ill a turn as to cause it to be supposed that he had induced his master to sign a firman without any object; which could not fail to be believed to be the case if Mehemet-Pasha, on appearing in obedience to the decree, had handed in a document such as that which he wished to obtain from me. It might follow that the Grand-vezir would be dismissed from office owing to such an incident; but whether he preserved his power or lost it, none the less should I be exposed to the just resentment of a man who had shown himself full of kindness towards me. I therefore rejected the proposals that had been made to me.

The cause was called on, and, through my advocate, I put in a statement of the jewels, diamonds, articles of *vertu*, furniture, carriages, etc., constituting my personal property, and comprising both what I had of my own, and the presents that had been made me; the whole amounting to upwards of four million piastres (forty thousand pounds). In spite of all the subterfuges that my husband's agent could employ, his client was ordered to make over to me everything I claimed. When the decision was pronounced, I only required, in order to secure its execution within three days, the approval of the Sheik-ul-Islam, or supreme religious dignitary, as decisions in civil matters are given by interpretation of the Koran.

But at this stage of the proceedings a political turmoil sprang up which overthrew my fair prospects and gave the upper hand to my adversaries. Within forty-eight hours, from a triumphant suitor, I was reduced to the condition of a victim of' despotism.

Reshid-Pasha, satisfied at having administered this severe check to my husband, resolved to deal a blow against his other rival, Mehemet-Ali, whose case with the banker was still pending. The latter, notwithstanding the Imperial firman laying the commands of the Sultan upon him, had not made his appearance before the Porte to answer the claim lodged against him by his banker, Djezaïrli-oghlu. The Grand-vezir hastened to inform the Sultan of this circumstance, representing the Prince's disobedience as an act of rebellion of most dangerous example against the supreme authority of the Padishah, and obtained an order of banishment against Mehemet-Ali-Pasha, who was on the point of retiring to rest when his attendants came to inform him that the palace was surrounded by troops, and an officer was inquiring for him on the part of the Sultan. He went down, was arrested, roughly dragged away, and hurried on board a steamer, which only waited for him to put out to sea.

The Sultan's sister went next morning to the palace, but her brother refused to see her. Knowing how little able he was to refuse anything to the ladies, he feared to run the risk of listening to the supplications of the Princess. She was not discouraged, but set in operation all the means of influence she had at her disposal, and before the end of the day obtained from the Sultan, who was indignant at the manner in which his authority had been abused, and the hatred displayed by his Grand-vezir, the dispatch of a vessel appointed to bring back Mehemet-Ali-Pasha.

On hearing this news Reshid-Pasha resigned office. Ali-Pasha, friend of the exile of a day and of my husband, was chosen to fill the place of the retiring Grand-vezir, and Mehemet-Pasha was appointed president of the Tanzimat, a supreme court of appeal lately established at the request of the European Powers.

The Sheik-ul-Islam, seeing these changes, refused to ratify the decision pronounced in my favour under the fallen Grand-vezir. I was obliged to recommence the proceedings ; but the defendant, Kibrizli, by a privilege attaching to his rank, was entitled to be believed on his oath respecting my demand. He declared himself ready to swear that nearly the whole of what belonged to me was the property of my daughter, then eight years old. He did not acknowledge my claim to more than thirty thousand piastres (about three hundred pounds).

On the day that the oath was to be taken I was brought to the house of the Pasha, where the highest dignitaries of the Empire were assembled, to be present at the taking of the oath. On a table were laid out numerous documents and a copy of the Koran on which the Pasha was going to swear. When I entered, instead of acknowledging by a bow the presence of Kibrizli, who stood now as my adversary, I merely saluted the bystanders, and took my place facing him. When invited to state my claim, I rose and sharply reproved Mehemet-Pasha for the perjury which he was ready to • commit.

"I should never have thought," I exclaimed, "that one who occupies your high position would come to-day to take an oath respecting the poor ornaments of a woman. How can you lower yourself

to the pretence that necklaces, bracelets, robes, and
ear-rings belong to you ? "

At these words the Pasha, overcome with rage,
rose and rushed upon me, while shouting :

" Bring me my sword ; I will kill this wretch who
dares thus to insult me ! "

" Do not hesitate," said I, without displaying any
emotion. " To complete your conduct it only remains to assassinate me."

Numerous persons then threw themselves upon
him and held him back.

" Let him alone," I added. " He has abandoned me in a cowardly manner, but he would not
dare to commit a cowardly action in my presence."

This scene of violence came to an end by the
interference of the Sheik-ul-Islam, who had us both
removed out of each other's reach.

Next day, about sunrise, my house at Sari-Guzel
was surrounded by a detachment of police, who
forced an entrance and compelled me to follow
them. A carriage conveyed me straight to the
office of the Minister of Police, where I was imprisoned. The reason they gave me for the commission of this arbitrary act was that, it was a
punishment for the want of respect I showed for a
vezir of the Sultan.

My imprisonment lasted five or six days, and the way it ended was sufficiently whimsical. The Minister's employés gave me to understand that the only means of obtaining my liberty was to sign a declaration renouncing all my effects, and accepting the conditions my husband imposed upon me.

"Mind what you are about," they told me; "if you show any obstinacy, the Pasha will have you packed back again to Koniah."

"I am in your hands," I retorted, "you can do with me what you like."

Accordingly, on the ninth day of my imprisonment I was conducted under escort to the Court, and there I was compelled to sign a mandate, in virtue of which I acknowledged to have thankfully accepted whatever the Pasha had consented to give. This signature once extorted, the agent of police left the Court, thus setting me at liberty.

The Shiek-ul-Islam sent me that day what had been awarded to me by a decision without appeal; that is to say, three hundred pounds, and the extremely modest pension that it had pleased my husband to allow me—only two pounds sterling, *per annum!*

I must here say, however, that jealousy more than meanness incited Kibrizli-Pasha to refuse me my rights. He dreaded that once in possession of my property I should leave for Europe. The idea that I should show my face to the Ghïaurs made him mad.

CHAPTER XXII.

AFTER my litigation had been disposed of in the manner above mentioned, I went to live at Jalova. It was very pleasant, after all the troubles I had undergone, to remove to some little distance from the scene of my sufferings. Separated from a husband for whom I had vowed unbounded affection, parted for ever (as I thought) from a beloved daughter, deprived of fortune, and fallen from a position of the highest rank, I found retirement necessary for me.

Jalova is a town situated on the Gulf of Ismid, only three hours' voyage by steamboat from Constantinople. I bought a house and four horses, and engaged a woman to manage the first, and a man-servant to groom the horses and attend on me. In the neighbourhood, which was agreeably diversified by hills of most charming aspect, were several villages, which I proposed to visit. Attended by my servant, I travelled without fear, by night as well as by day. The warnings of the mudirs, who endeavoured to make me more circumspect, by telling me how greatly the country was infested by robbers, did not restrain me in the least. Exercise was indispensable to drive away the thoughts of despair which, without it, would have been the death of me.

In my retirement I always kept up some intercourse with the capital. Reshid-Pasha, and, after his death, the ministers of his party, frequently wrote to me. An old lady also took care to give me news of my daughter, as to whose lot I had great uneasiness, given up, as she was, to a woman who could not but hate her, and who seemed to dread my vigilance to such a degree that, she had taken the most rigorous measures to deprive me of the possibility of seeing my child, to whom she passed me off as dead.

Hitherto my life had been passed in the highest spheres. Except on my excursion to the Druses and Bedouins, I had rarely come in contact with the people. It was, therefore, an entire novelty to me to find myself in the heart of the country, and to observe the inhabitants. I visited in succession

all the different villages in the neighbourhood;
sometimes I remained for twenty days without returning home. I was everywhere received with a
degree of cordiality and respect that were quite
touching. These good people, knowing who I was, -
did their best to be accommodating. My arrival
in any place was announced beforehand, and the
wealthiest inhabitants disputed the honour of receiving me. Wherever I presented myself, I always
found a lodging and a repast prepared for me.

Notwithstanding the fears with which it had been
attempted to inspire me, I was never attacked by
any evil-disposed persons. It would, however,
have been a profitable undertaking to have robbed
me, for I usually carried the greater part of my
remaining property in a bag hooked on to my saddle.
One night, as I was going to Sulus, a village, the
charms of which I had heard highly spoken of, I
climbed a mountain, on the other side of which was
the spot I was going to visit. My servant was
obliged to dismount and lead my horse, and it was
with difficulty that he could get him to make the
ascent. Suddenly there appeared before us a horseman, wearing a large turban, with a gun in his
hand, his belt furnished with pistols, and a sabre at
his side. Of the middle height and thick-set, his

face covered with a black, bushy beard, and his limbs powerfully formed, everything about this man betokened more than common strength. At this sight, my attendant began to tremble from head to foot, and could scarcely continue to guide my horse. For my part, I attributed his demeanour to the effect of a long and troublesome journey. The horseman of whom I spoke drew near to us, looked attentively at me, and readily saw by my dress that I was a stranger to the country.

"Welcome, madam!" he exclaimed in a loud voice.

"God protect you," I replied. "It would appear that you are an inhabitant of this neighbourhood."

"Yes," said he, "I live on this mountain; but it seems to me that you don't belong to the country."

"No," I rejoined; "I am from Constantinople, and some time ago I came to take up my abode at Jalova; but Sulus has been so highly commended to me, that I am on my way to that place. The night, however, is so dark, that I don't know whether I shall be able to reach it easily."

"If you will suffer me to accompany you," said my strange interlocutor, "I know a Greek priest in this village, to whom I propose to conduct you."

I accepted his offer; he led the way, and we soon

arrived at our destination. My guide knocked violently at the door, and the priest at once came to open it.

"Father, here is a lady whom I have brought to you. Take care of her; I insist upon it," he added in a menacing tone.

The poor priest asked us in, gave me his best room to sleep in, woke his wife and daughters and ordered them to prepare dinner, while he himself took our horses to the stable.

"Madam," cried my servant as soon as he was alone with me, "I don't understand your object in giving yourself into the hands of a robber. If you wish to perish, that is your own look-out; but you ought not to get me into such scrapes."

"Take courage," said I. "I don't know whether or not that man is what you think him; but if he had any bad intentions, he would have executed them already. There is nothing to fear from him."

Soon afterwards our host came in. "How came you, madam," he asked, "to fall in with the man who brought you here?"

"He accosted us on the mountain," I answered; "and on my telling him that I wished to make my way to Sulus, he conducted us to your house."

s

"You little know," said the priest, "that this man is our ruin. He lives in a den in the neighbourhood, and comes unexpectedly, from time to time, to the house of one or other of the inhabitants, and makes a demand for whatever he pleases —money, oil, or silk. As he is known to be a desperate character, they hasten to satisfy him. Many times the authorities have sent troops after him, but they have never been able to seize him. He has an astonishing scent to escape a meeting with the Zaptics when, his depredations having passed all bounds, they have been sent in quest of him. As soon as they are withdrawn, he exercises most atrocious vengeance on those whom he suspects to have made complaints of his misdeeds."

I partook of the repast which my host's daughters prepared for me, and then came my brigand friend.

"Are you satisfied with the reception that has been given you? Have you any complaints to make?" he asked.

"On the contrary," said I, "I am quite satisfied, and know not how to thank you for having conducted me to the society of such obliging people." He then sat down near me and began to converse as follows :—

"I live on the summit of the mountain, with a

young girl whose mother refused her to me, and
whom I carried off five years ago. We are very
happy and comfortable ; she has made me the father
of several children. I have a beautiful garden, and
when you are pleased to set out on your travels I
hope you will pay me the honour of a visit. I
assure you that you will not repent it ; I will display
all my possessions, and you shall take away whatever you please. Will you come and see me to-
morrow ?"

"I cannot come so soon," I replied. "It is known
where I am. I have sent word to Jalova that I shall
return to-morrow, and if I delay they will at once
send out in search of me ; but when I come again
into this neighbourhood I will pay you a visit."

I used this language in order to excite his alarm,
lest the police should be sent in pursuit if he ventured to attack me. He did not press the invitation, but withdrew.

Early next morning I mounted on horseback, and,
after admiring the beauty of certain cascades which
fell down the mountain-side with considerable noise,
I followed the sea-coast on my way back to Jalova.
When I saw myself near the water I was not free
from uneasiness, for if the idea occurred to my
obliging robber of assailing me at that spot, he could

easily kill me, plunder and throw me into the sea. It was with considerable satisfaction that I returned safe home again.

I did my best to make myself agreeable to the villagers near whom I lived. I voluntarily interposed between them and the mudirs before whom they were summoned. These functionaries, knowing the terms I was on with some of the Ministers, stood in awe of me, and complied with all my requests. They even went so far as to send me presents of considerable value, from fear of my invoking some superior authority to take cognisance of their doings.

The usual grounds of my interference were the prosecutions entered against the people for the recovery of imposts, and I generally compelled their prosecutors to grant them reasonable time for payment.

The two principal branches of industry to which the inhabitants devote themselves are the culture of the olive and extraction of the oil ; the rearing of silkworms and winding off the cocoons. The two products are ready for the market at about the same time of year, following by a fortnight or a month the period when imposts are payable. The well-disposed mudirs wait patiently for the sale of the stocks, before demanding from the tax-payers their dues to the *mahlieh* (treasury). Those who act thus are beloved by those under their jurisdiction, but they find themselves reduced solely to their salaries, and therefore they are rarely to be met with.

The great majority of these officials conduct themselves in the following manner:—As soon as the oil has been extracted, and before it is sufficiently clarified to be offered for sale, and when the cocoons are ready to be unwound, they send their cavas with an order for immediate payment. The poor creatures upon whom this demand is made, having just then none of their resources realised, see their products seized, and sold by auction, at an absurdly inadequate price, to usurers who have an understanding beforehand with the mudir as to making a profit out of these executions. These miscreants promise that official a fixed sum, in order to induce him to bring about these iniquitous sales. They agree among themselves to have no competition, and they are well assured that the people of the country, being very poor, have no money available for the redemption, by process of law, of that of which they cannot prevent the seizure. There are even officials so monstrously unjust as to bring to sale everything, including the furniture, stewpans, and agricultural implements belonging to the poor, thus reducing them to beggary.

The tax-payers cannot get the superior authorities to listen to them. In the vicinity of Constantinople the mudirs are all servants, secretaries, or grooms of Ministers in office, who put them in these places to recompense their services. The complaints of the inhabitants receive no attention from the Ministers, who are naturally disposed to favour their old servants, and are maintained in this disposition by constant supplies of butter, silk, fruits, and vegetables, extorted from the peasants. In the provinces distance is an additional obstacle, to which must be added the circumstance that the applications, to reach the ears of the Ministers, must go through the *valis*, who are all more inclined to favour their subordinates than the complainants.

I sometimes amused myself, after the evening repast, by sitting in a rustic dwelling, before the huge fire round which the rough but peaceable country folks assembled, while they offered me hospitality. It was on such an occasion that they expressed, with charming simplicity, the sufferings they had to endure from their oppressors.

"We see perfectly well," said my host (a well-to-do agriculturist and indefatigable workman), "that we have nothing to hope for. The Padishah desires only the welfare of his people, but he is surrounded by subordinates who rob us of the gold that is drawn from our tears and our toil."

"It will not do to lament over all that," replied a brave and robust woodman, named Hussein. "Something worse may happen. The *ghïaurs* (Christians) may come and take possession of our country."

"Well! and do you think they will treat us worse than we are? On the contrary, fearful of a revolt on our part, they will endeavour to conciliate our good-will, and will govern us far more gently than we are governed now."

"But," said another, who was a confirmed Mussulman and a pilgrim at Mecca, "they will try to make us Christians, and will persecute us on account of our religion."

"It is true that they hold our creed in abhorrence," observed my host, "but they know that our faith is everything to us. They will dread to make themselves our mortal enemies by attacking what we have most at heart. You see that the English allow their Mussulman subjects to practise their rites unmolested; the Russians, also, never attempt to convert the Tcherkesses (Circassians) and other Mussulmans within their dominions."

I was much astonished, as may readily be supposed, to find these peasants reasoning in such a manner on subjects to which I had thought they would have been strangers ; but the desire to ameliorate one's condition tends to enlighten the most limited capacities.

CHAPTER XXIII.

Death of Abdul-Medjid—Kibrizli-Pasha raises Abdul-Aziz to the Throne —Character of the new Sultan — Consequences of the protection afforded by the Consuls—Disgrace of Mehemet-Pasha.

I HAD been five years at Jalova, or in its vicinity, when I heard that the Sultan, Abdul-Medjid, was ill. Kibrizli-Mehemet-Pasha, my husband, was Grand-vezir, and it was feared that a revolution would break out on the death of the Sultan. The discarded Ministers got up an agitation in order to bring to the throne the Prince Mourad-Effendi, son of Abdul-Medjid. They thus acted in defiance of the Mussulman law, which conferred the sovereignty on the brother of the dying Sultan, viz., the Prince Abdul-Aziz, whose favourable disposition towards Mehemet-Pasha and his party were well known.

I returned to Constantinople, in order to be in a position to take advantage of the new state of affairs which a fresh reign could not fail to produce. Mehemet-Pasha, meanwhile, took his measures to secure the rights of the legitimate heir. The chamberlains

were devoted to him. Very few persons could contrive to penetrate to the chamber of the sick man,
whose state was much more serious than was allowed
to be known.   The new Valideh-Sultan, mother of
Abdul-Aziz, was apprised of it, and the Prince, her
son, kept himself prepared for any emergency.   It
was towards evening when the Padishah breathed
his last, and the news was kept secret all that night.
Next morning the public only learnt the fact from
hearing the funeral chants given out by the muez-
zins from the tops of the minarets and seeing the
Prince Abdul-Aziz going to the Mosque to be proclaimed Sultan.

The new Sultan, on ascending to power, showed
himself animated by the best intentions.   He
desired to remedy those abuses that had deeply
affected him while he was only a private individual.
His accession was hailed as the presage of an era of
prosperity for Turkey.   He was known for his
kindness, without ever carrying it to the verge of
weakness, as did his predecessor.   It was known
that he had led a retired life ; that he had married
only one wife, whom he had promised he would
never take any other but herself; that his tastes
were simple, and his expenditure moderate, without
avarice ;   and after the excessive prodigality of

Abdul-Medjid this latter quality was especially appreciated. It was believed that he would occupy himself independently with the interests of his people, without yielding to the influence of the Seraglio. His mother, the Validch-Sultan, had a profound dislike to business, and he regarded all women with equal indifference.

He began by lodging in the Old Seraglio all his predecessor's wives, and put a stop to their disorderly conduct; and next he busied himself with improving the condition of the troops. He wished to see the distribution of stores punctually performed; the salaries paid when they became due; the soldiers' clothes made of good materials; the bread and other provisions of good quality. All the Ministers were in a state of consternation. They saw the contractors, with whom they had private agreements to sanction waste, compelled faithfully to execute their contracts with the Government.

Some time after his accession to the throne, however, his sister having made him a present of a young slave, Abdul-Aziz could not refuse such a gift, for he would have gained a deadly enemy by so doing. Subsequently being struck with the charms of another slave, he made her also his odalisque. At present he has three wives: this is

not much, compared to the brilliant and crowded
• Seraglio kept by his predecessor. However, the
Sultan's wives and odalisques lead very simple
lives ; their luxury does not much exceed that of the
Ministers' wives. Abdul-Aziz finds his chief pleasure in taking trips on board a steam-boat. Twice
a month, he goes to pass two or three days alone in
a small country-house of his own, on the sea-coast,
two or three leagues from the capital, which affords
him the gratification of making a short voyage.
When he was only heir to the throne, he used to
spend nearly all his time on board a pleasure yacht,
on which he frequently took a voyage of several
days' duration.

As is usual on taking possession of the throne,
Abdul-Aziz had his palaces refurnished. This furnishing on such a scale is an important undertaking,
and must produce an outlay of several hundreds of
thousands for the benefit of those employed in the
work, or those whose duty it is to procure the
furniture. This incident affords an opportunity of
pointing out by what means Europeans contrive,
under the protection of their ambassadors and
consuls, to make a rapid fortune in the East.

Whoever offers the largest sum to the Minister
who has the control of the work obtains the con-

tract.   It is usually signed without being read; his Excellency looking to one thing only—how much he is to receive.   The furniture, of the value of five or six hundred thousand francs, is purchased at Paris or Lyons, on account of the Sultan, by the contractor; and the latter presents a bill for four or five millions, which is approved by the Minister.

The contractor obtains, by dint of continued applications, the payment of instalments, amounting to seven or eight hundred thousand francs—probably the cost price of the furniture and the allowance to the august signatory.   The latter refuses to pay more; alleges the poverty of the treasury—that to pay such a large sum as claimed would compromise him—that by-and-by he will be able to make up further instalments, etc.   The contractor then waits for a change of Ministers.   As soon as a new vezir is appointed he calls upon him, and demands payment of the balance.   His Excellency flies into a passion; declares that he who allowed such an account has participated in a most iniquitous robbery.   "It is impossible," says he, "to pay so enormous a sum as that claimed for a thing of so little value as the furniture supplied."

If the creditor is a Frenchman, he goes to his ambassador or consul, who communicates with the

government of the Porte, and protests against the
course taken by the new Minister. "It is impossible
to admit," says the diplomatic agent, "that a claim
is to be rejected under the pretext that it has been
approved by a vezir who is not now in office. Such
a proceeding is robbery. The cabinet which I
represent cannot suffer the Porte to treat with such
contempt the interests of the French who are
established in Turkey." In spite of all his efforts,
the Ottoman Minister is obliged to yield, and to
satisfy a claim advanced in so peremptory a fashion.
Of course the affair ends at last à l'amiable, and
both the Minister and the dragoman get out of it
their little pourboire.

Abdul-Aziz had now held sway for two months,
and was still animated by an ardent zeal for the
repression of abuses. Riza-Pasha, Minister for War
in the previous reign, was charged with numerous
frauds; moreover, he had made every effort to get
the Prince Mourad appointed in succession to his
father, to the detriment of the new sovereign.* The
Sultan called upon him to make restitution of
sundry large sums, of which he told him the
amount. Riza-Pasha shut himself up in his house,
and refused to pay anything. The Sultan thereupon appointed him Governor of Smyrna, as a

means of removing the culprit to a distance from Constantinople, where his wealth had gained him a great number of friends or accomplices interested in supporting him, and well able to give trouble if any attempt were made to gain forcible possession of the person of their patron.

Riza-Pasha was obliged to obey, but he went away very unwillingly. He had not resided for many days at Smyrna, when he received the order to go into exile ; instead of submitting to it, he took refuge on board a French frigate. The Sultan demanded his extradition from the French government, whose *protégé* he was. The reply was, that the prisoner would be given up, but only upon the condition that prosecutions were to be instituted against all the former Ministers, as Riza-Pasha had only acted in conformity with their usual proceedings.

Very shortly afterwards, the enemies of Mehemet-Pasha succeeded in depriving him of the high position which he had hitherto occupied. Insinuations were made to the Sultan that his Grand-vezir considered himself to be the real master of Turkey. If he were listened to, it was said, one would suppose that it was to him alone the Sultan owed his throne, and that he would be quite unable to retain it without the powerful support of his servant. Fuad-

Pasha, who was the originator of these reports, succeeded to the inheritance of the individual whose disgrace he had procured.

The Sultan, perpetually haunted by the dread of a conspiracy, was determined not to leave to Mehemet-Pasha the possibility of joining himself with the discontented factions. He intimated to him the order to repair immediately to Adrianople. Under Abdul-Medjid these orders were rarely carried into actual execution; it was considered sufficient if the individual who received one confined himself to his own palace, and was careful not to mix himself up in any political intrigue; if he strictly adhered to this line of conduct, he was left in peace. The new Sultan, accidentally passing before the palace of Mehemet-Pasha, two days after the order had been given for his departure, was very indignant at seeing that it was still inhabited. He sent a message to the disgraced Minister, that on the day after the morrow a steamboat would be in readiness to receive him. The Pasha was compelled to obey; he took with him his wife, but left behind my daughter Aïsheh, whom he had married to Shevket-Pasha, the son of my rival. This exile to Adrianople lasted two years.

CHAPTER XXIV.

As I have already had occasion to narrate, in the course of this history, when I was separated from my husband, I had left with him a son and a daughter. My daughter was called Aïsheh-Hanum; when the catastrophe occurred which parted us, she was in her eighth year. Her lot was as cruel as my own,—I may even say that it was worse; for I, though in exile and poverty, still enjoyed a certain liberty of action. My unfortunate Aïsheh fell into the hands of a mother-in-law, whose cruelty and malice far exceeded what is universally attributed to mothers-in-law in general. This quintessence of evil qualities was called Ferideh-Hanum; her first husband had been a certain Reshid-Effendi, a renowned writer, notorious for his drunkenness. The malice of the one, and the drunkenness of the other, rendered any agreement between this ill-assorted couple impossible: they in consequence sought to recover

T

liberty and tranquillity by a divorce. By this husband Ferideh had a son called Shevket, who accompanied her to her new home; she endeavoured to have
him recognised as the adopted son of his Highness.

Ferideh, once installed in my husband's house,
sought by every possible means to establish her
authority in it. She was entirely deficient in the
ordinary grace and beauty of her sex ; in default of
these she had recourse to all kinds of intrigue, and
brought into play every influence which she could
command. She availed herself of the protection
accorded to her by the Grand-vezir Reshid-Pasha,
and the numerous friends and relatives of her own
brother, Bessim-Bey. By a clever employment of
these means, the shrewd and cunning woman succeeded in obtaining complete ascendancy over
· Kibrizli-Pasha, who was compelled to submit to the
yoke imposed on him by all these tricksters who
surrounded him. Sometimes it was the wife who
had him in hand, sometimes it was Bessim ; sometimes their slaves, or the relatives who took up the
game. In the midst of all these intrigues the unhappy Pasha grumbled, became irritated, but in the
end he was always either worked upon by flattery
or cajoled by intrigue into yielding. In every dif-
ference, in every struggle which took place, it was

always he who was in the wrong, and who was in consequence compelled to give way. But so adroit and skilful were those who pulled the strings, that Kibrizli never saw through their game, and, whilst obeying them implicitly, believed that he was acting according to his own will. So great is the power of • intrigue in the private circles of Oriental society !

Ferideh, who aspired to universal rule, looked with • an evil eye on the presence of my daughter Aïsheh in her harem. Aïsheh was the daughter of her rival, and was the one strong link that bound the heart of the Pasha to mine. She was, in consequence, the natural enemy of her mother-in-law,— the one standing menace against her happiness and against the realization of her dreams of complete power and of complete absorption of the Pasha's property.

From the first moment that Ferideh set foot in my husband's house, she strove, by every possible means, to separate the daughter from the father, so as gradually to weaken the bonds of affection which united them. With this object in view, she took most particular care to place every obstacle in the way of any meeting between father and child, and carefully endeavoured to prevent any • tête-à-tête, the consequences of which she dreaded.

To that effect, she confined Aïsheh to a distant apartment, where she remained surrounded by slaves and
out of sight of all comers. For years my daughter
continued to be completely forgotten, and it was only
by accident that any visitors at the house ever
observed her.

A girl, who was thus entirely neglected in regard
to all the ordinary details of family interests, would,
of necessity, be brought up in the grossest general
ignorance. The Turks, as a rule, have a dislike for
educated persons ; they prefer those who are ill-
informed and ignorant, for they feel sure of being
able to manage them and to mould them to their will.
Ferideh perfectly understood what she was about, and
it was with good reason that she determined to bring
up my unfortunate Aïsheh in the most profound
ignorance. It thus happened that, during the eight
or nine years which preceded the marriage of my
daughter, she had been taught nothing but to read
the Koran, to be able to scrawl a sort of writing,
and to do the sewing which is indispensable in a
household. The remainder of her time was passed,
as is not unusual in a harem, in gossip, always useless, and not unfrequently hurtful.

My readers will, I am sure, with difficulty believe
that a girl belonging to one of the princely families

of Turkey, the daughter of a man who had in his own person experienced the advantage of a European education, could have been so completely neglected as regards instruction. Nevertheless, this phenomenon would be easily intelligible to any one who was acquainted with the disposition and character of Kibrizli-Pasha, and with the habits and manners of the highest classes in Constantinople. It is true that Kibrizli had received a certain education, of which a part had been acquired in Turkey and a part in France ; but this education consisted of a thin surface of knowledge veneered over a thick mass of ignorance.

Kibrizli resembled the greater number of those who have been sent to Europe to be educated, in having only acquired a smattering of learning, and having just mustered sufficient of the rudiments to enable him to pass through the indispensable formalities of an examination. He had never advanced sufficiently far to acquire any real love for science, or to enable him to recognize the positive necessity and importance of instruction.

Besides this, he had never been able to shake off the ideas which are innate in all Turks, and which lead them to believe that there is no such paramount requirement of knowledge amongst women as to

• make its requisition a necessity. Kibrizli had pre
served below the varnish of civilization the stam]
of the old Turk ; as such he looked down on womei
as inferior beings. He was one of those who, when
ever speaking of women, would exclaim with an ai
of self-sufficiency, " Oh ! women have long hair anc
short wits."

And yet no man was ever so thoroughly unde
the thumb of women as himself, as between mysel
and Ferideh we did with him what we liked.

From this tendency of opinion arose the indif
erence which was one of the causes of my unfor
tunate daughter's education being so lamentabl
neglected. But independently of the small valu
which his Highness himself attached to instruc
tion, the customs and habits prevalent amongs
Turkish grandees, as those already observed
exercised in this matter a most perniciou
influence.

Family life is, in reality, unknown amongst th
Turks. The law of the Koran, which divides man
kind into two distinct classes,—men and women,—
does not admit of the existence of a family in whicl
each member can live the same life and form a par
of one harmonious whole. In Mussulman societ}
the men have separate ideas, habits, and interests

whilst, on the other hand, the women have others, which belong exclusively to them. Thus persons who pretend to form a part of one and the same family, have, in reality, nothing common amongst themselves,—neither apartments, nor goods, nor furniture, nor friends, nor even the same hours for taking rest. The selamlik (the apartments of the men) and the harem are, in consequence, two separate establishments, placed side by side, where each one does what pleases him or herself,—the men on one side, the women on the other. The authority of the head of the family, when he is in a position to exercise any at all, is the only connection and bond of union between these two halves of the same household.

This separate system, upon which Mussulman family life is based, acted upon by the paramount law of self-interest, gives rise to a singularity which cannot escape remark by an attentive observer. It becomes evident that the degree of separation which exists in Turkish households between the men and the women can be measured by the greater or less amount of affluence in which the family lives. A poor Mussulman has only one or two rooms for himself and his family ; he is compelled to study economy, and on this account he, like a good father of a family, eats, drinks, and sleeps with his wife and children. The well-to-do middle-class man establishes his household after a much more orthodox fashion, and begins by drawing a more palpable line of demarcation between himself and his harem. Two or three rooms are completely divided off from the remainder of the house; these form the selamlik—the apartment for men and place of reception; the remainder of the house constitutes the harem, the forbidden ground.

If we now go to the rich—to the Pasha with three tails—or to the minister with a portfolio, we shall find his palace installed in grand style, and the separation between men and women more complete. The selamlik of a grandee comprises an entirely separate building, and the harem has the proportions of a colossal palace, with iron gates, grated windows, and a garden surrounded by high walls. The men and women shut up in these two divisions of the household remain completely isolated from each other, and have no means of communication except through the eunuchs, or through the female Christian servants who are attached to the harem. The Pasha, his sons, and near relations, who alone have the privilege of free entry into the harem, can only enter it by a sort of bridge, enclosed with iron gratings—a kind of secret passage, which is traversed under the escort and charge of a eunuch.

This complete separation between the harem and the selamlik gratifies the vanity, and satisfies the pride, of the grandees of Constantinople. The higher they rise in station, the more absurd they make themselves in taking useless precautions, and in enforcing ridiculous formalities as means of elevating their wives by withdrawing them from the eyes of the lower orders. The natural results of this complete separation of the two establishments is the existence of diverging habits of life. The women on their side have their own private affairs, their own household management, and their own intrigues; they entertain their friends, have their receptions, and amuse themselves in their own fashion. In the selamlik the Pashas, with their friends and domestics do the same thing; there they receive their visitors and guests, and spend their time intriguing and gossiping, or in setting themselves up as puppets to be admired by their parasites and flatterers.

If on the one side the men are spendthrifts, and dissipate their means, on the other the women fail not to do the same. The efforts made on both sides to get the upper hand, and to surpass each other in magnificence, give rise to a sort of rivalry between the two elements. The master of the house—Pasha or Effendi, whichever he may be—generally plays the part of moderator between the different members of the seraglio ; but this part, originating rather in egotism than in any real wish for moderation, is generally confined to two points—to assure to himself the full enjoyment of the harem and to maintain the splendour of the selamlik. If the Pasha obtains his aim in the enjoyment of the one, and in satiety of the other of these worldly pleasures, he makes light of all else, and shuts his eyes to the robberies committed by his domestics, and to the extravagance and excesses of his wives.

The Pashas, caring for nothing but their own pleasures and gratification, leave the entire management of their households in the hands of an intendant—kïaïah,—who does much for himself, and very little for anyone else, and often ends in plunging the Pasha into debt up to his neck. Those Pashas who are shrewd hold the opinion that it is much more advantageous to occupy themselves with robberies on a large scale in the administration of affairs than to trouble their heads with the petty thefts in detail made by their intendants and domestics.

Thus a sort of tacit understanding grows up between master and servant, by which each robs to the best of his ability—the one wholesale, the other retail.

A Pasha, having thus disembarrased himself of all care and trouble as regards his private establishment, becomes, so to say, a mere guest in his own home. During the day he generally passes his time at the Porte, where he discusses questions of justice and politics with all comers ; then he makes his rounds in the town, visits his friends and partisans, and stretches the lines which are to form the nets of his political intrigues. Towards the evening, at five or six o'clock, his Excellency makes a solemn entry into his palace, accompanied by his aides-de-camp and the gentlemen of his suite. Arrived at the top of the staircase, he does not enter his own apartments, but without loss of time turns towards the great gate which gives entrance into the harem. A eunuch, who stands as sentinel at the door, throws it open with all the requisite ceremonials, and introduces the Pasha into the Dwelling of Bliss. In the hall of the harem he is received by his wife, or by the directress or superintendent of the harem, and to her belongs the honour of introducing him into the inner chamber.

The Pasha, as a general rule, does not remain

more than a quarter of an hour in the harem; that is to say, the precise time necessary to undress himself, and to put on his dressing-gown and pelisse of ermine fur. In this costume, which is not wanting in elegance or comfort, he again returns to the apartments of the men, and proceeds to occupy his customary place on the divan. He has hardly had time to install himself here before the entry of a procession of his friends, his flatterers, and of persons who desire to ask favours of him; these, one after the other, kiss the hem of his robe, and take their places in line before him.

Surrounded by these people, the Pasha drinks his bottle of *raki*, eats some dried raisins and filberts, and smokes several pipes. When the hour of dinner arrives, his Excellency places himself at the head of the hungry troop around him, and conducts them to the dining-hall. All who have the honour of sharing his repast do not fail to give loud expression to their gratitude; and at each mouthful which they swallow they never omit to make a profound reverence. The great man, on his part, seeing how injurious his august presence is to the satisfactory digestion of his guests, does not cease during the repast to encourage them, and urge them on by the powerful stimulus of his voice.

With this view, at each occasion of a new dish appearing, he never fails to request them to attack it in earnest, crying out continually in a loud and sonorous voice, " *Buīurun, buīurun* "—" Eat, my friends, eat."

When the dinner is concluded, the Pasha and his friends return and place themselves in the same seats which they occupied before it commenced ; then begins a course of coffee and pipes, and a renewed course of social and political gossip. Sometimes, but rarely, as a variation, cards are played ; but tric-trac is more in vogue : the great world at Constantinople have a preference for this kind of diversion. The Pásha and his circle spend their evenings in this fashion amongst themselves, without caring what their wives may do in the harem. These, on their part, endeavour to amuse themselves as best they can, by assembling round them their friends and all the gossips of the neighbourhood, and with these companions they laugh, they feast, they play games, and sometimes have a little music with tambours — *tef*.

It is generally half-past eleven before the Pasha definitively retires for the night to the harem ; he is received at the threshold by the eunuch, who waits his approach, standing with lights in each hand,

and who precedes him through the entrance-hall to the apartment of his wife.

At the time of rising in the morning, the Pasha is attended by slaves, who assist at his toilet and ablutions ; when these are completed, and he is ready to leave his room, he remains a few minutes and talks with the members of the harem on any subjects which may interest them. It is usually at this early *levée* that his daughters and female relatives take the opportunity of presenting themselves and enjoying his society. When this short space of time has elapsed, he hastily takes his departure, in order that he may not keep too long in suspense the crowd of worshippers who are waiting for a sight of his august countenance.

The description which I have now given of life amongst the Turkish grandees sufficiently explains the kind of intercourse which exists between members of the same family, and what little care parents take of their children. It is true that for boys the case is different, because the latter have the power of going out, and can enter the harem when they please ; and, besides, as their education is much more cared for, the separation from their father has not such a disastrous effect. The daughters are those who really suffer from this entire absence of

family life and of a father's care, whom they do not ✔
see, perhaps, more than once or twice in a month.
Confined entirely to their own apartments, they
depend solely on their own resources, having no
society but that of slaves and old women, who surround them, and amuse and manage them as they
please.

My poor Aïsheh was not treated with greater distinction than the ordinary children of a family,
either as regards instruction or in the general tenour
of her life. If any exception was made, it was
decidedly to her disadvantage, as every means
and trick was employed in order to withdraw
her as much as possible from the eye of her father
and of the world, and to keep a constant watch over
her. The cunning Ferideh was well aware that she
was much beloved by her father. Influenced by an
ignoble feeling of jealousy, she constantly interposed
between them, never ceased to spy on my child, and
took unceasing precautions to prevent any acci-
dental meeting with him.

CHAPTER XXV.

THE complete isolation to which Aïsheh was condemned, and the strict surveillance to which she was subjected, had for their object the prevention of the development of her intellectual faculties, and it was hoped thereby to retain her in a permanent state of mental degradation. But even if this object had been fully attained, it would not have satisfied this savage mother-in-law, whose jealousy and cupidity knew no bounds. By keeping the daughter of her rival in a brutalizing state of ignorance, she succeeded wonderfully in her designs, for a brute is never to be feared ; but a brute has a heart, and knows what the love of a mother is. This notion flashed across Ferideh's mind, causing her serious apprehensions, and making her fear that filial love would find a response in the heart of the unfortunate Aïsheh.

"Never," said she, "never! Aïsheh is in my power. She must belong body and soul to me alone. If the voice of nature calls upon her, I will stifle it; for I and my rival can never be on an equality. Aïsheh must forget even the very name of her mother."

Impelled therefore by blind passion and a boundless jealousy, the mother-in-law set to work to attain her aim, which was to cause every trace of me to disappear from her mind. For this purpose she took care to surround the girl with people who were devoted to her wishes; and in addition to them she began a systematic attack, in order entirely to drive away any remains of filial love which might still remain in her heart. There was no atrocity or calumny which could be devised against me which these people did not repeat to Aïsheh, enlarging on and bringing them forcibly before the tender spirit of my unfortunate daughter.

These clever tactics, as I had foreseen, did not fail to obtain a complete success; for, sharp as she was, poor Aïsheh was forced to feel all the influences which they brought to bear upon her. So, by dint of lies and continual efforts, the clever emissaries of Ferideh succeeded in making my daughter believe all sorts of absurdities against me, and impressed

U

her with the idea that, like the mythological beings, she was the child of a monster in flesh.

Having succeeded in poisoning and perverting Aïsheh's mind, the wily Ferideh thought it would be better to endeavour to efface every trace of her rival from the daughter's mind ; by this means she fancied she would remain absolute mistress of her destiny. In causing the last vestiges of a past domination to disappear, she calculated to consolidate her own. An order was therefore given to the people about the house that they were to spread the report of my death, and never to mention my name again. The same order was also given to those who came to the house, so that none should mention the name of Melek-Hanum in the presence of the girl. Further, as a precautionary measure, all those who had frequented the house in my time, and who knew me, were dispensed with. Ferideh evidently feared lest kindly disposed or indiscreet persons should reveal the truth to her whom she desired so ardently to deceive and mystify. Amongst the persons who were excluded can be enumerated Atidjeh, Hanum-Effendi, Zekieh-Hanum, the Hanum Sultanas, and several others.

Owing to these plots and endless intrigues, Ferideh and her worthy brother, Bessim-Bey, a downright scoundrel, made my poor daughter their slave, only allowing her to see what they liked, and hear what suited them. Aïsheh had to submit to this slavery in the midst even of her family and under her father's eye for seven years, until she had attained her sixteenth year. Having reached this age, when girls in the East are considered marriageable, Aïsheh began to excite notice, owing to the freshness and beauty of her face and her youth. Aïsheh's charms, at the same time that all remarked them, equally impressed Ferideh, who, in her quality of mother-in-law, had to think of her future. What will be the fate of this girl? is a question which Ferideh and her accomplices must often have put to each other. Owing to every sort of intrigue, they had succeeded up to that time in doing what they liked, and in keeping her in the most complete dependence.

In Turkey, girls of good family usually marry at sixteen, and that because aspirants to obtain the hand of a great Pasha's daughter are never wanting. This grand question, namely, to know to whom would be intrusted my daughter's future, became the topic and question to which all the policy of Ferideh and her clique had resort. This question became a fixed idea for them in the day-time and a nightmare during the night; but a real and tangible nightmare, for they were forced to decide one way or another. In fact, the question which arose before them, like an insurmountable mountain, was truly one of the most difficult which a set of scoundrels and rogues had ever to solve.

Two courses presented themselves to Ferideh's and Bessim's consideration, by which to resolve the problem of marriage. Either they had to give the girl to a young man who was able to keep her in the ease and comfort to which her birth entitled her, or they had to seek a suitable *parti*, who would be admitted to the house in the capacity of son-in-law to his Highness Kibrizli-Mehemet-Pasha.

The first of these two aspirants did not suit Ferideh at all, and that because the idea of separating herself from Aïsheh and giving her her liberty made her tremble with fright. "How," said she, "can I allow this girl to leave the house, away from my superintendence, in leaving her to the care of the first comer whom it would be folly to fight against, and who would kiss my hand to-day that he might betray me the next? No, that cannot be! And if, unluckily, my rival, on hearing that her daughter is free and settled, should find her out and unfold to her our misdoings—how we separated her

from her father—how we despoiled her of all she
possessed—how we declared she was dead, the better
to assure her death,—if this were to happen, I am
lost for ever! But what am I saying? The union
of the daughter with the mother would inevitably
lead to the union of the husband. Eh! eh! eh!
that is a fearful dream, a dream to make my hair
stand on end; and if his Highness, drawn into
their midst, should see once again the woman he so
loved . . . and whom he loves still, the triumph
of my rival is certain, and I should be for ever
lost!"

Terrified by such a terrible occurrence, Ferideh
turned her attention to another method which still
remained for her to dispose of Aïsheh, which was to
marry her to a man of her choice, who would keep
her under the paternal roof. This was the only
means which offered a certain guarantee, and it was
to this that the perfidious mother-in-law had recourse. But, even whilst deciding on this last,
Ferideh's troubles appeared only to increase; the more
she surmounted, the more appeared to arrive. Being
determined not to let go of her prey, she sought for a
husband — a sort of make-believe husband — an
ignoble being, who would lend himself to play the
rôle of accomplice, and who would be transformed

into the jailer and even the executioner of his victim.

Amongst people who wish to make their fortune at one stroke by marrying a girl, there are some of all sorts; thus Ferideh had not far to go before she found the individual who would suit her, had she been simple enough to rely on the first rogue who presented · himself as suitor. But Ferideh was too cunning to trust too indiscriminately to anyone. She sought for a sure husband, one who would be proof against all exterior influence and romantic sentiment, one who would be hired to do anything. To judge by the absurd requirements and pretensions advanced by this mother-in-law, one would have decidedly thought she was choosing a husband for herself and not for another.

And yet all this was simply mere play-work, but serious play-work too, by means of which the players sought to blind everybody, more especially Kibrizli, the father, in whose eyes they threw dust. Whilst Ferideh, Bessim, and the rest appeared to be considering the future of Aïsheh, and were carrying on all sorts of intrigues, they had already passed sentence on their victim, and were considering the means by which they could put it into execution. Kibrizli had no other issue but two daughters; one was Aïsheh, my child, and the other by his second marriage. These two daughters were therefore the successors to his fortune; for at his death his possessions were to be equally divided between them. It was evident that at the death of the Pasha, with the remainder of this fortune Aïsheh would have acquired her own portion, which she would have been able to dispose of as she liked, even to sharing it with me, her mother.

To prevent this, and further to render it impossible for her to share and enjoy it with me, Ferideh and her relations decided on taking possession both of Aïsheh and her fortune. But this could only be done by keeping the unfortunate girl to themselves—marrying her, in fact, to one of their relations.

As often happens amongst rogues, several of Ferideh's relations who had come forward as suitors fought between themselves and intrigued to obtain the girl and her fortune. Each thought he was the favoured individual, and did his best to keep in the good graces of, and conciliate himself with, Ferideh and the father of the girl. Ferideh had, however, already chosen her man, which she concealed all the more carefully because she feared lest anything should compromise her success. The handful of suitors which the mother-in-law kept by her, included three principal ones, Bessim-Bey, her eldest, Shakir, her youngest brother, and Shevket, her son by Sarosh-Reshid. The two former were only lay-figures : the latter was, as it were, the trump card by which she hoped to win the game.

Having made up her mind to drag Aïsheh into her family, Ferideh began insensibly to alter her manner towards her, by taking her out of the solitude in which she had been left. Thus the unfortunate girl was subjected to the trial of a complete transformation, for her usual habits and surroundings were suddenly changed, and she was drawn, as if by enchantment, out of the cell where she had been kept. By Ferideh's orders, her wardrobe was immediately filled with rich clothes, her apartments were luxuriously furnished, the number of her servants and slaves was augmented, whilst several carriages and horses were put at her disposal.

Thus at the age of fifteen my daughter was withdrawn from this prison, where her intelligence and bodily health had languished for the long period of seven years, and she made her first appearance in the society of ladies. Having been gilded by the rays of Ferideh's favour, from that time Aïsheh became the object of the adulations and attention of all the acquaintances and friends of the house. The guests, who came in great numbers to solicit the patronage of his Highness's wife, began to turn their steps towards the apartments of the Pasha's daughter, whose goodwill they also desired to obtain.

From this time, whenever Ferideh wished to go out paying official calls, or, better still, ceremonious ones, she took care to be accompanied by Aïsheh, whose beauty only added brilliancy to the cortége. After having exhibited her in the houses of the different ministers and nobles of the empire, the mother-in-law took her with her when she was received into the Imperial palace, and on this occasion she did not fail to present her to Abdul-Aziz, who at this time was on the throne.

The description of the ceremonial, and the curious incidents which took place on the occasion of this reception, such as they were repeated to me by my daughter, offer such a striking interest that I cannot refrain from giving an account of it here.

CHAPTER XXVI.

As it may be remembered, Kibrizli-Mehemet-Pasha, the father of my child, was at the head of the Ottoman cabinet, at the death of the late Sultan, Abdul-Medjid. In his capacity as head of the government, like a sort of *ad interim* Sultan, it was he who had the upper hand in affairs during the interregnum. It is to him, too, that the empire is indebted for the inauguration of the new reign, and the installation of Abdul-Aziz on the Imperial throne; for the fidelity and energy of Kibrizli contributed enormously to the maintenance of order and respect for the laws and dynastic traditions.

This period (1862) was assuredly the most brilliant epoch of the political career of Kibrizli-Pasha, for Providence had reserved for him the rôle of supreme umpire, who, on the one hand, could consign the mortal remains of a Sultan to the tomb, and with the other, aid his successor to gird on the sword of Osman. Being first amongst the vezirs, he rallied them all around the throne, and his voice was law from one end of the empire to the other. His power and authority, which threw their rays over all, were shared to a certain extent by the woman who served him as companion, and that was Ferideh. Notwithstanding the complete separation of the two sexes in the East, the woman who shares her life with the man ends by also sharing, to some extent, his power and honours ; bound together as they are by common fate, this division becomes inevitable.

Ferideh was then, at this time, the first amongst her fellow-women, the grand vezir of the women as her husband was amongst the men. She was at the head of the vezir's wives, surrounded by the highest class of women, for her protection and good graces were sought after by all those who found any allurement in her power.

At the period of the inauguration of the new reign, Kibrizli's wife also played a part, and, being the first amongst the women, she considered it her duty to be present at the ceremonies, fêtes, and receptions which were given to celebrate the succession of Abdul-Aziz to the throne. On the occasion of the official reception, which took place at the palace of the Dolma-Bagtcheh, Ferideh presented herself at the head of the feminine branch of diplomacy to swear fidelity and congratulate his Imperial Majesty on his accession to the throne.

Accompanied by my daughter Aïsheh, and surrounded by a numerous suite of ladies in waiting and slaves, who vied with each other in the beauty of their faces, the elegance of their figures, and the magnificence of their jewels,—in the midst, I say, of a brilliant staff, Ferideh approached the golden doors and marble staircases which, on the shores of the Bosphorus, give access to the interior of the Imperial harem.

Hardly was the arrival of the *caïque* signalled which bore the harem of the Grand-vezir, than a crowd of guards and eunuchs in full dress arranged themselves in two lines, so as to render the honour due to the wife of him who held in his hands the seal of the Padishah. Supported under her arms and elbows by numerous masters of the ceremonies, Ferideh had to walk the whole distance between the banks and the entrance-door, trampling under her feet the rich shawls which had been spread out the length of the quay in her honour.

Once arrived at the entrance-door, Kibrizli-Pasha's wife was received by the first mistress of the ceremonies of the Imperial harem, who awaited her standing; with the ladies and slaves of her retinue.

As separate chambers had been prepared for each of the guests, where they were to remain during the reception, the mistress of ceremonies hastened to show Ferideh into the room which had been reserved for her; after which she and her suite were regaled with splendid refreshments, including Eastern sherbets and Neapolitan ices. The refreshments were served during the interval which was accorded to the ladies to arrange their toilettes and make themselves worthy of the Imperial glance.

The mistresses of ceremonies having announced the time was come for the ladies to pass into the reception-room, the whole number of guests arose with measured tread, and took the attitude required by the court ceremonial, crossing their hands before them. This attitude or position is known to the Turks under the name of "*pencheh-divan*," and it is in this posture that the women pray. On presenting themselves before the Sultan, who is a man and a mortal like any other, Ferideh and her companions were not veiled.

This incident demands a moment's pause and also a little explanation, for my readers will feel naturally curious to know how it is that the Turks allow their wives to appear before any one with their faces uncovered. "Decidedly," they will say, "that must be a sign of progress amongst the Turks." My readers must beware of arriving at premature conclusions on the faith of such an occurrence. The Turks may change, it is true, but never will they change on the point of jealousy : the most refined Turk, he who passes for a Europeanized being, once returned to his home, is certain to eclipse all his compatriots on that one point of jealousy. As regards woman, the Turk is jealous of his own shadow ; he would never allow a profane gaze to fall on her. But, at the same time, the Turk is a curious being, with whom contrasts of every description are possible. For example, the Turk who would shudder to hear his wife's name on the lips of another man, the same irascible, quarrelsome and jealous being, consents, with a light heart, to let his wife present herself unveiled before the Sultan.

One can trace to two distinct causes this apparent contradiction—this act which, for the Turk, is an act contrary to nature and the divine law : the first is religious sentiment; the second, a servile mind. Religious feeling is that which compels a Turk to commit an action which the Koran condemns most decidedly : in his opinion, the Sultan is a being placed above all mortals ; he is the Prophet's Vicar, the shadow of God upon earth — "*Zil-ullah.*" These divine attributes evidently raise the Sultan above human creatures, and elevate him to that height, that none can think of putting him on the same footing as the rest of created beings.

Such a profound respect for the sacred person of the Padishah, clearly explains how the Turks put aside their jealousy, and how they ever consent to allow their wives to appear unveiled before a mortal. Thus, since the Sultan has taken the title of Mahomet's Vicar, the Turks have tacitly accorded him the privilege of looking on the wives of his subjects. One thing which I do not know, and which I am very curious to understand, is, owing to what theological effort the Ulemas can reconcile the laws of the Koran upon marriage with the right of *carte blanche* allowed to the Sultans. According to the Koran, the moment that a Mussulman woman shows her face to a stranger, the marriage instantly becomes null and void.

Servitude is the second cause to which must be attributed the existence of this privilege in favour of the Sultans. In fact, the marked disposition shown by the Turks in making themselves the very humble and obedient servants of those who govern, added to the total absence of independent feeling, are reasons which can explain the extraordinary abnegation of the Turk towards Mahomet's Vicar and the reigning power. In the struggle between the ruling passions of his soul, fanaticism and covetousness bear the palm, and jealousy remains powerless : then he consents that his wife shall present herself in all her beauty and attractions before the Sultan. " Padishaha yassak yok dur " (" to the Sultan nothing is forbidden"), says the Turk, shaking his head ; and upon that he permits his wife to go.

It must be allowed that if subjects, on their side, give such a signal proof of their loyalty and veneration for the sovereign, on the other hand, the Sultans have never abused the confidence placed in them.

At the request of the grand mistress of ceremonies, all the ladies who were going to be presented, with Ferideh at their head, advanced towards the throne-room. On entering the hall, she and my daughter were conducted close to the Sultan, who stood upright and looked with surprise at the number of his faithful subjects. In accordance with the etiquette used at such ceremonies, Ferideh knelt down, and, bending forwards, kissed the feet of his Imperial Majesty. Aïsheh, and all the other ladies

or girls who followed her, imitated the example
which the Grand-vezir's wife had set them. Having
achieved this act of adoration, they retreated, walking backwards, so as not to turn their backs on the
Sultan, and then they ranged themselves in a line
along the wall.

This latter ceremony was succeeded by a promenade, which the Sultan made round the hall—a sort
of review, in fact, which gave him an occasion to
address a few words and compliments to the wives
of his Ministers. Ferideh, who had precedence
over the others, was the first to whom Abdul-Aziz
spoke. When the Sultan came near her, he said
graciously, "Madame, I am highly satisfied with
your husband, and the whole nation appreciates his
high merit."

After this Abdul-Aziz continued his promenade
without failing to speak a few words to the wives
of Ali and Fuad Pasha, besides other high dignitaries of the land.

From what I have heard my daughter say, it
would appear that her mother-in-law completely
lost all presence of mind when once she was con-
fronted with Mohamed's representative. But when
the Sultan spoke to her, it was all over with
Ferideh : the poor woman was seized with such a

x

palpable convulsion that her head nearly sunk within
the huge mass of her shoulders.   When once the
Sultan had passed, Ferideh became more tranquil,
and, taking courage, determined to repair the bad impression she must have given him.   She decided,
therefore, on making an ample apology by a master-
stroke, which would put her on a level with her
position.   From this resolution of hers there arose
an incident which unfortunately made her fall from
the sublime to the ridiculous, and which proved
very annoying to her husband.   Such things often
happen to persons who insist on occupying a position for which they are not intended, and, in seeking to repair a fault, they end by making a much
graver one.

On quitting the throne-room the great ladies of
the Ottoman aristocracy were conducted to the
Valideh-Sultan, who, under the title of Empress-
Mother, occupies a very high position.   The ladies
received a very courteous reception from the
Sultana, and each took the place on the divan
which was assigned to her.   Ferideh, at the head
of the troop, sat cross-legged near the Valideh, to
whom she hastened to address a few respectful
words.   After having congratulated her on the
accession of her son to the throne, Ferideh thought

it time to conciliate the favour of her Majesty by
making the following speech :—

"Your Majesty, no doubt, is aware how Kibrizli-
Pasha, my husband, has been ever one of the most
devoted servants and sincere partisans of your
august son, our lord. It is owing to his efforts and
fidelity that the nation has to-day the happiness of
celebrating Abdul-Aziz's accession to the throne."

The Valideh-Sultan could not refrain from receiving, with visible signs of coolness this doubtful
compliment, in which the speaker clearly informed
her that her son and herself were indebted to Ferideh's husband for the throne which they had begun
to occupy. The Sultana, however, restrained herself,
and with much presence of mind and good taste
sought to turn the subject.

But Ferideh, with her usual want of tact, did not
notice the effect which the first part of her speech
had produced on the Sultana. Absorbed by political pre-occupations, she continued in the same
strain, and began to unfold the programme of the
reforms which she and her husband intended to put
into execution.

"Yes," said she, " it is time to put an end to the
abuses, the thieves, and wickedness which made the
last reign one of infamy. The Pasha is determined

to put a stop to such a state of things. All thieves must be summarily dealt with, the abuse of the Imperial harem must be reformed, and Mussulman society must be remodelled according to the precepts of our most holy prophet and the primitive laws of Islam."

The effect of such a tirade can be imagined on the Valideh's mind. No doubt at first she felt undecided whether to laugh or be angry; for such language could only belong to an insolent or a foolish creature. However, the Sultana gave her the latter preference; and she justly appreciated her, for one must be truly mad to dream of making such wounding speeches, concerning the honour of the Imperial family, before the mother even of the Sultan, and to pry into strictly private affairs whose solution only depends on the good pleasure and will of the sovereign. The Valideh, having estimated the speaker for what she was worth, contented herself with simply turning her back on her and beginning a conversation with the other wives of the different Ministers.

No sooner was this done than Ferideh opened her eyes; but that only caused her to measure the gulf which she had made between the Imperial family and her husband. On her return to her home she found that this unlucky incident had already gone round the town, and had even reached Kibrizli's ears. Several scenes were naturally the consequence, in the midst of which the Pasha could not refrain from saying to his wife, "When God gave fools mouths, it was not that they might talk, but eat."

This diplomatic failure of Ferideh's was enough to cause her many bitter regrets, and to take from her any further wish to meddle in politics. But, like a philosophical woman, she resigned herself to her fate, and decided on taking things as they came.

It is an ancient custom in the Ottoman court to give gifts to those who are present at the official receptions. These presents are given to the guests when they are about to leave. As a rule they consist of rich brooches and other ornaments in diamonds, the beauty and value of which vary according to the importance and position of the people for whom they are destined.

Thus, at this reception, the Ottoman court did not derogate from its traditional liberality and munificence, for care is taken to satisfy all the guests by the quantity and value of the gifts which were bestowed on them.

Ferideh, in her position of wife of the Grand-vezir, received the lion's share, which ought to have satisfied her. The ornaments presented to her from his Imperial Majesty were all in brilliants to the value of one hundred thousand francs. Other similar things were also given to the ladies of her suite; and my daughter Aïsheh received a costly *parure*, which was barely inferior to that of her mother-in-law. Contented and joyful on account of the reception, and still more so because of the presents which they took away with them, the mother-in-law, daughter, and attendant ladies returned to their home. Once there, they barely gave themselves time to take off their veils than they rushed up to Ferideh to obtain possession and revel in the sight of the jewels which belonged to them.

They pushed each other about in their impatience, and on all sides arose cries of " Where are my ornaments ? where are my jewels ?"

By degrees all these exclamations ceased, each one received what belonged to her, and all, wild with excitement, contemplated with avidity their rich presents.

But, in the midst of this general excitement, there was one who clamoured in vain, and who had all the trouble in the world to make herself heard. That one was Aïsheh, my daughter, who had vainly endeavoured to get possession of her jewels and could not find them.

On finding that her case was not there, they began to search for it everywhere, and to question everybody, but without any success.

Fear and suspicion seized them all, and they began to say aloud, " How could the ornaments and their case both disappear ? "

And this occurrence threw alarm and perturbation into the harem, as much amongst the strangers as its inmates.

But whilst they were searching everywhere, a voice made itself heard, it was Ferideh's, who called out in somewhat troubled tones, " Here is the case ! Come, come, I have found it !"

The haste with which every one ran up can be imagined, and the impatience with which they pressed round her who said she had discovered the lost object.

But on opening the case, what was the surprise of every one to see it empty ? It was difficult to believe one's eyes, and the case became an enigma to them all.

" Where is the ornament ? Where did it fall ? "

Such were the questions which arose on every side, without any one's being able to answer them.

Up to this day the case incident has remained a mystery.

As for my poor Aïsheh, a few tears were shed and then she forgot all about it.

What is assuredly worthy of remark, is the fact that this occurrence of the stolen jewels is similar to what happened on a subsequent occasion.

At the time of the marriage of Mustapha-Bey, brother of Kibrizli-Pasha, who was consequently uncle to my daughter, the Sultan Abdul-Aziz sent as wedding-present a rich set of brilliants destined for the bride. The jewels were placed, by the chamberlain to his Majesty, in the hands of Ferideh who had taken upon herself the office of godmother.

The beauty of these jewels, the light which burst forth from this mass of brilliants, the exquisite taste of the setting, all produced on Ferideh an effect so bewildering, that it is not wonderful that she should have lost her head whilst contemplating it. After that she was no longer mistress of herself, and the giddiness which seized her was such, that the good woman on going to visit her future sister-in-law, instead of the superb ornaments she ought to have taken, brought another set, without being aware of her mistake. It was true that the parure of jewels she gave her sister-in-law was very inferior to that sent by the Sultan, but when a mistake has been made it must be supposed that the value of the objects exchanged has nothing to do with the mistake. Nevertheless, Mustapha-Bey was not of this opinion at first, as he decided on rectifying the error; the fear, however, of troubling his brother made him keep silent on the subject.

CHAPTER XXVII.

A YEAR was thus passed in receptions and visits of all sorts, in which my daughter Aïsheh took part in order to become initiated in the habits and customs of society at Constantinople. But whilst she was thus engaged, Ferideh had her own plans, and paved the way towards the realization of the dream she cherished more than all else in the world, and this was the marriage of Aïsheh with her son Shevket. The first step she took towards forwarding this project was to present to the Pasha her eldest brother, Bessim-Bey, and, immediately afterwards, Shakir; but on the refusal of her husband to listen to such aspirants for the hand of his daughter, Ferideh raised her mask and proposed her own son. It is averred that Kibrizli at first absolutely refused the proposition, for the reason that the two young people having been brought up together as brother and sister, he could not consent to their being united by conjugal ties.

This first rebuff did not discourage the woman, who, to obtain her ends, did not hesitate to put the Pasha in a very difficult position. In fact, Ferideh managed things so skilfully, that she led him to think that having confiscated all my property, there was no alternative left for them but to keep my daughter also. For if Aïsheh should ever get beyond their surveillance, all the chances were in favour of a meeting between me and my daughter, and, if so, the question of the confiscation of my property would inevitably have come on the *tapis*. The marriage with her son Shevket would render such an hypothesis impossible, for not only would the girl remain under their direct surveillance, but also she would never be able to hear or know anything of her mother.

With such arguments, and thanks to the skilful intrigues of Feridch's coterie, she succeeded in obtaining the hand of Aïsheh for her son. As for the poor girl, no one troubled themselves to obtain her consent. In Turkey, it is the parents who arrange all these matters; if the parents think the *parti* a good one, the girls can only bow their heads.

Thus one fine day the Pasha and his wife called

my daughter into their presence, and notified to her their intention of giving her in marriage. On leaving the chamber, the slaves surrounded the unfortunate girl, drew her into another apartment, and there attired her in robes of ceremony, and covered her head and neck with jewels. The preparations for the betrothment finished, they conducted Aïsheh into the middle of a large room, where were assembled the wives of the Ministers and the aristocracy of the country. Before the ceremony commenced they laid at the feet of the betrothed cashmere shawls and embroidered carpets of great value.

The ceremony had nothing in itself worthy of interest; for it consisted only of a prayer that the Imam read in a loud voice, and which was followed by the reading of a deed before witnesses of the conditions of the matrimonial contract. In the middle of the reading of this deed the witnesses sent by the future husband require the consent of the *fiancée*. But this consent, which the law of the Koran requires, is in reality only a pure and simple farce, for as the witnesses and the *fiancée* are separated by a large folding-door, they could never know who the person was who uttered the fatal *Yes*.

The last act of this comedy was the crowning of my daughter by her step-mother, who was now about to exchange that title for the sweeter one of mother-in-law. The *finale* of all this ceremony (as is the custom nearly everywhere) was the *magnificat*, for no sooner is the *fiancée* crowned than the guests immediately attack the refreshments, sweets, and sherbets that are placed before them.

Four months passed between the betrothal and the celebration of the marriage. This period was much longer than usual in the generality of cases. It appears that the resistance of the girl, and her aversion to the proposed union, was the cause of this delay. Nevertheless, by means of menaces and cajoleries they succeeded in overcoming her and fixed the day for the marriage.

I was at this time at Kadjik, a village in the vicinity of Constantinople, situated on the borders of the gulf of Nicomedia at the foot of Olympus. I had gone there in order to find amongst the good and simple shepherds of Bithynia that repose of mind and body that the hatred of my enemies in the capital so greatly troubled.

Whilst all these plots were becoming developed, with a broken heart I was, as I have said, retired from the world, and keeping a strict neutrality as regards all that concerned the interests and future of my daughter. In my deserted position, deprived

as I was of all means, it was the best thing I could
do ; for any effort of mine, with the object of inter-
fering in favour of my daughter, would have had
no other result than that of making her position
still more difficult.

Resigning myself, therefore, to inaction and
silence, I had but one consolation in my solitude
—the thought that the animosity of my enemies
would lead one day to a crisis that would deliver
my daughter from their hands, and re-unite us for
ever. Until this moment should arrive I considered
it my duty in nowise to trouble the tranquillity of
my child by revealing to her that, contrary to what
had been told her, I was still alive, and that I was
not even far from her.

Such a proceeding would have brought about
complications that I had no desire to provoke.
Whilst desiring ardently the well-being and liberty
of my daughter, I did not wish to attain this end by
upsetting the whole of my husband's establishment.
Besides, the course followed by her mother-in-law
and her associates showed clearly that a crisis
was inevitable, and that the emancipation of my
daughter was only a question of time.

My enemies, on their side, took courage from my
silence and inactivity ; and brought things to a

conclusion by the celebration of the marriage, which took place without once asking my consent, or even acquainting me of it.

The marriage of my daughter Aïshch with Shevket took place in the autumn of the year 1857. The wedding was not celebrated, however, with all the pomp that the public of Constantinople expected to have seen on the occasion of the marriage of the daughter of his Highness Kibrizli-Mehemet-Pasha. This circumstance did not fail to raise murmurs amongst the population, and comments of all kinds were circulated, from which one could learn that the sympathies of the public were not for this union. They thought that the two did not make a pair, and that a daughter of Kibrizli might have found a husband more worthy of her than Shevket, whose exterior was far from attractive, and who, besides, was penniless.

In Turkey the mass of spectators do not spare their remarks on the bridegrooms; for, as they are exposed to the gaze of the public, everyone picks them to pieces, and points out all their defects. If a pretty girl falls to the lot of an ugly fellow, the spectators show him no mercy, and from one end of the town to the other they denounce him as being a monster. The Turkish lower classes are very unruly as regards this matter, and if they once take an aversion to anyone they do not easily change. Thus, in this case, the public hoped to bless with its sympathy the newly-married couple.

On the day of the marriage, the apartments and gardens of the summer residence of his Highness at Gheuk-su were decorated and put in gala costume, in order to receive the guests who came to attend the wedding. The guests of the Pasha and his son-in-law were received in the selamlik, which is the apartment of the men ; there, at midday, the tables were prepared, on which were arranged all the most delicate and expensive dishes, the finest wines and the best *raki*. Troops of musicians, seated under the shadow of the trees, made the air resound with their pathetic songs, and thus encouraged the merriment at which Bacchus presides. Between Mohamed and Bacchus the last prevails, for after the third or fourth glass, the guests give themselves up, without reserve, to a wild and disorderly mirth.

But let us leave the men in the middle of their joy and drunkenness, and turn our steps towards the harem, where since the morning many interesting scenes had taken place. Marriages are, after all, fêtes for the women, and it is only just that they play the most important part in them. What

I say is true for all countries in the world, but still more so in the East, where for the woman the wedding day is the one on which her future depends whether it be for good or evil. As for the man, the day of his marriage does not occupy so important a place in his life; if a first marriage does not turn out well, he can repeat the experiment as often as he pleases.

Thus the position of the woman is the reason that in a marriage she attracts the attention of everyone, and is an object of pre-occupation to all, and consequently all that occurs in a harem on a wedding day is a subject of general interest.

Several weeks previous to the celebration of the marriage, preparations on a vast scale had been made in order to decorate and furnish the bridal chamber in a manner worthy of the daughter of a Grand-vezir. The arrangements made to this effect were such that nothing was omitted, neither trouble or expense, in order to show to the public an apartment that might truly be called sumptuous.

In the nuptial chamber the divan with its cushions were all in rich red velvet, embroidered in gold from one end to the other; besides which, the cushions had at each corner tassels composed of pearls. The windows and doors were ornamented with rich silk

Y

curtains, the fringe of which was also of gold. The carpet was one of those rich and soft gobelins whose design and colour surpassed everything that could be made of this kind in the East.

The reader will have remarked in this description of the nuptial chamber that no mention has been made of chairs, sofas, and the furniture which in the present day is considered indispensable even in Turkey. The fact is, that chairs and tables are excluded from the nuptial chambers; for, according to custom in this chamber, there is nothing else but the divan and a curious article of furniture that they call the *aski*.

This *aski* is a thing which requires some explanations, and even detailed explanations, for this article of furniture belongs to the bride, and it only remains there during the ceremony of the marriage. The *aski* is neither more or less than the throne of the bride, the throne on which she is placed to receive the homage of the crowd. They give the name of aski to a sort of tent or canopy of rose-coloured net, which being suspended from the ceiling descends gracefully on to the floor ; this canopy is sprinkled with gold stars, and surmounted with a wreath of flowers which reach to the bottom in the shape of festoons. It is in this fairy-like niche that (as I have said) the young bride is seated to receive the homage and congratulations of the inquisitive crowd. The day after the marriage the *aski* naturally disappears, in order to make way for more useful furniture.

After having described the bridal chamber, we must pass to the other room which is also the apartment of the bride. This one is the chamber for the trousseau, which the Turks call djeiss-odassi; it is here where the exhibition of all the riches which belong to the bride takes place. These riches consist of all sorts of things, such as toilette-table, massive silver dinner-service, linen embroidered in gold, mirrors, slippers, and cups covered with diamonds and other precious stones, clocks, and costly velvets. All these articles were in this instance spread out with much care and art, for in all Turkish houses they make a point of dazzling the eyes of the public by the display of the riches they possess.

All Turkish women without exception pride themselves so much on the subject of the riches that were exhibited in their honour on the day of their marriage, that one frequently hears old women boasting that on the day of their wedding the crowd remained wonderstruck in contemplating the splendour of their trousseaux. These good old creatures forget thirty or forty years of their existence, and their misery; but it is impossible that they should forget the diamonds, the bijoux, and the silver services that were displayed the day of their marriage. I have met some who had even forgotten their husbands; but none who forgot the djeiss-odassi, the chamber of the trousseau.

It is needless to say that great precautions are taken to prevent pilfering. A gilt railing is arranged in the chamber at a sufficient distance from the trousseau, and by this means they succeed in protecting the property of the bride from the effects of too indiscreet admiration. This precautionary measure is supported by a system of efficacious surveillance, which is rendered all the more necessary, because on this day the doors of the harem are open to all sorts of people. Following the ancient custom, a wedding day is a day of universal hospitality, and all women who wish to see the bride, and admire her trousseau, are free to enter without invitation.

Thus, on each occasion of a wedding, numbers of women flock from all sides to see the spectacle. There are some women who seem to have a sort of madness after weddings; there is no fear of their remaining at home when they once hear that there is a wedding anywhere. With or without invitation, they rise, dress themselves, and run straight to the house where the celebration of the marriage takes place. Once there, the poor things content themselves by making remarks on the bride, criticising her toilette and her *trousseau*, eating *pilaf* and some sweets, and return home to recount to their neighbours all they have seen.

Let us take up again the narrative of what took place at the marriage of my daughter, and thus will be seen in what manner they celebrate marriages in Turkish high life.

On the eve of the marriage a grand reception was held in the harem, at which were present all my daughter's friends and acquaintances. The name given to this reception is that of *Khenah guiedjesi*, for the reason that the *fiancée* is conducted that night to the bath by her friends, who paint the tips of her fingers and the extremity of her feet with the Khenah.

By this festival the bride is meant to give a sign of the joy she feels at the approach of her marriage. The friends and acquaintance of the bride then conduct her with lighted candles in their hands all round the harem, making her at the same time a sort of ovation. A good supper completes the evening.

I must here make a remark on the singularity of
Turkish customs. The evening of the Khenah
which precedes the marriage has been instituted to
mark the passage of the bride from celibacy to the
matrimonial state. It is on this evening that she
quits the friends and customs of childhood to enter
into a new existence.

But this fête which precedes the marriage has its
counterpart in the receptions given on the day
following the marriage. On this occasion the bride
makes her entry into the society of married women
as one of themselves.

On the morning of the great day my daughter
was attired in a long dress embroidered with gold,
and trimmed round the skirt with heavy fringe ;
this dress had two long trains, which were held up
by two Circassian slaves, remarkable for their beauty
and grace. Aïsheh was then crowned with a heavy
diadem of diamonds. It is useless to speak here of
the necklaces, bracelets, ear-rings, etc., with which
they ornamented her, it suffices to say that her
shoes were embroidered with gold, pearls and diamonds. Evidently this profusion of diamonds and
precious stones were intended to dazzle the girl and
astonish the crowd, for they only figured provi-
sionally during the solemnity, for immediately it

was over all these gems were locked up in the treasure chamber.

Attired in this manner, Aïsheh was conducted into the presence of her father. According to custom she knelt down to kiss his feet, but the Pasha raising her gave her his blessing, and placed round her waist a belt of diamonds, a symbol of the dignity of a married woman to which she was about to be raised.

With the Turks, a woman must not wear this belt before the day of her marriage; and the act of clasping the belt is a species of investiture that the father ought to confer on his child; it is the symbol of womanhood. This custom is also used for young men, for in former times it was usual amongst the Turks to buckle the sabre on to the young warriors. The investiture of the sabre was made with a pomp not inferior to the celebration of a marriage. This institution is even in the present time occasionally used; thus when a Sultan ascends the throne, instead of being crowned, according to the custom adopted in the East, he receives the investiture of the sabre, the emblem of authority and force.

In ornamenting the waist of his daughter with the nuptial belt, the father invokes the protection of heaven on her, and prays that she may be fruitful and happy. In receiving the belt a daughter ceases from that moment to depend on the paternal authority. This ceremony is the last adieu that the father makes to his daughter, when she is on the point of entering into the marriage state.

The moment Aïsheh left her father a shower of gold and silver money fell on the heads of the female spectators, who tumbled one over the other in their anxiety to catch some of it. This money is held in great consideration in Turkey amongst superstitious people, of whom there are many ; it is said that these coins bring happiness, consequently they are kept as long as possible by their fortunate possessors, so as not to let their good luck leave them.

As for the master of the house, who distributes this metallic manna, he is more than convinced that in throwing away money in this fashion, he brings good luck on the purse of his daughter.

On leaving her father the bride was again brought into the presence of her mother-in-law, who gave the finishing touches to her toilette—fastening on to Aïsheh's forehead, cheeks, and chin diamond stars and flowers. This done, there only remained to cover her face with a rose-coloured veil, which completely concealed her features.

Enveloped in this manner, my daughter was conducted to the top of the stairs, there to await the arrival of Shevket. Naturally he soon made his appearance, and presenting her with his arm, they directed their steps to the bridal chamber. Once there, he handed her to her place under the *aski*, which I have already described.

After having installed her under the canopy, Shevket left the chamber, without having dared to raise the veil from the face of his bride. As will be seen further on, the veil is only raised in the evening after the benediction of the Imam.

The bride, after her husband's departure, remains seated in her niche, while the inquisitive crowd press round her on all sides, and shoals of admirers stand open-mouthed before her trousseau.

As the bride could not remain exposed to the gaze of the crowd for any length of time, after one or two hours of this martyrdom they generally allow her to retire into the guest-chamber. Here the bride mixes with the rest of the society, and partakes with them of the repast which is served in the harem.

We must now endeavour to give an account of

what takes place amongst the men. After twelve o'clock they meet in the salons of the selamlik, where, as I have said, they pass their time in tasting of the delights of the table, and the charms of music. The hour for evening prayer and the voice of the Imam all at once terminates the orgies, and interrupts the songs. Everyone hastens to take his place in the ranks of the faithful who go to invoke the heavenly benediction on those who this day are united by the sacred tie of marriage.

In the first line was Kibrizli, the father of the bride; by his side were several Pashas and people intimately connected with his Highness. In the second line was the bridegroom, Shevket, and by his side were his relatives and friends. The other line was composed of invited guests of less importance and the members of the household, and all who wished to offer prayers like true and good Mussulmans.

When the prayer was ended, all the company rose and formed a circle round the Imam, who, turning towards the bridegroom, recited a short prayer in order to invoke the divine blessing on the union he was about to make. But scarcely were the last words of the prayer finished, before the bride-

groom slid away from the midst of all the guests,
and quickly ran towards the door of the harem.
Many of his companions followed him, and being
quicker than he was, they overtook him and administered to him several blows on the back. These blows
are the last adieux that young men make to a com-
rade who is about to enter on married life. This is
a very ancient custom with the Turks; sometimes,
however, instead of giving the bridegroom blows
on the back, they throw old slippers after him.

At the door of the harem the bridegroom was received by a eunuch, who, with a torch in his hand,
conducted him to the nuptial chamber. When there,
however, the bridegroom has by no means finished
with the ceremonies and formalities that custom
imposes. He sees his bride, who, covered with her
veil, awaits him at the end of the divan; he gazes
at her, and, full of impatience, desires to approach
her; but behold! to augment the troubles of Tantalus
the mistress of the ceremonies of the nuptial chamber (*yenghieh-kadin*) makes her appearance, and
spreads before the bridegroom a praying carpet,
embroidered in gold. The bridegroom, obeying this
invitation, recites a prayer, which is very short, for
in this supreme moment each minute appears to him
to be a century.

This short prayer finished, and the mistress of the ceremonies having taken her departure, the bridegroom approaches his bride. It is not the custom for the bridegroom to raise his bride's veil without a good deal of ceremony and finesse. Oriental manners do not tolerate that the husband should be guilty of rudeness. It is true that he has now become absolute master, and that the woman is there to obey his will; nevertheless, a delicate and romantic sentiment imposes on him respect for the woman he has made his wife. It is only, therefore, after praying and beseeching, that the bridegroom succeeds in overcoming the modesty of the bride, and that he obtains the favour of admiring her countenance for the first time.

Having repeated his petition three times consecutively, the bridegroom raises her veil, and hastens to show his recognition of the favour he has received by fastening a diamond pin in her hair. Custom makes this present obligatory, for the husband has to pay for the happiness of seeing his bride's face : *Yuz-gurumluk* is the name the Turks give to the present that a girl requires for showing her face.

It must be understood that it is only girls who have the right to demand a price for showing their faces; women who marry for the second time are not allowed to have this privilege. On the contrary, if a woman who has already been married unites herself with a person who enters for the first time into the married state, it is she who has to make a present to her bridegroom as the price of seeing his face.

The day after the wedding is also a day of solemnity. On leaving the nuptial chamber, Shevket went, according to custom, to kiss the hand of his father-in-law, who gave him a beautiful diamond ring and an Arab horse. The mother-in-law on her side made the bride a present when she went to pay her respects, and acknowledge her as being her mother-in-law.

Towards noon, the banquet of *legs of mutton* took place, at which the bride and the married women, friends of the family, took part. As for the *legs of mutton*, it must be said that on such occasions they are very recherché by the Turks, who attribute to them hygienic and exceptional qualities.

The fête of the legs of mutton (*patchah-guiunu*) is the counterpart of the fête given on the eve of the marriage. By the former the girl made her adieux to the companions of her childhood: by this one she is introduced officially to the society of matrons.

CHAPTER XXVIII.

THE account I have just given of the fêtes which
took place to celebrate the marriage of my daughter,
suggests to the mind reflections which can only
sadden my heart. How can persons who have
taken upon themselves the grave responsibility of
insuring the future of an innocent creature, make
her contract an alliance in which everything con-
spires towards discord and unhappiness? Nevertheless, to render the farce complete, they do not
hesitate to fête with all possible pomp and ceremony the sacrifice of their victim! While they
purposely neglect everything really necessary to
make her a worthy wife, they throw away handfuls
of gold and diamonds in order to dazzle the eyes of
the crowd with puerile and fantastic ceremonies.

And in fact this marriage was only a derisive
fiction, an atrocious deed. By this marriage nothing
was changed in my daughter's position, who continued

to remain dependent on her father and mother-in-law. The husband they had given her was only used as an intermediary to keep up this servitude; in other words, this husband was nothing but a sham, who had neither position, fortune, or personal charms of which he might boast; his only value consisted in his falling in with all the designs and inspirations of those who employed him as their alter-ego. It is generally understood that the woman plays an important part in the matrimonial state; in this case, however, the unhappy Aïsheh was considered of no account in the matter; she was simply to serve the interests and good pleasure of those who had her fate at their disposal.

A marionette has but one string by which it is put in motion; my daughter on her entry into conjugal life found herself influenced by three separate sources of motion; the string of one of the sources was in the hands of the Pasha; the second was in the hands of the mother-in-law, and the third was held by the husband. It was not necessary to possess any extraordinary amount of foresight to prophesy the downfall of an edifice which rested on a foundation as little firm as that on which the establishment of my daughter was based.

From the earliest period of her married life she

found herself placed at the mercy of the caprices of a mother-in-law, who pretended to dictate her conduct in every point. The constant grumblings and complaints which arose from these caprices, left the unhappy bride a prey to continual changing and mischievous impulses. Tossed about by conflicting interests, placed in the midst of intrigues and plots of all kinds, she no longer knew what to say or what to do.

Continually exposed to discomforts and the most wearying annoyances, Aïsheh made desperate efforts to set herself free, and to place herself on a level with women of her position in life. But all her endeavours proved useless, for both husband and mother-in-law were there to stop the road, using paternal authority as their weapon. Had this authority been employed sparingly, Aïsheh would have yielded, for she loved her father, and nothing in the world would have induced her to displease him.

Meantime, this continued struggle, which went on between the woman who wished to secure her just rights and those persons who desired to impose their authority upon her, at length resulted in a crisis, which took place in the following manner :—

Aïsheh, seeing herself at the mercy, and subject

to the caprices of everyone, began in her despair to consider how she could obtain her deliverance, and from whom she could hope to receive aid and protection. To count upon her father was useless, for he himself, being a prisoner in the hands of Ferideh and of her numerous relatives and adherents, was in no state to offer any succour to his daughter; it was, in fact, from him that most was to be feared, for the wily Ferideh did with him what she chose.

My unhappy daughter, being thus deprived of all hope, naturally turned her eyes elsewhere. But whither could she look when she was in the last agony of despair, but to her mother? A mother who, as she well knew, had tenderly loved her; and from whom she had been by a cruel destiny separated.

"I am despised, trodden in the dust, tyrannised over, and no one will protect me! Where is my mother?"

Something of this kind Aïsheh must have said in the midst of her tribulations. The mere name "mother" must, in her moments of desperation, have appeared to be the one plank to which she could cling for safety from shipwreck in that stormy sea, in which she was being tossed; and having

z

once uttered the name of mother, my child's memory would naturally turn to the happy days of
her early childhood, when she was the object of constant tenderness and caresses; her mother's image
must have appeared like a living reality before her
eyes, and with sobs and tears she must have recalled
the bitter consequences of our separation.

"Where are you, mother, where are you? Shall
I in my life ever see you again?"

It is easy to conceive, that when her thoughts had
for some time taken this direction, the poor child
would have her eyes opened to the state of cruel
and deceitful usage to which she had hitherto been
subjected.

In uttering those words, "Shall I ever see her
again?" Aïsheh conceived a doubt of the truth of
what had been told her respecting my death. The
enmity and ill-will showed to her by her mother-in-
law had naturally filled her with distrust, and this
distrust instigated her now to make inquiries. The
experience of the past having taught her that she
should not believe one word in a hundred of those
that were spoken to her, it was only natural that
she should say to herself, "They tell me that my
mother is dead; have they not deceived me in this,
also?"

When this suspicion had once entered Aïsheh's mind, she could not rest until she had caused inquiries to be made, in order to satisfy herself whether I was really dead, and to discover traces of me if I was alive. The person to whom she applied to carry out this delicate mission was a woman who had long been in her confidence. But how great was her surprise when she heard this good creature announce to her with a timid voice, "Your mother is still living, my child."

These words made Aïsheh's heart bound with a mad joy, which her ardent and affectionate temperament could not control. Her first excited emotion had scarcely passed before she had entreated this woman to commence her search for me at once, to find out my abode, and to place her in communication with me. The woman did in fact seek me in my place of retreat; she communicated to me my daughter's message, and gave me a detailed statement of her position. At the same time the messenger brought me an invitation from my child, who was awaiting me in a retired part of her park, for she felt she could no longer live without seeing me.

The meeting which took place between my daughter and myself in a sequestered portion of the park, situated behind the residence of his Highness,

is one of those scenes which it is impossible for me
to describe. The emotion which I felt on embracing
my child after so many years made me quite beside
myself. The account which my daughter then gave
me of her own sufferings nearly broke my heart.
Nevertheless I considered it my duty to try to
soothe the irritated condition she was in, by showing her what the consequences would be if she were
to oppose the will of those on whom her future
prospects depended.

These counsels which I gave my daughter were
the counsels of a mother who has at her heart the
happiness of her child. Unfortunately, these counsels came too late, and when the alarm had already
been given to those who wished for our destruction.
Having been informed of what had passed between
my daughter and myself, Feridch and her accomplices suspected that a secret understanding would
take place between the daughter-in-law and their
rival. The fear of this made them alter their
tactics.

Up to this time, these people had nourished the
hope that by giving Aïsheh to their Shevket, they
secured for themselves in a lump the inheritance of
Kibrizli-Mehemet-Pasha's property. But suddenly
they discovered they were brought face to face with

obstacles whose possibility they had not foreseen even, and which were the ever-increasing resistance made by Aïsheh and also her renewed acquaintance with myself. Thus, believing their project would get noised abroad, that project whose realization had cost them so many intrigues and troubles, Ferideh and her relations said to themselves :—

"In appropriating for ourselves the fortune, we should have been willing to spare Aïsheh ; but since she will not have anything to do with us, well, she also must be sacrificed."

From that very day sentence of death was passed on Aïsheh !

With implacable hatred, Ferideh and her associates then began to persecute the poor girl by displaying a refined and subtle art. Concealing themselves from view, these people employed agents of different kinds, so as to compromise Aïsheh before her father, while they secretly excited the fierce anger of the latter. These designs did not fail to meet with the results which they expected.

Profiting by the inexperience and want of tact of the young wife, her enemies circulated all sorts of rumours about her, and sought to put her in a false position with her father. His mind having been poisoned and excited by all kinds of evil reports, violent quarrels followed, in the midst of which the Pasha's anger blinded his good sense. On one occasion things went so far, that he, in a passion, seized his daughter and struck her several times. This most deplorable incident was caused by a rumour which attributed to Aïsheh the design of escaping and coming to me. The rumour having taken a firm hold, the Pasha declared that to prevent such a catastrophe, he would not hesitate to bind his daughter to a tree and have her beaten till she died.

"I would far rather mourn her death for forty days than live dishonoured for the remainder of my life."

Such were the words which, in a moment of rage, they say, escaped from his mouth.

Whether these words really came from the Pasha is a point on which there are some doubts; but whichever way it may be, whether the Pasha pronounced such a threat or not, the fact is that the unfortunate girl was terrified and fancied herself on the eve of a bloody catastrophe. Seeing herself, as it were, between life or death, Aïsheh decided on finding a refuge by flight; gaining from her despair and delirium almost supernatural strength, she did not hesitate to risk everything sooner than fall beneath the blows of her enemies.

The violent emotion, the fear, the panic which seized on Aïsheh caused her terrors, to which the silence of the night gave more strength and intensity. Her bewildered imagination made her think of her end as inevitable, amidst tortures and cruel sufferings. But if, on the one hand, her excited imagination disordered her reason, on the other she could not be deluded as to the instigations of her enemies, who wished to provoke acts of violence, whose consequences would be fatal to her and her father. These instigators had nothing to lose by such a catastrophe; by these means the whole heritage of Aïsheh must fall wholly into their hands. They did not care how much misery befell either the daughter or the father. At first they had sought to appropriate the daughter and her large fortune by means of a farce of marriage; now they wished to attain the same aim by sacrificing her who would not do as they wished.

Those terrible words, "If she died, I should mourn her loss, but at least I should not be dishonoured," made Aïsheh believe that it was only by flight she could prevent a catastrophe whose consequences would have been terrible for her and her father. Having thus resolved on seeking her safety in flight, my daughter decided on her plan of evasion, a plan in the execution of which she met with every description of dangers. First, she had to decide on the easiest method of escape; then she had to think of some way in which to deceive the vigilance of the guardians and slaves of the harem.

In order to deceive the latter, Aïsheh decided to flee towards the dawn of the day, for at this time everyone is sound asleep, and none were spying out her movements; besides the darkness was also favourable to her after she had made her escape, whilst she was wandering about the neigh-bourhood. An attractive young woman, and bear-ing the stamp and the manners of a lady of conse-quence, would naturally have attracted the notice of the sentinels and patrols who wandered about during the twilight.

As the easiest place from which to make her escape, Aïsheh chose a window opening on to the roof of a wing of the harem, where the eunuchs and the guardian lived; this roof ended in a boundary wall, by which one could drop himself down into the street. The height of this wall was about fifteen feet.

Towards four in the morning Aïsheh arose quietly, avoiding the least sound, gave a last kiss

to the child she was abandoning, took the few,
diamonds she possessed, and climbed unperceived
on to the roof.   Once on the wall she did not.
hesitate, but sprang into the road, without consider-,
ing the risk she ran of being lamed for life.

Fortunately the jump succeeded wonderfully
well, and Aïsheh, finding herself free, began to run.
in the direction of the Eau Douces (gheuk-su).
When she passed through this smiling plain the first.
glimmer of dawn was making its appearance, and
the song of the birds announced the awakening of
nature.   On the other side of the plain was a
barque, which served to maintain communication
with the village of Anadolu-Hissar.   It was on this
barque that Aïsheh traversed the small river of the.
Eau Douces d'Asie, and it was by the little door,
with its iron chains, that she managed to penetrate
into the interior of the old château.   In this village
lived one of his Highness's slaves, who had been
married to one of the villagers.   Aïsheh, not knowing to whom to turn or how to procure a barque,
decided on going to her, and imploring her help and
succour.

She went straight to the house of the slave, and
after having knocked at her door several times,
succeeded in making her jump half-frightened out

of bed. One can imagine what an impression the sudden apparition of her master's daughter, at such an early hour, made on the slave; also her pitiable condition, without servants or slaves. Her face even was in a fearful condition, for Aïsheh, after having jumped from the wall, had rubbed mud and dust over her face. This excessive precaution she had considered necessary so as not to attract the attention of any one.

Once informed of the details of this adventure, the slave and her husband believed it their duty to counsel the fugitive, by making her understand the gravity of the step she had taken. Seeing, however, that their words were of no avail, and also that the time for advice was passed for ever, husband and wife offered their services to the unfortunate girl, and put her into a barque which was going down the Bosphorus. Owing to the strength of the current the distance between Anadolu-Hissar and Stambul does not take very long : in about three-quarters of an hour one can accomplish this voyage and arrive at Un-kapan, the nearest port for those who wish to visit the centre of Stambul. It was towards this part that Aïsheh turned, for she counted on going on from thence to Balat, where she knew I lived when I was in the town. In fact, when she disembarked, she got into one of those carriages called in the country *coutchi*, and told the driver to take her quickly to Balat. That also was the only thing she could say, for she was ignorant of my address, and in her precipitate flight she had not been able to learn it. Evidently her mind was so unsettled that she had never given a thought to the danger she was running in throwing herself into the streets without knowing quite where to go, or to whom to address herself. Whilst Aïsheh, seated in her carriage, was wandering about the streets of Stambul, a strange coincidence occurred which led her to the door of the house where I was staying. This was such an extraordinary event that it cannot be accounted for in any other way than as a striking instance of Divine assistance.

Now it happened that hardly had they perceived in his Highness's harem the flight of the daughter, than the alarm was given so that the fugitive might be found, and brought back to the bosom of her family. Not only were numerous police agents put on to her traces, but Shevket, the husband, at the head of valets and house servants set off in pursuit of her whom he was pleased to call his rebellious wife.

Provided with peremptory orders, all these people began to rush about the town and its suburbs, searching every place where they thought it likely their master's daughter might be concealed. My house was naturally the first to be visited by these zealous emissaries, for they knew well that in her misfortune Aïsheh would not have implored other protection than that of her mother.

In fact Mustapha, the *valet de chambre* of his Highness, accompanied by two or three other individuals, presented themselves at my door and questioned me on the subject of my daughter. As may well be imagined, the unexpected apparition of all these people, and the news they brought, caused me great uneasiness. Being in complete ignorance of what was going on in the house of the Pasha, I did not know how to account for this unexpected event.

"How did it happen? For heaven's sake, tell me, what my poor daughter will do?"

Such were the exclamations with which I replied to the search made by Mustapha and his companions, exclamations which made them perceive that they must go elsewhere to fulfil the mission with which they had been charged.

Mustapha having seen that my daughter was not there, sent away those who accompanied him, giving them instructions to pursue their researches elsewhere, and himself went towards the port, and the most frequented portion of the town, hoping to learn by so doing if any of the others had succeeded in hearing anything about the fugitive.

But whilst he was walking towards the sea, he saw a closed carriage approaching, from the interior of which a voice proceeded who called "Mustapha! Mustapha!" There could be no doubt, the voice was certainly that of Aïsheh, who signed to him to draw near, and then begged him to lead her to my abode.

Nothing could have been more imprudent than this step, taken in such a critical moment by Aïsheh. It is true that not knowing how to find me out, she was constrained to take this means, and to show herself to Mustapha; but in doing so she played a hazardous game on which her fate depended. What guarantee had she that the *valet de chambre* on perceiving her would not employ force to reconduct her to her step-mother. Aïsheh, however, did not act on this occasion without discretion, for she well knew with whom she had to deal, and she was sure that Mustapha would never betray her.

In fact, Mustapha was the only man in the house of his Highness who was attached to our cause after my fall. In my time he had been my *valet de chambre*, and the kindness which I had shown him had made him remember me well. But independently of these bonds which attached him to our cause, other reasons prevented him from lending himself as a servile instrument to the designs of people who were capable of everything. These were his honesty and chivalrous sentiments. For nothing in the world would the brave man have consented to betray a woman, the daughter of his late mistress, who implored his succour at such a moment. The worthy Mustapha, on seeing the unfortunate girl in such a condition, turned to the driver and told him to go to my dwelling. He began to follow the carriage, and reached the door at the same time as Aïsheh ; once there, he turned and hastened to inform the Pasha of what had taken place.

This act of kindness cost Mustapha his situation. As soon as it was known in the harem how the meeting had taken place between him and Aïsheh, the old servant was treated as a traitor, and told to leave immediately. According to them, Mustapha ought to have seized the girl with the help of the police, and given her over, bound hand and foot, to those on whom her fate depended.

CHAPTER XXIX.

As may well be believed, the news of the flight of
Kibrizli-Pasha's daughter soon spread, and produced
great sensation amongst the Mussulman world.
Everybody talked about it, and the strangest ver-
sions were said to be authentic. Our enemies did
not hesitate to seize on this occasion to circulate the
most scandalous tales on the subject of my daughter
and myself. But the Pasha's friends and ours
expressed their regrets on the subject of these pitiable scenes, which rendered the incompetence of his
Highness in his private affairs so visible.

Amongst these colleagues of the Minister, there
was not one voice which was not raised in blame
against the conduct of Kibrizli, who permitted family
quarrels to attain the proportions of a public scandal.
Fuad-Pasha and Ali-Pasha, who were his rivals,
found these tales and scandals very useful in darken-
ing Kibrizli's reputation, and making him lose the

prestige and moral force which rendered him redoubtable.

From the manner in which the public regarded my daughter's flight and party feeling, there resulted a state of things which were favourable to the interests of Aïshçh, and which saved her from the hands of her enemies.

In Turkey, as in every other country where the arbitrator takes the place of the law, society is at the mercy of the powerful and of the greedy. In such countries everything is permitted to those who have power. The divine law, public opinion, all are nil; the only recognized law is the caprice of those who govern.

My daughter's flight, according to the Koran, was a perfectly legal act; for by that a married woman cannot be compelled to live in the society of other women with whom she refuses to associate. The woman in such a case has the right to demand of her husband a separate dwelling, and she can forbid the entry into it to anyone. Further, the woman recognizes no other authority than that of her husband; she can renounce her father, mother, and certainly therefore her mother-in-law.

On escaping from the paternal roof, Aïsheh had only protested against the oppressive authority imposed on her by her mother-in-law, who made use by turns of her husband's or father's name to enforce it. This protest gave her the right to be installed by her husband in a house to herself, where she would be allowed to do as she liked independently of her mother-in-law. But in insisting on that, Aïsheh put herself in open hostility with her father's wife, who would not relinquish the power she possessed over her ; for she knew that once removed from her sight, Aïsheh would associate with whom she liked, and naturally with me, her own mother. It was just this that the malicious Ferideh wished at any price to prevent, by instigating Aïsheh's husband to make an abuse of the paternal authority.

The motives of Ferideh's hostility against any arrangement which would have rendered Aïsheh mistress of herself and household, are of such a description that they merit being disclosed. Such a revelation is all the more necessary since it serves to reveal the secrets of family life in the East.

All Ferideh's reasons and motives arose from the instinct of her own preservation ; that of covetousness was only secondary. It was the instinct of preservation which made her fear a separation from her daughter-in-law ; for, according to her ideas, this separation could only be the prelude to her loss.

A A

Ferideh foresaw that combined action on our part would have for result the estrangement of her husband and her expulsion from the home into which she had succeeded in insinuating herself.

Her fears were only too well founded on this point. In fact it was plain, that Aïsheh once established, it would become impossible for her father and mother not to meet some time or other. Thus the daughter's house would have been transformed by force of circumstances into a species of rendezvous, where her rival and her husband would be able to meet and indulge in affectionate *tête-à-têtes*.

The bare idea of these meetings was enough to make Ferideh tremble with jealousy. One such was enough to give her the *coup-de-grace,* for as the divorce between his Highness and myself was of the first degree, it only needed a simple encounter of a few seconds to renew the marriage and do away with Ferideh.

Divorce with the Turks is, as I have just said, of three sorts ; the first degree of divorce is the weakest, for the husband who wishes to do away with it has only to recite a formula, and pass his hand over his wife's head to render the marriage valid again. The second and third degrees of divorce demand special formalities and ceremonies in order to renew the marriage. I must also add that the first degree of divorce may suddenly become irrevocable. This happens when the husband showers upon the wife a battery of three combined divorces, which he rapidly discharges upon the woman's head; then it becomes very difficult to renew the matrimonial bond.

The divorce by which I had been separated from his Highness was not of this dreadful description, stigmatised by the Koran under the name of *Telaki-salisseh*; it was a simple divorce, which a spark would have sufficed to re-kindle. And this is explained by the fact that this divorce was not actuated by internal disputes, but by the wiles of those who wished to destroy me at any cost. In other words, the Sultan's mother, her eunuchs and servants, with my husband's political enemies fell upon, and obliged the Pasha to separate from me. The Pasha, over-ruled by his enemies, made the sacrifice demanded of him; but this divorce was only a mere formality, his sentiments really remaining unchanged towards me.

Ferideh who had nominally taken my place, could not deceive herself on this point; her tranquillity and happiness depended on keeping Aïsheh to herself. Aïsheh's flight was therefore a mortal stroke to her, which she sought to parry on all sides, even by means of brute force. Happily for us, but unfortunately for Ferideh, the employment of strength was out of the question, for an essay of that description would have had sorry consequences for her and her husband.

The Pasha was not in full possession of power, and that suffices to explain the moderation which he had to show under these circumstances.

Fuad and Ali-Pasha had the real direction of affairs. Kibrizli at this epoch was a minister without a portfolio, an unenviable position, which only left him a very limited influence. Independently of that the relations between these high personages bore a certain stamp of coldness and bitterness, for Kibrizli was far from wishing Fuad and Ali overmuch happiness, and the latter well knew he considered them as rivals.

Such being the relative relations of the parties, it is not difficult to understand that any illegal attempt or false step would have seriously compromised the position and reputation of Kibrizli-Pasha and his associates. His political adversaries would have been enchanted to find an opportunity of compromising and paralysing him for ever. They would have fallen upon him, making use of his wives' quarrels and family scandals. They would not have hesitated to say that Mussulman society was tired of the endless gossip and squabbles which were taking place in Kibrizli-Pasha's house.

The force of circumstances, therefore, obliged the enemies of Aïsheh to set to work softly and with circumspection. Every coercive measure being out of the question, they decided on winning over the rebel by ruses and wiles. The first measure which Ferideh and the Pasha thought fit to adopt was that of entering into conversation with us, to try and find out our designs, to know whether they were to look upon my daughter's flight as a protest against her father or husband's authority. In other words, they wished to find out whether my daughter had decided on getting rid of her make-believe husband, Shevket. This point once clearly defined, they would have decided on the part they wanted to take; for if Aïsheh appeared to desire to live under the matrimonial yoke, Shevket would then have served as spy to watch over Ferideh's interests; if, on the contrary, Aïsheh wanted to break off with her husband, they could have pursued her by bringing forth the conjugal rights invested in the son.

From the second day of Aïsheh's flight negociations were set on foot. Emissaries of the Pasha

presented themselves to us in the hope of obtaining
a categorical answer on the subject of her husband,
and to assure themselves whether my daughter was
disposed to submit to his authority. Having received a satisfactory answer to this cardinal question, the negociators took a further step, and invited
Aïsheh to Hadji-Bekir's house, where her husband
would rejoin her.

This proposition gave us some cause for reflection
—a refusal would have hastened the crisis, whilst
by accepting it we should have placed ourselves
completely in the power of our adversaries.
Situated in such a dilemma, I did not hesitate to
accept a proposition which could not compromise
materially my daughter's interests. I therefore
informed the envoys that my daughter would go to
the rendezvous which had been agreed upon to meet
her husband. This having put an end to the negociations, the emissaries joyfully returned to their
master, being the bearers of what they believed to
be good news.

But hardly had they left than I hastened to enter
into a treaty with the ministry, to inform them of
the state of things, and solicit their protection.
Evidently, by entering the house of one of the
Pasha's domestics we were risking our lives, it

was as though we had put our hands bound in those of our enemies. It will, therefore, be understood that these precautionary measures were not altogether superfluous. My overtures were received with kindness by Fuad, who assured me that we were under his protection. This assurance was followed up by secret instructions sent to the head of the police department, ordering us to be guaranteed against any attempt which might be made to take us away from Hadji-Bekir's house.

Having thus done all that he could to prevent us falling into the snares of our enemies, we went to Hadji-Bekir's house, where we found Shevket, who was impatiently waiting for us. After having exchanged a few words, Shevket told us he was the first to regret what had recently occurred, and that in spite of his mother he had resolved on living apart with his wife. Further, he informed us that his Highness, ceding to his wishes, had authorized him to choose a house and furnish it in a manner worthy of his daughter. The Pasha, continued Shevket, was resigned to such a sacrifice in the hope that his daughter would understand how much he desired her happiness, and that she should continue to live with her husband. Then, turning towards me, he said affectionately, that he could not permit

me, his mother-in-law, to live anywhere but with
my daughter.

From the next day, in fact, all the necessary
measures were taken to find a convenient house,
and decide on the necessary furniture required for
it. The house on which Shevket's choice fell was
one opening on to Shekh-zadeh's mosque; its position offered certain strategical advantages, one, for
example, being that it was surrounded by the
friends and abettors of Shevket and his mother;
another, equally great, was that on the side of the
mosque it was easy to attempt a master-stroke—a
forcible abduction. By scaling the house on the
court side during the night it would be easy to carry
off any number of women without the neighbours
on the right or left being at all the wiser.

Pleased at having found such a house, Shevket
hastened to finish furnishing it. Everything having
been arranged, he invited Aïsheh to install herself in
the new residence which her father had provided.

This new household, as may be seen, was only a
clever device by which they could better destroy
their adversary: we were not once deceived about
it. An arrangement situated on such a volcano
had no chance of lasting long; each side understood the intentions of the other, and yet feigned

ignorance. We each held the tinder in our hands fearing to set fire to the mine; as for myself I did not dare to hasten a separation whose responsibility would fall on myself.

From the first days of our residence at Shekh-zade-bashi, Shevket altered his manner, and became cold and distant; his prayers were changed into peremptory commands; nothing pleased him; and the slightest incident was enough to cause alterca-tion and disagreement. One week was enough to disgust Shevket, and make him hasten his designs.

In fact, on the eighth day, the first act of the master-stroke was disclosed beneath the form of a supreme decree, in virtue of which the entry to the harem was forbidden to all who were not possessed of a previous authorization. At the same time he adopted this measure, Shevket provided himself with a reinforcement to aid him at the given moment. This reinforcement consisted of an over-seer, Hadji-Ibrahim, and of five or six individuals, sbires and bandits, used by the Pashas to do any decisive deed.

But the most dreadful of all these preparations was the attempt made by Shevket to imprison us by closing all the issues which might have favoured our flight. There was one small door which served to afford communication between the harem-kitchen and the stables. Shevket understood that it was an important point which must be guarded at any risk. He, therefore, ordered some masons to come and close it up, and raise in its place a small wall. After having made the personal inspection of these places, Shevket went away, enjoining his people to keep in readiness for the evening.

He was much deceived, however, in his calculations, for he might have known that some women have more perspicuity than men give them credit for. In fact, since I had put my foot inside the prison which had been prepared for us, I had never once been deceived on the subject of Shevket's intentions. I instinctively knew that we were living on a volcano as it were, on the bosom of which violent eruptions might be expected. Thus, during these seven days of worry, I was continually on the *qui vive*, ready, like a sentry, to seize on the slightest sound or index.

The lucky star which presided over my birth, so arranged that the very day when the masons began to dig the foundations of the walls, I went down to the kitchen to see what was going on. Hardly had I been there for a few seconds than the sound of workmen struck my ear. Having been informed of what they were doing, it only needed a few minutes' reflection for me to see through Shevket's designs and decide on what measure to take in order to upset them. Evidently the only thing was to escape before the iron circle closed in on us. With a heavy and beating heart I ran to my daughter, told her what I had seen, and declared that there was no time to be lost, for if we waited till the evening we certainly should be done for. Whereupon my daughter and myself set to work to collect everything we could in the way of silver or jewels. We made it up into large packets, and we filled our pockets with everything that could be carried conveniently.

I must here observe that the feradjehs (mantles worn by Turkish women) are very useful for such purposes : for when wrapped in one of these mantles it is easy to conceal a quantity of merchandise. This was what my daughter and myself took care to do on this occasion. We well knew that everything would be taken from us, and that it was folly to leave Shevket what we could adroitly conceal. Besides, both legally and morally, we had more right than he had to consider everything in the house as belonging to ourselves.

Once these preliminary measures taken, I had to

have recourse to some cunning in order to disarm any suspicions amongst the slaves of the harem. As I could not conceal our clandestine *sortie* by the small door, I said that as we had no money in the house we had decided on selling some of our things, and that with the results we should buy what we most needed. In order the better to conceal my game, I promised them each beautiful silks and pretty presents. These promises did not fail to take effect, for the slaves entered into our designs, and helped us in our flight and in getting out of the little door.

Whilst all these events were passing in the harem our guardians were outside smoking and chatting. Hadji-Ibrahim, their chief, amused himself by giving {instructions to his subordinates on the way in which they were to watch over us. He had been heard to say—

"Our master is resolved to make those people behave."

On leaving the house my daughter and myself got into a carriage and went straight to one of the court ladies, who was a friend of ours, and she put her house at our disposal. Once in safety, we hastened to send a message to Shevket, in which my daughter declared that she no longer consented to live with him, for she was tired of him, his mother, and their intrigues.

This move on her part was the result of the conviction she felt that in their midst she should vainly search for tranquillity or happiness. Several years of experience only confirmed her in this conviction.

Towards evening, Shevket returned to the house, the bearer of fresh instructions which his mother and the Pasha had given him in the conference he had held with them during the day. But barely had he entered than our messenger, Ressim-Bey, approached and informed him of the letter of which he was the bearer. This announcement quite overcame Shevket; he was thunderstruck; for if, on the one hand, he resented the humiliation of the rôle which had been imposed on him, on the other he trembled at seeing himself for ever compromised in the eyes of his mother and of the Pasha.

Shevket was the pulley by which they sought to keep my child under their control, and that explains all the importance they attached to him. Unfortunately Shevket did not sustain the attack with that courage which might have been expected from him; for on learning his wife's flight he lost every vestige of the sang froid for which he had been famed. Furious at finding himself so humiliated and debased, Shevket sought to forget in drunkenness the insult which had been offered to him.

Turning to his servants he bade them bring arrack, and the accessories which charm the drinkers of this chosen beverage. Then surrounded by his boon companions, Shevket got so drunk that he lost every sentiment of honour, and the respect he owed to himself and the daughter of his benefactor. It was in the midst of this orgie that Shevket pronounced the formula of divorce according to the Mussulman law—*Shart olsun.*

Barely were the words uttered than emissaries were sent to inform both ourselves and his Highness. This news was the very best we could have had, whilst in the Pasha's palace and the harem it caused sorrow and consternation. Shevket was disgraced, for neither his mother nor the Pasha could forgive his having betrayed their interests.

THE first excitement produced by the news that Aïsheh was at last free having been appeased, agents were immediately sent in the hope of regaining the ground lost and enticing Aïsheh once again. These agents were the bearers of propositions and counter propositions whose aims were to renew the marriage. They sought to touch my daughter's heart by relating the agony and distress felt by Shevket when, on coming to his senses, he understood the harm he had done. He was inconsolable, and his repentance was sincere and in earnest they said. For the future he was determined to allow his wife to do as she pleased, and neither his mother nor the Pasha should meddle in their affairs.

As may be well imagined, after what we had suffered from the hands of our adversaries, such proposals and words were far from touching us in the least. The only reply vouchsafed to these envoys was a decided refusal to pay any attention to the proposals, menaces, or promises of Shevket and his associates.   This ultimatum was the signal for the commencement of hostilities, which continued during a period of seven years.   This new miniature seven years' war only terminated with the death of his Highness, the 9th September, 1871.

The first thing done on receiving Aïsheh's refusal to accept for the second time a husband she never cared for, was to empty Shekh-Zade's house of all the furniture which had been given to her.   Two days after the divorce had taken place, a crowd of domestics were sent to empty the house of every thing, even the clothes and linen belonging to the unfortunate Aïsheh.   To render this cruel act still more insulting, they took care to send her a few old dresses shut up in an old broken box.

I must here observe that this dastardly act of vengeance was further a violation of the law and established customs.   According to Mussulman law and Turkish usages, the effects and furniture given to a girl at the time of her marriage become her unalienable property.   Now, at the period of Aïsheh's marriage, half her trousseau had only been given her.   The Pasha, on furnishing her house, had only acted as he ought to have done before.

So every thing employed in furnishing the house belonged by rights to his Highness's child, and even he had no right to seize upon it. According to the Mussulman law, this act was equivalent to a confiscation. But it did not only end with Aïsheh's furniture and clothes, for her money underwent the same treatment. My daughter had some time before bought a large farm in the neighbourhood of Aleppo ; this property belonged to her in her name, and the title-deeds were in the hands of Shevket, who kept them.

Eminent economists, like Stuart Mill, have brought forward a theory, according to which it appears that women's rights are better established under the Mussulman than under the European law. When one considers that, according to the law of the Sheriaht, a woman is not for a moment sure of what she likes best in the world, her husband and children, of what use to her are the few possessions she may have ? But if from the written law we turn to the living one, from theory to practice, it is there one sees of what little use for the woman are her pretended rights.

The confiscation of goods made by Kibrizli-Pasha and Shevket was one of those deeds carried out every day by those who feel powerful enough to execute them. Now, where are women's rights amongst this fight between the strong and the weak ?

My daughter having failed in her attempt to regain possession of her furniture, there was nothing left for us to do but to settle at our own cost somewhere. We sold our valuables and jewels, and the few thousand pounds they realized permitted us to face the expenses of re-settling and leaving a little reserve.

I must here say that this sort of arrangement did not receive my approbation, for the initiative in money affairs remained entirely with my daughter. Prudence, therefore, recommended the strictest economy, for the clouds were dark and the tempest imminent. My daughter did not believe in a storm, and she hoped still that her father would relent and furnish her with the means of subsistence. Truly one might have said that the mother's experience ought to have dissipated the daughter's illusions, but, unfortunately, a feeling of delicacy prevented my taking the law into my own hands. I did not wish her or any one else to reproach me with having profited by the abandoned position of my child in compelling her to submit to my will in money matters.

The house we hired in the suburbs of Scutari for

the summer of 1864 was a beautiful residence, admirably situated, offering the advantages of a charming view over the Bosphorus and a garden full of oranges and lemon trees. Our existence in the midst of this beautiful scenery ought to have been very pleasant; but the charms of the country were spoilt by the ceaseless worry caused us by our adversaries. Our door was literally besieged by emissaries, men as well as women, sent in the hope of preventing us feeling a moment's repose. Now it was the Pasha who sent to find out some means of bringing us under his domination; now the ex-husband Shevket who sent women to plague us; then agents, who came to spy upon us on the part of the tribunal and to annoy us in every way.

The law-suit we were obliged to bring against Shevket in order to reclaim the property and marriage-portion of Aïsheh was our principal occupation during our stay at Scutari. Aïsheh could not obtain any of her goods or property, for the Cadi or Judge told her openly that he was not powerful enough to compel her husband to give up what he had taken. As for her marriage portion, no obstacle was raised to oblige her husband to refund the sum he owed; yet, when the question of paying the nafakah, or the husband's marriage present, came, Shevket turned Jew, and the tribunal helped him to play this part.

The nafakah, or its equivalent in money, is what the husband ought to give for his wife's maintenance during the three months following after the divorce. The amount which the husband ought to give his wife is agreed on by the tribunal, which takes into consideration the social position and means of the parties concerned, as well as the price of food, and such primary matters. Where the lower classes are concerned, the divorced woman is only allowed for *nafakah* two or three piastres a day. There are often even people who refuse to give as much to their wives, under the pretext that their means do not allow them to be extravagant; then they merely give them bread and a candle a day. In such cases they take care to leave the candle and bread before the woman's door, by which means they escape all legal pursuit.

Amongst the middle classes the husbands allow their wives something like two or three hundred francs a month; whilst in the higher classes it is generally agreed upon to give either a good round sum or nothing at all. We came to a compromise of this sort with Shevket; he never attempted to give a farthing, and we never mentioned the nafakah.

With autumn the charms of the country begin to depart, and the approach of winter is the signal for the flight of those who like the luxuries of Stambul. At the close of the season we hastened therefore to re-enter the town, and for this purpose hired a house in the part of Stambul called Jussuf-Pasha. This house was large and spacious, but time and poverty had reduced it to the condition of a dilapidated palace. Formerly it had belonged to a Grandvezir, Selim-Mehemet-Pasha, who, having been sent to quell the revolt at Damas, was killed by the insurgents. This Selim was the same who had been famous for the carnage he had made amongst the Janissaries, in company with Agha-Hussein of Viddin and Kara-Djehenem. Selim had escaped the reign of terror at the time of his vezierate, but at Damas he had to pay his debt to the revolted population.

These events happened in 1824. Before his departure for Damas, Selim had built the house we had hired. He did not neglect anything which might render this residence worthy of a Grandvezir : large halls and kiosques, grotesquely ornamented, marble baths, in fact nothing was omitted which could please his family in the comforts and luxuries of Oriental life. At his death all this disappeared as if by magic. Selim's riches, honours, and property were divided amongst his friends and attendants; as for his heirs, they only got what the others could not take from them, which was their father's house and a small amount to live on.

This is truly Selim's history and that of his descendants, but by changing the name to that of Mehemet or Mustapha, it would be equally that of every great family in Turkey. The father may have been Grand-vezir, but the sons and daughters do not inherit much. I can truly say that in Turkey there are not more than four or five great families who count over sixty years of nobility. The greater number of *soidisant* noble families only date back one generation; in fact they are noble so long as the person who elevated them exists; at his death his sons maintain themselves for a few years and then disappear; and by the third or fourth generation the name of Vezir, which ennobled the family, is completely forgotten.

The constitution of Mussulman society and the Turkish system of government are the causes of such a state of things. As amongst Mussulmans society is composed of several families, only distinguishable the one from the other by their proper

names, it so happens that a family is first represented by Hassan, then by Mehemed, his son, and
after by a Mahmud or Selim. These heads of families having thus no family name to transmit to each
other, their proper names fall into oblivion, and their
genealogy is forgotten. The Arabs endeavour to
remedy this organic defect in their society by means
of a genealogical tree, which they religiously preserve in their families. The Turks do not attach
any importance to blue blood : they consider the
Sultan and his dynasty as alone being noble ; the
rest are plebeians. Their system of government is
also incompatible with the aristocratic system and
the maintenance of noble families.

The actual proprietor of our house was
Mahmud-Bey, sôn of the Grand-vezir, Selim-
Pasha ; he was a little fellow, whose exterior did
not reveal his high birth. Mahmud had a face, on
which was visible the traces left by great trials and
suffering ; his sorrowful and gloomy appearance was
the reflection of an over-burdened spirit, whilst his
worn and mended clothes were the heritage of a
Grand-vezir. Whether owing to misfortune or prodigality I know not, but the fact was that Mahmud-
Bey was at his last farthing. All the property left
by his father had disappeared, except the house,

which was left because the deceased Selim had had the good idea of making it an entailed property.

In order to satisfy his most urgent needs, Mahmud had cleared his house of everything, so that nothing but the four walls were left; at last he was compelled to let it, for it would have been foolish to stay in a large house, which he could neither fill nor furnish. Mahmud-Bey retired, therefore, with his family into a distant part of the harem, which was his last stronghold against utter misery. There he meditated on the vicissitudes of human life and on fate, whilst strong doses of arak served to soothe the despondency arising from poverty and want.

The winter which we spent with Mahmud-Bey passed somewhat sadly, and in the midst of all sorts of torments and worries. Kibrizli-Pasha did not cease to impose Shevket again upon us, and we did not feel disposed to accept his conditions. Things were pushed to such an extent, that they sought to buy over and corrupt our servants and slaves, so that they might make scenes and scandals in the house. Our coachman got drunk one day and brought back with him two or three scoundrels, who made a great noise before the door of our house and caused much scandal in that part of the town.

These people evidently did this under the instigation of those who were endeavouring to defame our house and worry us. They tried every way in which they could find some pretext to exile us from Constantinople. Ferideh trembled with passion when she saw her rival going about in her equipages and with her servants. When she heard us called by our names, as the wife and daughter of Kibrizli-Pasha, she shook with rage and spite.

Therefore she sought to compromise us, and for that purpose every means seemed good. One must have lived, as I have, amidst the Turks to form any idea of their anger and vengeance. Thus our enemy, Ferideh, thought of nothing but how to defame and despoil us of the little we possessed, and to exile us from Constantinople. Seeing that her husband's authority was not enough, she began to work upon his Highness and try to make him solicit the favour of Fuad-Pasha. This step, as may be imagined, cost Kibrizli very dear: for no earthly consideration would he have wished to humiliate himself before his rivals. That his self-respect and interests must have suffered there could be no doubt, for the *rôle* of chief of the opposition forbade him to make any advances to those in authority. Besides, the cause which he pleaded had something

repulsive about it ; for in begging the Government to
help him in his troubles with his wife and daughter,
Kibrizli played a pretty part, which could only
spoil his reputation amongst his colleagues and with
the public.

But Kibrizli-Pasha (or his counsellors) put such
scruples aside, and showed themselves ready to carry
it out at the price even of political concessions.
As for Fuad, it can be understood that he did not
disdain to negotiate on the basis of a *quid pro quo.*

For us, we only needed such an understanding
between Kibrizli and the Grand-vezir to place us in
a most critical position.   Imprisonment, exile, even
death was to be feared, for our enemies had reached
to such a pitch of exasperation that nothing could
appease them but our ruin.   When I was informed
of what was passing, I had no doubt as to the
gravity of our position, and we took counsel
together on the best way to escape the hostile
intentions of our enemies.

My plan was to go straight to Europe, leaving the
Turks to their jealousies and intrigues.   "Fleeing
the pleasures which were mixed up with fears," as
the saying is : this forcibly struck me amidst the
dangers in which we were placed.   In fact, of what
use to us was a seductive climate, hospitable people,

and the luxuries our means allowed us, when our enemies treated us like wild beasts? It was useless, after what had passed, to think of any compromise with them.

The Pasha said that the marriage with Shevket must be renewed; the woman, on her side, preferred death rather than to consent to such an arrangement. Neither side would yield; therefore a collision was inevitable, and this shock could have no other result than my ruin and that of my child, as I never would have consented to leave her with those who were conspiring against her life. To flee from Constantinople was naturally the first thing which came into our minds; but where to go? That was the question on which we had to think seriously before undertaking any further steps. There was no place in Turkey which could shelter us; for if Constantinople could not, the provinces were certainly still less likely to do so. Egypt offered certain advantages; for its internal government served us as a guarantee against any persecution. Long experience had taught me the wiles of Eastern policy, and I knew that in this policy there is one chapter called that of Betrayal. An arrangement like that which had just been established, occurring between the Ministers at Constantinople, would have sufficed to place us in the underground prisons.

Europe was the country which alone could shelter us, for there neither the Padishah nor his vezirs would be able to reach us. In Germany or France our enemies might mock at us, but we should soon forget envy and persecutions amidst civilized races. The small property which still remained to us would have assured to my child a peaceful and happy existence. Unfortunately, my daughter could in no wise comprehend the importance of the counsels I gave her, and my efforts to overcome her opposition ended in nothing. The reasons which prevented Aïshch from resolving on a flight into Europe were the following :

Aïshch, like other Turkish children, had been educated amidst the most absurd doctrines, of which the principal taught her was that the Mussulmans are the elect race, and that other peoples are a mass of impure and filthy beings. Imbued with these ideas, the Turks feel an insurmountable repugnance towards Christians, towards their habits and their persons. This repugnance is so strong, that if one asked a Turkish woman as a joke whether she would consent to become the wife of a Christian, she would hasten to show her horror and disgust by

spitting upon her own clothes. Aïsheh had a similar horror of Christians, and the idea of going to
live amongst them produced a resistance that I could
not overcome.

The love she bore her father was another reason
which prevented her adopting this plan. In fact,
when I pressed my arguments upon her, and showed
her that in her position she had no other choice, she
sighed from the very bottom of her heart and said,
" No, I love my father too well ; I could not cause
him such a sorrow in his old age. If I went among
the Ghïaurs, he would die of a broken heart."

My child's noble sentiments imposed silence upon
me ; for there are moments when affection carries
away all before it. That in this circumstance my
previsions were just, the future will prove. My
readers will soon see how Aïsheh herself decided on
taking refuge in a Christian country, and abandoning for ever the country of her birth. But, to arrive
at such a climax, she had to be reduced to the last
extremity, and, as one might say, almost to have
the knife at her throat.

We finally agreed upon a flight into Egypt.
Egypt has from all time been the polar star of the
unfortunate, the country which offered them an
asylum, and protected them from the hatred and

persecutions of their enemies. In our days also, any one who wishes to ameliorate his position finds in Egypt a hospitable country. Let us therefore take flight into Egypt; for once there our enemies would find it difficult to seize us, and the people of the country would surely have pity upon two unfortunate women.

CHAPTER XXXI.

OUR preparations for departure were concealed with care until the day we started for Alexandria. Towards evening our small caravan, which consisted of six or seven persons, comprising slaves and domestics, directed their steps towards the steamer which leaves the Golden Horn at seven o'clock. During the voyage between Constantinople and Alexandria, nothing occurred worthy of remark, if it were not a meeting with a certain Abib-Pasha, a friend of our enemies, who was going to Egypt to get some money out of the Viceroy. This sort of operation is much in vogue amongst the Turkish Pashas, who fly to Egypt every time they find themselves penniless. In the time of the Romans, Egypt was the granary of the empire ; at the present time the Turks have converted it into a mint, where everybody runs to fill their purses.

Abib-Pasha was a good fellow : his career was a singular one. He had commenced by being a writer, but soon changed his vocation to that of a buffoon. His buffoonery procured him several patrons, amongst others Bessim, the brother of my rival, Ferideh. It was Bessim who in a fit of drunkenness made his buffoon a Pasha, and sent him to govern Croatia, Macedonia, and some other provinces. But, though a Pasha, Abib did not find himself any better off, because he would continue to be Pasha and buffoon both at the same time. The truth is, that no amount of money was sufficient for his extravagances, and he was over head and ears in debt. Nevertheless, his debts were the least of his anxieties ; for, with surprising good humour, he fancied he could pay his debts with the same money that he employed to gain his patrons, that is to say, by means of his buffoonery. But his creditors would not let him off with such payment, for they strenuously opposed the departure of his Excellency, and would not let him leave Travink or Drama until they had placed his wife and secretaries in security as pledges.

Abib, on his arrival at Constantinople, went everywhere beseeching his patrons to raise the money for their release, and succeeded in doing so. He then took a voyage to Egypt, where he hoped to get into

favour with Farahon, whose generosity he hoped
would soon fill his pockets. Abib was not altogether
a bad fellow, and showed us every attention and
kindness during the voyage. On our arrival at Alexandria, Abib-Pasha hastened to warn the Egyptian
authorities, and gave them information regarding
us which was not, however, inspired by hostile sentiments. This was all the more honourable to Abib
that in the East it is the custom to turn the back,
and even to kick those who are persecuted or in any
misfortune.

In all countries, it is true, the wretched are
shunned like a pestilence ; but in Turkey this is
done without the least reserve or delicacy, and in
such a manner that one need not be surprised if one
receives a box on the ears from him who the evening before had kissed your slipper.

The moment Hafiz-Pasha, Governor of Alexandria, heard that the wife and daughter of Kibrizli-
Pasha was on board, he hastened to send us a
carriage, with an invitation to alight at the hotel
that the Egyptian government places at the disposition of travellers of distinction. This establishment is called the *Musafir-Khaneh ;* it contains
apartments sumptuously furnished, where persons
of rank who visit Egypt are lodged. They gave

c c

us the first floor of the hotel, and twice every day they served us with an exquisite repast in the Eastern fashion, with patties, sweets, and everything that one required.

But the attentions and zeal that the Egyptians displayed, in order to render our visit to Egypt agreeable, soon gave place to an unexpected coolness, which suddenly manifested itself the fourth day after our arrival. Our friends at Constantinople, having learned that we had left for Egypt, sent, without loss of time, a despatch to the Viceroy, to let him know that his Highness Kibrizli-Pasha having disgraced and disowned us, he felt wounded by the attentions that had been shown us.

Having had my suspicions of what was passing, I asked for an interview with the governor, Hafiz-Pasha, in order to assure myself of his intentions regarding us. Hafiz made me understand the bearings of the instructions that had been sent him, and informed me that his Government, whilst offering us hospitality, did not desire to offend his Highness by giving him, or the authorities at Constantinople, any cause for annoyance; and he wound up his remarks by counselling my daughter and myself to do everything in our power, and by any sacrifices to endeavour to regain the favour of his Highness.

The diplomatic and reserved style employed by Hafiz-Pasha sufficed to reveal the intentions of his Government on our behalf, and to show me the danger which menaced us. A plain and simple language, without compliment, would have inspired me with confidence; whilst this enigmatical manner of speaking proved that the Egyptians were not people on whom one might count Evidently they would not have hesitated, had they been pressed from Constantinople, to handcuff us, and send us into the subterranean prisons, from which we should never have escaped.

Terrified by the ideas that the interview with Hafiz-Pasha had suggested to me, I hastened, on my return to the hotel, to give the alarm to my daughter, notifying to her my intention of returning to Turkey by the first steamer. I made her understand that, if we were once imprisoned in a distant country, I should never be allowed to return again; for the Turks were so angry with me personally, that they would lose no time in getting rid of me once for all. It was true that, in going back to Turkey, we were both of us in danger; but we should also have there some chances of safety. Being in Turkey, we could rely on the sympathy of the people, and at the worst find means to escape. In Egypt and in the Sudan we should have no one to help us, and, once there, we should most likely have to remain for the rest of our lives.

It did not require much persuasion to convince Aïsheh that my fears were but too well founded, and the same day she decided on returning to Constantinople. Nevertheless, during the few days which preceded our departure we set ourselves to think what we should do after our arrival at Constantinople, and endeavoured to trace out a line of conduct which would assure to us the advantages of a retired life, and protect us from violence.

It was impossible to disguise from ourselves the fact that, in going to Constantinople, we placed ourselves in an abnormal position; for it could not be in the proximity of our adversaries, who hunted us everywhere, that we could hope to find that tranquillity and security which we longed for. Besides, from an economical point of view also, the capital was not exactly the place where one could dream of economising: the name of our family, the expensive habits of my daughter, the example of others, were so many obstacles which would prevent our leading a quiet and retired life.

After having considered various projects, we at length agreed on a plan which appeared full of the required conditions. I had heard it said that the island of Mitylene was a charming place, where the inhabitants passed their lives in the midst of enjoyment and plenty. From the accounts I had received, house-rent was at a relatively low rate, food was abundant, whilst the gardens and country offered all the pleasures that nature could procure; and, besides, it was said that the trade in corn and olives prospered there.

The information that I acquired at Alexandria on the subject of our safety, taught me that the different Powers had consuls residing in the town, the chief place of the island. This fact was of a nature to encourage and reassure us, for it is well known that everywhere, where there are foreign consuls, the Turkish authorities are circumspect, and a certain restraint is placed on their arbitrary actions. In a place like Mitylene they would not dare to touch us with impunity, for public opinion would to a certain extent protect us.

The decision which we adopted was, then, that we should first go to Constantinople, from whence, after having realised the money which we required, and after having made the necessary preparations, we should leave for Mitylene.

Our arrival at Constantinople greatly surprised our adversaries, and this surprise on their part favoured the execution of our project. Whilst the Pasha and the Ministry discussed amongst themselves the coercive measures that they proposed to decree, we had plenty of time to make our arrangements for the voyage, and to start for Mitylene.

On our arrival at Mitylene we at once occupied ourselves with getting a house, and procuring all that was necessary for our subsistence. The house we hired was a beautiful residence, situated on a height, from which we had a magnificent view of the port and of the mountains which surround it. Our nearest neighbours were the consuls of Italy and Greece, whilst in our immediate neighbourhood the consuls of the other Powers and the Greek Archbishop of Mitylene resided. We had, indeed, as may be seen, neglected no precautions, and our position, in the midst of the diplomatic corps, was, one might almost say, unattackable. Nevertheless, these very precautions hastened the catastrophe.

Some days after our arrival in the island, I thought of entering on some speculations, of the sort which were most in vogue amongst commercial people, with the aim of increasing the small amount of capital we still had at our disposal. The speculation which I entered upon was that of importing flour from Salonica, in order to sell it to the inhabitants of the island at an opportune moment. To this effect I associated myself with a Greek merchant, and I ordered a large cargo of flour, which was warehoused.

These commercial operations, the administration of which I left to an overseer, a man called Hadjii, did not prevent my entering on friendly relations with my neighbours, for in our position it was an advantage that everyone should know us, and that we should know everyone. When one has nothing to conceal, and can carry the head high, one has everything to gain by being sociable and mixing with one's equals. Thus we frequently visited the Italian consul, M. Marinucci, M. Delaporte, the Greek consul, as also other families on the island; but the society which charmed us more than all the others was that of Monseigneur the Archbishop of Mitylene, a venerable old man, full of goodness and courtesy.

The archbishop had a magnificent garden, where he reared with the greatest care the rarest flowers and shrubs, amongst which the oranges and lemons were so numerous that they formed a thick forest, the scent of which perfumed the air. In this garden my daughter and I used frequently to walk and enjoy the freshness of the evening, and the amiable society of the archbishop. One day, whilst seated near the kiosque in company with the archbishop and his attendant priests, our servant Abdullah entered the garden, and with a terrified air informed us that the soldiers had sur- rounded our house, and were seeking us every- where.

This unexpected news, coming into the midst of the circle of friends in which we found ourselves, threw consternation amongst us all, and, as was but natural in a case of such a critical nature, the old archbishop and his attendants surrounded us at once to offer their counsels and good offices. To the kindness of these worthy priests I replied by thanking them in my own and daughter's name for all the attentions they had shown us, and prayed them to be witnesses before God and men of the barbarous acts that were about to be committed against women. Turning then towards my daughter, I endeavoured to raise her spirits by exhorting her not to be afraid; for if our last hour was come, it would not be remedied by our showing ourselves cowardly.

Having said these few words, I turned towards the garden door; but scarcely were we outside, when the gendarmes, who were waiting for us, seized us and led us away to an old fortress, situated about two miles from the town. The gendarmes who conducted us remained taciturn the whole way, and did not say a word as to what was going to be done with us; only in reply to an observation of mine that I supposed it was owing to the receipt of an order from my husband that they acted in this manner towards us, the commandant of the detachment said dryly,—

" You know it, Madame ; well, then, march."

When we reached the fortress, they made us pass through three small iron doors, and led us into a vaulted room, only partially lighted by an opening close to the roof. This dark and damp prison had for its sole furniture two wretched beds with a woollen coverlet. No sooner had we entered when the guards, locking us in, left us to meditate on our position and on the fate which awaited us.

Whilst the orders that the Ministry had sent from Constantinople were being executed on our persons, our house and goods were seized by the detachment which were charged with this operation. Amongst all our property and furniture, our clothes were the only things given over to us; everything else, comprising the flour and other merchandise that we kept warehoused, and also our ready cash, was confiscated, and passed into the hands of persons greedy for plunder.

The three days we passed in the fortress were days of misery and anguish; each time the door of our prison was opened, or that we heard a noise from the outside, we fancied that our last moment had arrived, and that the executioners were come to strangle us. This dread which seized us was not the result of an excited imagination or terrified mind, but it was caused by the conviction that our enemies, Feridch and Bessim, were persons who would not draw back from any enormity in order to get rid of us. It was their inability alone which had paralysed them; but now that the authorities appeared to lend them assistance in their aims, we might expect everything from them.

Nevertheless, at the end of the third day of our detention, one of the officials of the government of the island came to inform us that we were to be exiled to Koniah in Asia Minor, and in consequence we should have to embark on board the steamer which was to leave that same night for Smyrna. The Pasha's officer did not fail to give us some words of consolation, and made many excuses on the part of his master, who, he said, greatly regretted having had to perform so sad a duty, but, as a servant of the State, he could not do otherwise than obey the orders that had been sent him.

Thus again escorted by gendarmes we were conducted on board, just as though we had been condemned to the galleys, or like people who had conspired against the life of the Padishah and the safety of the country. Our arrest took place in the beginning of December, 1865.

CHAPTER XXXII.

On our arrival at Smyrna, we were conducted under an escort to a Turkish house, where we were kept for three more days under strict surveillance. The preparations for our journey being then terminated, we were placed on horses, and took the road which leads from Smyrna to Koniah by way of Sparta. Our escort at this time was not a very formidable one; it only consisted of two gendarmes. Evidently the Smyrna authorities did not fear our attempting flight during the journey. Besides, with bad horses, bad cavalry saddles, and the snow which covered the mountains of Aidin, we had need to be men of exceptional strength instead of women, in order to attempt such a flight.

Poor unfortunate creatures as we were, we had barely strength to keep ourselves on our saddles, for we shivered with the cold, which almost deprived us of the use of our limbs. Aïsheh, who never ought to have been exposed to such trials, had to undergo some great hardships; her condition was truly pitiable. The privations and sufferings to which she was exposed told upon her strength with greater force, owing to her mind and spirit being so crushed, and being deprived of all the comforts and luxuries to which she had been accustomed in her father's house; but what rendered her more inconsolable than all besides, was the knowledge that she owed all this dreadful treatment to a father whom she tenderly loved.

The sufferings of my daughter, and the state of the roads, did not permit us to take long marches, or to enjoy any of the pleasures of the journey. Our stages were generally from three to four hours a day, so that it took us a fortnight to reach Koniah, the place of our destination. On the way we rested in many towns and villages: the most important places we saw were Aidin, the country of the famous *Zeibecks*, the troubadour warriors of Asia Minor. Aidin, or Guzel-Hissar, must be a charming place in summer time, as it is surrounded by gardens and orchards, and offers a beautiful view of the adjacent plain. Sparta is another town whose smiling appearance somewhat enlivened the dreariness of our journey. This place, like Aidin, commands a fine view over a valley covered with fine plane trees: the waters flow plentifully through the beds of the streams and torrents; while the houses seemed to us elegantly and well built in the midst of gardens.

But in the midst of our sufferings, seeing ourselves exiles and outcasts, the beauties of nature and the sight of towns and villages could not produce any great effect upon us; so that it often happened that we entered inside a place and came out again without even thinking to ask our gendarmes or the country people any questions about it. In the midst of our anxiety the predominant thought which engrossed our minds was, "And what next? What will they do with us when once we reach Koniah?"

After a march of fifteen days, we at last arrived at Koniah, which is situated in the middle of a vast plain. I will not say anything here on the subject of Koniah, of its houses, its mosques, and the gardens which constitute its suburbs; for, as the reader will remember, I have already made mention of this town, in speaking of my first exile here. Nevertheless I do not hesitate to say that in approaching the town I could not prevent feeling a lively desire to see it again, and to meet my old

friends and acquaintances once more. It seemed to
me at this moment that in all misfortunes there is a
charm, and that the recollection of a sad past has
in it also something to soothe and please the mind.

Our arrival at Koniah did not fail to produce a •
lively sensation amongst all classes of the population, amongst the men as well as in the harem.
They were astonished to see a daughter sent by her
father into exile in the midst of ice and snow. The
Pasha-Governor was a certain good and fat old man,
called Izzet-Pasha : when the gendarmes placed in
his hands the *firman* which condemned us to exile,
the poor Pasha remained stupified, and, seizing his
long beard, cried out—

" Tchok shei ! Tchok shei ! bunudah giurduk !"
signifying, " Zounds ! one must live to my age to
see such things as these."

Izzet-Pasha took care to settle us in a house,
where we were no sooner installed than we were
besieged by a mass of visitors. Every one who had
formerly known me came at once to see me ; some
of my friends hastening to express their regrets for
the misfortunes that had befallen me and my
daughter, whilst my most intimate friends could not
conceal their joy at seeing me again in their midst.

The wives of the Mollah-Unkiar, as also those

of several dervishes, hastened to send us hot dishes and sweetmeats, as a proof of their cordiality. In our private conversations as between mother and daughter as regarded our position, we came to the conclusion that it would be folly to think of returning, at least for some time, to our own country, and that for the moment we could not do better than resign ourselves to our fate, and to try and render our exile as agreeable as we could possibly make it.

Evidently the only hope we could entertain of returning to our home was based on the possibility that the voice of nature might make itself heard in the heart of him who had not hesitated to persecute his wife and child. Nevertheless, Providence, which watched over us, had in its hidden designs ordered otherwise; for without our knowledge, or even thinking of it, it was about to open the road of our deliverance.

Three months had scarcely elapsed since our arrival at Koniah, when one fine day a certain Hadji-Kadin, the mother of a dervish, came to visit us. In the course of conversation the worthy woman said, that if she had been placed in a similar position to ours, she should have escaped and returned to Constantinople.

"You have not committed any crime," added

Hadji-Kadin. "What do you suppose they can do to you? If I were in your place, as Allah is my witness, I would not remain a minute longer here."

These exhortations produced an extraordinary effect on me and my daughter; for we felt our courage and strength reviving at every word. The question of our flight was then fully discussed, and between us three we talked over the means we must employ to carry out our enterprise successfully. Hadji-Kadin offered with the best good-will to provide us with horses for the journey, and proposed that her son, Dervish Ahmet, should accompany us in secret outside the town, and put us on the road which leads to Mersine. The plan to be followed in our evasion having been decided on, it only remained to make the necessary arrangements.

Before relating the circumstances attending our flight from Koniah, I must give a few explanations on this event; for the explanations will throw a light on the causes which brought about our exile and our flight.

I must commence by saying that both our exile and our flight were neither more nor less than political farces, that the Ministry and Kibrizli-Pasha played one against the other. In the midst of these intrigues, it was we, poor unfortunates, who had to suffer. According to information which I gleaned on our return to Constantinople, which also bore out what I heard Fuad-Pasha himself say on the occasion of my interview with him at Nice, a short time before his death, I will now relate what the circumstances were which brought about our exile and our flight.

My readers will no doubt recollect what I have previously said on the subject of the instigations of our enemies, who, by their tricks and wiles, induced the Pasha to commit acts of violence on the persons of his wife and daughter. But Kibrizli, who was no longer in the Ministry, had no other means of satisfying the clamour of the people of his household, than that of asking the Ministers to aid him by means of their authority. The Ministers at first hesitated to give Kibrizli their support; for the intestine warfare which ravaged the family of a pretendant to the grand-vezirat, accorded completely with the wishes and interests of Fuad and of Ali Pasha.

The good-will which the Ministers at first showed us, and their refusal to lend themselves as instruments of vengeance, sufficiently explains their policy, during the first period of the conflicts which were carried on between Kibrizli-Pasha and ourselves. But an unexpected change in the aspect of affairs caused Fuad and Ali to alter their plans. Kibrizli having resolved at any cost to prevail over us and his political adversaries, presented an ultimatum to the Ministry by which he declared that if they persisted in refusing the arm of authority against his daughter, he would go straight to the Sultan, and get from his Majesty the *firman* he desired to have.

Seeing that Kibrizli would get the victory in spite of themselves, Fuad and Ali changed their tactics, by giving way to the demands of their adversary, in according him the firman for our arrest and exile. In acting in this manner, these two statesmen took into consideration our safety and interests; for it was evident that if Kibrizli-Pasha, Ferideh, Bessim, and our other enemies could have succeeded in procuring a firman according to their own wishes, our destruction would have been inevitable.

In giving therefore this firman, the Ministry, without our knowledge, rendered us a signal service. Nevertheless, as nothing is done in political matters without a motive, thus Fuad and Ali only consented to grant the firman with the aim of preserving the advantages that they could gather in the midst of our domestic quarrels. They both thoroughly well understood that it would be easy to annul a firman which emanated from themselves, whilst it would have been much more difficult to revoke a firman emanating from the Sultan himself. Briefly, Fuad and Ali said to themselves, "Let us give Kibrizli the firman he asks for; afterwards it will not be difficult to get the women back again, and things will go on in the same way as before."

This is exactly what they did in sending us two emissaries, such as Hadji-Kadin and Dervish Ahmet, her son. That these people acted from instructions received from head-quarters there can be no doubt; for if it was not the case, how can one explain these facts, that during our stay at Koniah no measure of surveillance was adopted on our behalf, and that afterwards, on our arrival at Constantinople, the Ministry took no notice of our escape?

Evidently they only wanted to shut Kibrizli Pasha's mouth by giving him the firman, whilst, in allowing us to escape, they wished to create new difficulties.

According to the plan we had laid down, Dervish Ahmet came and knocked at our door towards the dawn of day, accompanied by two guides and horses, which we had to mount. Without loss of time, we three, Aïsheh, myself and my

son, Djehad, took our places on our saddles, and
began to trot across the fields and solitary paths
that Dervish Ahmet had charged himself with the
duty of showing us. When at some distance from
Koniah, Dervish Ahmet confided us to the care of
the two guides, at the same time wishing us good-
by and a prosperous journey.

Now that I see things in a different light to what
I did at that time, I can but regret that they did
not spare us the fear, the agitation, and the fatigue
that this flight from Koniah caused us. If the
Ministry had decided on making us return to Constantinople to play out their game, for myself I
would have promised to play it out to perfection,
without any one guessing it and without causing us
real torments. But the complete ignorance in which
we were kept on the subject of what was passing
behind the scenes made us escape with all the
gravity and fear of dangerous consequences. At
every step we looked behind to see if any one was
following us. Instead of going along tranquilly,
we galloped like maniacs, and not being able to
sit well on our saddles, we fell off at least twenty
times.

As for my daughter, she displayed a great deal of
courage ; she astonished us by the skill which she

shewed in the management of her horse. Neverthe-less, she also fell off several times, but this did not occur till the moment when her strength failed her, and she felt herself worn out with fatigue and want of sleep.

Between Koniah and Karaman there is a distance of twenty hours' ride; we did the whole of it in two stages, and halted in a meadow on the banks of a rivulet. The truth is, that after a march of twelve or fourteen hours we were so knocked up that we could not go on without taking some rest. Leaving our horses to graze in the meadow, we and our guides lay down on the banks of the stream, and in a few moments fell fast asleep.

At daybreak Aïsheh woke : alarmed by the danger we ran in prolonging our halt in a place infested by Turkish marauders, she made us get up and continue our march. In fact, we were in a most dangerous position, for if evil-disposed people had presented themselves, we could not have offered them any resistance ; our caravan only consisted of two armed men, and they slept quite tranquilly on the grass. If thieves had made their appearance, they could easily have carried us all off—men and women and horses.

We continued our journey towards Karaman, but

were not able to enter it before sunset, on account of the by-ways we had to take, so as to avoid the most frequented paths. As I have already said, all these troubles and annoyances might have been spared us, if they had only hinted that we might escape by the public road and take our time about it.

After spending the night at Karaman, we continued our journey, following the valleys and keeping along by the sides of the mountains of Cilicia (the Ak-dagh). Before crossing this chain, our caravan passed the night at Khan, a small town situated on the road to Mersine. From Khan, on the following day, we mounted to the summit of the chain of mountains whose culminating peak the country people call Dunbelek-dagh. The road was a succession of zig-zags through the wooded sides of the mountains. The view was unexceptionably picturesque and grand.

The third night of our march we halted at a village on the other side of the mountain, and on the fourth day, late in the afternoon, we arrived safe and well at Mersine. As we feared lest the authorities of the town should take notice of our arrival, and in consequence raise difficulties and perhaps prevent our departure, we immediately on our arrival went to the French Consul, in order to put ourselves under his protection.

The Consul was absent at his country place, for in Cilicia, when the spring-time is much advanced, the inhabitants are in the habit of going for the month of March to their country residences, so as to enjoy the most agreeable season of the year. This tiresome circumstance necessitated our going in search of the Consul, and to have another half hour's ride. The *concierge* at the Consulate was gallant enough to offer himself as our guide, and walked at the head of our horses till we reached the Consul's door. The Consul's house was picturesquely situated in the midst of rocks, and commanded a large and beautiful vineyard, surrounded by fig and palm trees.

Having been apprised of our arrival, the Consul hastened in person to offer us the hospitality of his house, and, with an exquisite courtesy, assisted us off our horses, and did us the honours of his house. M. Geoffroy was a young man, about thirty years of age, of an agreeable exterior, and with manners which revealed high birth, and choice education.

The kindness which the chivalrous Consul showed us greatly surpassed the ordinary limits of hospitality and etiquette. According to Oriental custom, he

placed his bath at our disposal, and requested his
mother to see that nothing was neglected for our
comfort.   M. Geoffroy hastened, the first moment
we put foot in his house, to assure us that no one
shoud molest us whilst we remained with him, and
he would also give us a safe-conduct to put us on
board the steamer.

We remained for two days the guests of the
Consul, who charmed us by his manners, as also by
the attentions with which he overwhelmed us.   But
what pleased me more than all was the service he
did for us in giving us as a friend his best advice
and counsels on the subject of my daughter and
her father.   M. Geoffroy, who thoroughly understood the character of the Turks, did not hesitate to
say that, from what he had heard from us about
our affairs, our return to Constantinople was, under
the circumstances, an act of utter madness.   As for
the hope of bringing about a reconciliation with the
Pasha and our adversaries, it was an illusion that
the antecedents entirely contradicted.   According
to him there were but two courses open : either
my daughter must decide on a complete submission,
or else she must seek for safety in a foreign country.

In this M. Geoffroy and myself were of the same
opinion ; but unfortunately Aïsheh would not listen

to the counsels of her mother or a friend, for she still cherished the hope of arranging matters by means of a *mezzo termine*.

On the arrival of the steamer we took leave of M. Geoffroy and his mother, and went to take our places on board. As the vessel touched at the different ports along the coast, such as Rhodes, Smyrna, the Dardanelles, it took three days for us to reach the Golden Horn.

CHAPTER XXXIII.

OUR arrival did not fail to produce a certain effect on the mass of the populace of Constantinople ; but this sensation was not alone the result of surprise, for they knew that we were not women who would allow ourselves to be easily ruled. The news of our arrival naturally vexed our adversaries ; as for the Ministry, they rejoiced, for they knew the struggle was about to begin again between us and our enemies.

It will not have escaped my reader's notice that, whilst I do not hesitate to qualify Kibrizli, Ferideh, &c.; by the name of adversaries, I take care not to call the people in authority *our friends*: in fact, what title could I give Fuad and Ali-Pasha, who, whilst making use of us to attain their own political aims, nevertheless left us to the mercy of the strongest, and showed themselves totally indifferent to our sufferings and anguish ? If these people had had

really our welfare at heart, what they should have
done was very simple. They ought first to have
allowed us a sum of money for our subsistence, and
at once have intimated to our adversaries to keep
quiet, or otherwise the Government would interfere
in our favour.

Fuad and Ali took care not to follow such
a line of conduct, for they knew that by this
means an end would soon be put to our quarrels.
Naturally, if they had let us live in peace,
and if they had allowed us some thousands
of francs for our maintenance, we should never
have troubled ourselves about Ferideh and her companions ; we should have left them perfectly tranquil.

Wishing to put an end to a state of things in
which we had nothing to gain and everything to
lose, immediately on my arrival at Constantinople,
I begged my daughter to endeavour to regain her
father's good-will and favour. With this object in
view, Aïsheh went to see a *Khodja*, who was the
spiritual director of his Highness—a pious person
of great repute amongst the grandees of Constantinople, as well as the poorer classes of the people.
The *Khodja*, by name Ibrahim-Effendi, received
Aïsheh with every mark of kindness and consideration. He expressed his regret for the misfortunes

which had befallen us, and did. not conceal from her that he disapproved of the acts of violence from which we had suffered. Ibrahim-Effendi did not hesitate to say that he had remonstrated on this subject with his Highness, but that unfortunately he had not been attended to. The *Khodja*, in conclusion assured Aïsheh that he would not fail to seize the first favourable opportunity to intercede in her behalf; but he added, that we must keep very quiet, and avoid giving the least annoyance to the Pasha.

But whilst Ibrahim-Effendi preached these sermons to Aïsheh, and sent her away with fine words, we were rapidly hastening towards a crisis.

The fact is, we were reduced to the last extremity, having no other alternative before us than to surrender at discretion, or else to make a path for ourselves through the enemies' lines. Like a garrison which has used up its provisions, we were compelled either to lower our arms or to make a sortie.

Our means were entirely exhausted. Of the hundred thousand francs which my daughter had brought away with her in her flight from her father's house there only remained a few thousands. All this money had run through our fingers under one pretext or another. A part of it was expended by

Aïsheh in frivolities which she declared she could not do without; another portion was confiscated at Mitylene, or else was absorbed by the expenses of our exile and flight. Briefly, as I have said, all had been spent in one way or another, and two or three thousand francs was all we possessed in this solemn moment.

Under these circumstances it was impossible to think of continuing the struggle, or even to remain in the capital in which my daughter had been accustomed to lead a luxurious life. The only chance that was left us was to go and live in the country, where a small property which I possessed would have served us as a shelter, and would have saved us from the imminent danger of our dying from starvation. But after having solved the economical part of the question, the next thing to be considered was that of our personal safety. Should we be safe there? And if our enemies sent anyone to illtreat us, who was there to protect us? In the impossibility of solving this problem in a satisfactory manner, I bethought myself of a flight into Europe, in order to see if this course offered me more chance, or even a shadow of hope. But it was not necessary to rack one's brains to be able to understand that in our position it would have been madness to dream of a flight. I well knew that two women who dared to venture into Europe without money might expect everything, even death itself.

But whilst we waited with anxiety the result of our negotiations, and strove to come to a decision on the subject of what was best to be done, an incident occurred which decided our fate. We had a friend, a certain Hussein-Pasha, who was acquainted with Bessim, Shevket, and all that set. Hussein learnt, God knows how, that Kibrizli-Pasha and his counsellors had decided on getting rid of us at any cost, and with this end in view they intended transporting us to the fortress of Demitoka, from whence we could never hope to escape. The fortress of Demitoka is situated in Thracia, and it is there that the Porte sends those it wishes to be rid of. There is no place in Turkey more gloomy or where the surveillance is so strict as at Demitoka; this explains why this place is proverbially known as a sort of hell upon earth.

Hussein, on learning the intentions of our enemies, hastened to send us a secret emissary, to warn us of the danger which threatened us. The importance of this information could not be doubted, for after what had occurred to us at Mitylene, it was evident there was no outrage that our enemies were not capable of. As for doubting the veracity of the message sent us by Hussein-Pasha, this was quite out of the question, for we knew that Hussein cordially detested our enemies ; and if it was not entirely out of regard to us, at any rate his enmity to the others made him desire to be useful.

This news greatly alarmed us, but myself the most, for clearer than my daughter I could see that a gloomy future lay open before us. Aïsheh, on her side a prey to a consternation which bordered on delirium, implored me to leave for Europe, saying she preferred to die of hunger rather than fall living into the hands of her enemies. I did my best to calm her, and in this supreme moment to raise her spirits by making her understand that she must on no account despair of the future, for affairs had not yet reached the point she imagined, and that in some way or another we should obtain support and protection.

But all my prayers and exhortations were of no avail, she turned a deaf ear to them, for her terror was such that the unfortunate girl had lost all control over herself. After having fixed her wild eyes on the door, Aïsheh remained immovable for some seconds, then, turning suddenly to me, she said, in a terrified voice, " If you will go with me, well ; if not, I will go immediately to the sea, and embark in the first European ship I can find, for here I will not stay."

Having already had a hundred proofs of what Aïsheh was capable of, when once she had taken anything strongly to heart, and knowing that, in her excited state, she might even destroy herself, I gave way to her entreaties. Besides, a mother's feelings are apt to carry her away from the path of reason and common sense, and I felt as if a whirlwind was drawing me with my child into its vortex. I, therefore, at once promised to take her to Europe, and to place her in safety from those who conspired against us; at the same time I recommended Aïsheh to keep our intentions quite secret, for, if any one got the least suspicion of it, we should lose our lives.

In order to give the reader an idea of the dangers in the midst of which we found ourselves, I must mention that what Kibrizli-Pasha and the Turks most dreaded was, that we should escape into Europe. Fanaticism and jealousy are the two sentiments which predominate with the Turks; these sentiments are so violent, that no Turk can hear that a woman has escaped to the Ghïaurs without trembling with rage.

It is quite possible that the Turk who hears the dreadful news may neither know the woman or her family, or even her country : these things are perfectly indifferent to him; the mere fact that the daughter of a Mussulman has fallen into the hands of the Ghïaurs, and that these latter can look upon her features, is enough to make his blood boil, and make him rave. Should it happen, however, that the woman who has escaped is no unknown person of low extraction, but the daughter of one of the princes of Islam, the Turks are ready to declare in a body that such a fact is a national disaster ; some of them may in consequence even die of a stroke of apoplexy.

My daughter Aïsheh was the daughter of a Grand-vezir, of one who had three times held in his hand the seal of the Padishah ; besides this, she was an *Esseideh*, Emir, a descendant of the race of Mohamed... One can understand that the very idea that such a woman could escape, and be exposed to the unclean gaze of the Ghïaurs, would make the Turks furious to that degree that they would prefer to confine us for life in the fortress of Demitoka, or have us strangled, rather than cover Islam with so lasting a disgrace.

It is a grave error to suppose that jealousy

and fanaticism were extinguished at the epoch of
the destruction of the Janissaries, for even at this
date the young persons who have been sent to
Europe for their education take the infection of
these diseases on their return to their homes.
Fuad-Pasha made an exception to the general rule;
as regards Ali-Pasha, I can form no opinion, inasmuch as I am not acquainted with his ideas and
sentiments.　No one could ever guess what this
man really thought or felt; Ali was a real genius
in hypocrisy.

But to return to our flight.　I must mention that
the precautions which I took whilst I made my
preparations were in conformity with the gravity
of the circumstances, and of the risks which we
ran.　After having turned several projects over in
my mind, I finally decided upon the only one
which seemed to offer any chance of success; this
was, in the first place, to discover some one amongst
the Europeans at Pera who would procure dresses
for us in the European fashion—petticoats, bonnets,
mantles, and so on—and who would undertake to
secure places for us on one of the mail packet-boats
that sailed for Marseilles.

Under these circumstances it was natural that
I should turn my eyes towards my own relations

at Pera ; for to whom could I apply in a matter so dangerous and delicate, if not to my own sister ? The Perotes are so notoriously venal, that I had good reasons for fearing to confide in any of them ; there was a great risk that allured by the hope of making their fortunes, they would betray me to the Turks, who would readily have given an enormous sum for information respecting our plans. To say the truth, I for some time even hesitated to confide in my own sister, and for the reason, that her son Carlo Calix, was purveyor to the Imperial Court, and in consequence intimately connected with the Turks. " God knows," I said to myself, " how far money interests may prevail over family ties ; and Carlo Calix, who gains thousands and thousands by the Turks, may possibly betray his aunt, whom he scarcely knows."

But the honest Carlo proved the falsehood of my suspicions and fears ; no one in the world could have acted more nobly ; he took on himself, at his own cost and risk, to provide our means of escape. In fact, when I went to Madame Calix and confided to her our design of escaping to Europe, she immediately summoned her son Carlo, and we three held a consultation, in which we discussed the project in all its phases, and we decided on the plan of action which appeared most favourable. The eagerness which Carlo displayed in aiding us in this dangerous business took me quite by surprise, for I had no reason to expect it.

"Aunt," said Carlo, "as I see things, the only hope of safety for you and Aïsheh is in flight. By escaping to Europe, not only do you place yourself in safety, but you take a signal revenge on the Turks, who have ill-treated and tyrannized over you, and who now seek to destroy you.

"*Sacré-bleu*, leave us to act, and to-morrow everything will be ready for your departure."

CHAPTER XXXIV.

EVERYTHING having been made ready for our departure, we hurried to be off by the very first mail; which was to start for France that week. Our anxiety, our apprehensions may be, in a measure, imagined, but never fully realised. On the one hand we had already experienced the terrors of pursuit, the horrors of re-capture, the long torments of seclusion. A worse fate awaited us if our present project failed: an underground dungeon for life. On the other hand our success depended upon our taking advantage of the very first opportunity of attempting our escape. Should we be fortunate now? This was the momentous question the attempt could alone determine.

At Constantinople the Government and the police exercise a rather severe control over the passports of departing travellers. In the first instance, the docu-

ments must be viséd ; they are then presented at
the office of the Messageries, and are only returned
to the travellers a few moments before their departure.   Now these formalities threatened to be
for us a most serious business, for this simple
reason that we had no passports, and had no means
of procuring any.   But if our being without passports exposed us to the risk of being stopped by
the local police ; on the other hand the imminent
danger we were in, from the revengeful fury of my
husband, left us no alternative but to incur the risk
of being arrested by the local police, the chance of
bribing whom still remained to us.

Fully aware, therefore, of the immense advantage
to us of using diligence, we accomplished impossi-
bilities in these two days, in order to complete our
preparations.   Carlo hastened to bring us dresses,
prepared our trunks, and ordered the sedan-chairs
which were to take us through the streets of Pera
and from Galata to the place of embarkation.   I
for my part hurried off to tell Aïsheh that our
departure was fixed for the following day.

It was necessary to assign some reason for our
proceedings to our own household and neighbours.
We therefore gave them to understand that we were
only going to the quarter of the Ghïaurs to make

purchases. Our adieux were the last which we ever made to them—the last which my daughter made to her country, and to everything that was dear to her in the world. As for me, I made my last adieu to Mussulman society, in the midst of which I had passed thirty years—a whole existence.

On our arrival at Pera we went straight to Madame Calix, who was impatiently expecting us, for everything was ready for our departure. In such moments, when one is on the point of taking a final decision, a feeling of strong agitation must seize on all concerned, be they actors, accomplices, or witnesses ; and accordingly, on this occasion when we entered the house, we found my sister and Carlo in a great state of agitation, caused no less by the grave responsibility which rested on them, than by the decisive and irrevocable step which they knew we were about to take.

With the hurry and excitement which are inevitable on such occasions, we laid aside our Turkish dress, and put on the petticoats which are worn by Europeans. Aïsheh, with that light-heartedness which was the charm of her youth, did not appear to be much preoccupied with either responsibility or danger ; she was entirely absorbed in the operation of transforming herself from a Hanum ·into a lady.

The idea of approaching freedom made her forget the dangers which threatened her very life. When our toilet was ended, we bade adieu to my sister and her daughters, and went out into the street where the sedan-chairs were waiting for us. Carlo helped us in, advising us to be very careful to conceal our features by lowering our veils, and when everything was ready gave the order to start.

We passed through the most crowded streets of Pera and Galata ; whilst our chairs doubtless pushed against many who would not have hesitated to attack us, if they had only suspected that we were the individuals concealed behind those curtains.

Carlo followed in the distance, carefully watching our progress ; as soon as we arrived at the stairs, he joined us again, in order to give his assistance at the difficult office of embarking. The stairs to which we had gone were close to the custom-house at Galata, and not much frequented ; it was a spot admirably chosen for our embarkation, and here Carlo had stationed a Maltese boat under the English flag, which was to convey us to the steamer. On leaving our chairs, we bid adieu to Carlo, with heart-felt thanks for all that he had done for us, and took our places in the boat.

The Maltese boatmen rowed us in a few moments

to the steamer, and took us alongside. There was a crowd of Turkish boats and caïques before the ladder, which had carried merchants and merchandise to the steamer ; amongst the caïques were two or three that were there to watch the embarkation, and in each of these was a police officer. The gendarmes looked hard at us, made an inspection of our luggage, and allowed us to pass ; had they but known that one of these travellers was nothing less than the daughter of the Grand-vezir, who can say. what they would have done to us ? Probably we should have been made to measure the depth of the Bosphorus.

As soon as we got on board, we at once descended to one of the cabins reserved for ladies, and there we placed ourselves out of sight. It is a most astonishing fact, that none of the officers of the ship asked to see either our tickets or passports ; the clerk merely inquired how far we were going, and seeing that we had no tickets, he gave us the requisite number.

These were the circumstances under which we quitted Constantinople, in the autumn of 1866 ; and here I must conclude that portion of the narrative of my life, of which so large a part was passed in the harem.

The six years we have since spent in Europe, have been so many years of martyrdom. We have endured hunger, penury, abject misery. We have suffered persecutions of every kind, conducted with an ingenuity meriting the epithet of diabolical, and prosecuted with a degree of perseverance which indicates the intensest hatred. The object has been to discredit us everywhere; to isolate us from society; to drive us to despair—even to death.

Our vicissitudes in Europe, however,—and they have been of a most extraordinary kind,—must form the subject of a sequel to the present recital of our experiences and misfortunes in the East. I fervently thank God He has so mercifully preserved me thus far from my enemies, and I rely upon His good Providence to enable me finally to overcome them, and to obtain justice for myself and my children.

THE END.

BRADBURY, EVANS, AND CO., PRINTERS, WHITEFRIARS.